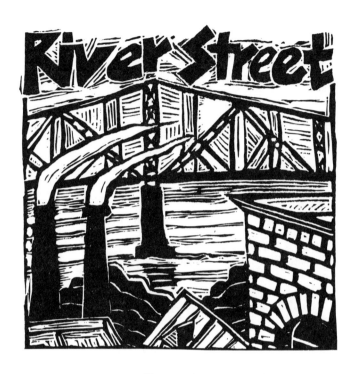

A Novella and Stories by
Phil Condon

Southern Methodist University Press
Dallas

These stories are works of fiction. Names, characters, places, and incidents are either the product of the author's imagination or are used fictitiously.

Requests for permission to reproduce material from this work should be sent to:
Rights and Permissions
Southern Methodist University Press
Box 415
Dallas, Texas 75275

Some of the stories in this collection appeared first in the following publications: "Starkweather's Eyes" in *Shenandoah;* "Seven" in *Prairie Schooner;* "Babyman" in *Cutbank;* "Insolence" in *New Letters;* "What Hurts the Fish" in *Roberts Writing Awards 1989 Annual;* "The Empty-heart Boy" in *Black Warrior Review;* and "River Street" in *Long Story.*

Grateful acknowledgment is made for permission to quote from *Preludes for Memnon* by Conrad Aiken. From *Collected Poems,* Second Edition, by Conrad Aiken. Copyright © 1953, 1970 by Conrad Aiken; renewed 1981 by Mary Aiken. Reprinted by permission of Oxford University Press, Inc.

Library of Congress Cataloging-in-Publication Data

Condon, Phil, 1947-
    River Street : a novella and stories / by Phil Condon. — 1st ed.
      p. cm.
      ISBN 0-87074-372-4 (cloth). — ISBN 0-87074-373-2 (paper)
    I. Title.
PS3553.04869R58   1994
813'.54—dc20   94-10530

Cover illustration and design by Barbara Whitehead

Printed in the United States of America on acid-free paper
10 9 8 7 6 5 4 3 2 1

For my mother, Marjorie

HELP BEYOND WORDS

Speak: and the ghosts of change, past and to come,
Throng the brief word. The maelstrom has us all.

CONRAD AIKEN

Contents

Starkweather's Eyes

MY FATHER disappeared the spring before Starkweather. One Tuesday night in April after dinner, creamed chicken on rye toast, one of his favorites, he went out for a quart of beer. He stood a long time at the door, smoothing the nap on his gray suede coat, as if it was important for it to be one uniform shade, staring through the diamond window in the front door at the '56 Fairlane he loved so much. When he wasn't home by my bedtime, right after the Jimmy Durante show, mother began making phone calls. He had left before, unexpectedly, for an hour or a day, one time even a week, so we waited. And waited. Mother and I always figured he was all right, hadn't come to any harm, but of course we could never be sure. I asked for a suede coat like his for Christmas the next year, but instead I got a fur-lined parka with a detachable hood. Mother said suede was impractical.

• • •

I keep wondering where his eyes went. Who got them. Starkweather's eyes, I mean. Whether it's true or not, I remember that in the last days before they strapped him in the chair in 1958, he signed a release saying they could use his eyes. I've read somewhere since that electrocution destroys the eyes, that they explode inside that thick black hood, the mask they use to cover death, but that must be sensationalism, because I recall the Omaha papers making a big deal about Starkweather doing one last good deed—donating his eyes. He wore thick glasses, I'm sure of that, and apparently something about his eyes was quite rare. He gave his eyes to science. Probably they're in pieces in sealed bottles on some medical school campus, long since dissected. But those eyes could be somewhere out there now. Or at least a part of them, maybe a slice of cornea or a tiny graft of optic nerve. Some little part of them could be out there, anywhere, right now.

Over and over, I tell myself: My mother's dead now, she's dead. I sit here, back home, comfortable in California with my wife and daughter, one week after my mother's funeral, my mind suddenly flooded with so much that I don't remember remembering before. So much about her and Starkweather and my father in the faraway 1950s. And my mother's probably the only one who could tell me if I'm dreaming or remembering. It's almost as if these memories had waited for this moment to appear, waited until I could never be entirely certain.

I'm pretty sure that if my father had been around, my mother wouldn't have been so afraid those few days in late October when Starkweather was on the loose. And maybe I wouldn't have done what I did either. The truth is, after my father left, I sometimes felt like I could float away, like there was nothing to hold me down anymore. I didn't even like to play outfield at the Little League in Hanscom Park that summer because I felt so exposed in center field, so far from trees and buildings. I figured if my force of gravity was ever going to fail me, that would be the place. I could see myself rising up over the ballfield, waving goodbye to the rest of the team who still had fathers, getting tinier and tinier in the eyes of all my former friends.

And yet I never saw things from up above, I saw myself from the perspective of everyone left behind. I'd try to concentrate on watching myself, like when you watch a chimney swift rise in the dusk, always thinking that if you just don't blink it will not be able to disappear, that if you concentrate perfectly you can follow it all the way up to wherever it goes. The coach let me play catcher when I lied and said I'd pulled a muscle in my leg and couldn't run well. I liked the comfort of the chain link backstop, the chatty umpire and the batter nearby, and the catcher's mask. The mask was the best of all. It was as if there was no danger of losing any part of myself, no danger in blinking, or forgetting, whenever I had the mask on.

Maybe you don't remember Starkweather. They made a movie about him in the seventies starring Martin Sheen, and Bruce Springsteen wrote a song about him, too. Both the movie and the song made him seem misunderstood, almost a hero, but he wasn't, I don't think. For me, he was the demon of childhood, of a lifetime.

Maybe all of us have our own mass murderer that we carry around inside, somebody whose unthinkable deeds struck us just at that certain vulnerable age, someone we never even met and yet who seems as vivid and close as a member of the family. I know I've heard people talk after a few drinks, talk about Juan Corona or Richard Speck or Son of Sam, tell how childhoods seemed to change all at once and a grown-up kind of fear started growing inside for the first time, a hard kernel of fear that keeps on adding layers through the years. And if I could take my fear apart, unwind it back to the very beginning, I believe I'd find him waiting there, still nineteen, still on the loose, never any older and never captured, my Starkweather.

I've always thought it was funny about his name, Starkweather, because he was just like that. For Nebraska in the late fifties, he was a storm nobody saw coming, some wild, aberrant weather that was impossible to prepare for. For that part of the country, Starkweather was a kind of turning point—something very modern—part of a disease, as pervasive as weather, that caused us all to realize how afraid we were of each other. He killed only eleven people, which isn't that many, no more than a bus crash or a building collapse, but it was the *fear* he caused in that green, quiet part of the country, the fear that surfaced as visibly as dark, thick sweat on everybody's faces, that seemed so new. People began pulling back, pulling in, retreating indoors as a way of life.

Of course, we killed him, I mean our State did, in our names, but we'd seen something unforgettable, and seen it in a different way, blown-up life-size on the TV news, in the newspapers, something nobody could explain with any of the old words or notions or formulas. Somehow, I don't think anybody *liked* anybody else quite as much after that.

My mother wore nylons every day. She was a receptionist at the County Services office building in downtown Omaha. "Nylons are something I've just got to budget for, just one of the hidden expenses of working," she would say. That and her Max Factor makeup and a row of different color pumps, each to match a different outfit. When I'd kid her about the time she spent in front of the mirror, she'd tell me, "No matter how well I do my work, I still have to look a certain way or nobody's going to take me seriously." I didn't believe her then, but I've learned since exactly what she meant. She worked for the County from two years before my father took off until 1984 when she retired. Twenty-eight years. Many, many nylons.

The last time I saw her alive, last year at Christmas, she'd taken to letting her nylons roll down around her ankles like folds of useless skin, not unlike the way my grandmother, her mother, had done in the hot Nebraska summers before air conditioning. I hate the way old women do that—wear their nylons rolled down.

Starkweather had a girlfriend. The first bodies discovered were her parents and her baby sister, dead in the chicken house on their farm outside Lincoln. She was only fourteen, four years older than I was. She went with him on the rest of what everybody came to call a killing spree. I don't think I'd ever heard that phrase before then. People debated about what to do with her because she was so young. They argued all over the state about when a child becomes an adult, for purposes of punishment.

Whether it's true or not, the thing I remember is that a gas station attendant from Fairbury swore she came into his station and bought a candy bar while Starkweather gassed up. People figured she should have run away then, should have been crying—instead of eating a candy bar. She spent thirty years in the State Penitentiary. They let her out finally in the eighties after she'd become very religious and changed her name. I remember seeing a photo of her right before her release—my mother sent me a clipping in the mail—and she looked like a different woman entirely. Without the incident of the candy bar, I think she could just as easily have received an outpouring of sympathy for the loss of her family. When I was a kid, that candy bar, the kind we all ate without thinking, the idea of that candy bar, haunted the hell out of me.

Sometimes I would watch my mother dressing and undressing, putting on and taking off her nylons that were like a thin, fine armor, like a second skin that could somehow protect her during her workday. Sometime after Starkweather, after that Christmas when I got the parka and she gave my father's slippers and robe to the Disabled American Veterans, I quit watching her. We became modest around each other, as mothers and sons should. The bathroom in the duplex we lived in had two doors,

5

one to her bedroom and one to the hall. We began closing both doors, which was a pain because so often she hung her nylons across the top of the doors to dry. I bought her stockings that Christmas though, silk ones the clerk at Kilpatricks said would make any woman feel like a queen. I did it partly as a peace offering. And I believe it worked because we never talked about that night in October. Although I did think about it again when I saw those damn nylons rolled down around her ankles last year, just months before she died.

Starkweather could have killed my father. Before his execution, he told several different stories about who he killed and where. He was convicted for only one out of the ten murders on his spree, because that's the way those things are done. Sometimes he said his girlfriend had done some of the killing, other times not. He even confessed to an eleventh murder, a traveling salesman in a small town a few months earlier.

I knew it would just worry my mother if I mentioned it, but I remember lying in bed at night and wondering if maybe that's where my father had gone, finally. Maybe he hadn't abandoned us after all, or if he had, he'd really intended to come back, but instead he'd crossed paths with Starkweather, long before anyone knew to fear him so, and ended up in a shallow grave somewhere in rural Nebraska. And only now do I realize my mother could have thought of it, too, and not mentioned it to me for the same reason. People do that—withhold doubts and fears from the ones they love the most. Because so much is possible in the imagination.

My mother always called them realms. She'd say this or that wasn't "beyond the realm of possibility" or that something was possible only within "the realm of imagination." I pictured those realms like the idyllic kingdoms in children's books, green rolling hills with stone walls all around to keep the magic of possibility and imagination inside. And within those realms, my mother's realms, it's just possible, even now, to imagine that the last thing Starkweather thought about, what he saw against the backdrop of the black hood, was the face of his first victim, the innocent face of my father.

I'm lucky. I've never seen anyone die, violently or otherwise. I've never seen a bad car wreck, or a knife fight, not even a dead body—until I saw my mother's. I wonder if down deep I hadn't always thought she would disappear as quietly as my father had, without leaving a trace, a shell, a husk. The service for her was quite large. My mother had made many friends as a lifelong receptionist; people I didn't know shook my hand and said she'd befriended them one day in 1972 or 1981 when they were down on their luck and waiting to see a caseworker or a social technician. My wife helped me get through the whole thing. It was much harder than I'd imagined; it made me feel more like a boy of ten again than a man of forty.

As stupid as I knew it was, I kept searching the faces of all the strangers at the funeral for a sign of my father, whom I was positive I would recognize, the way I recognize myself in the bathroom mirror even in the middle of the darkest night.

One of the hardest things was bringing the undertaker what he asked for—a set of clothes, the makeup she normally wore, the rings she'd taken off at the hospital. I couldn't stand the thought of going through her things at home so I went to a department store and bought everything. I don't know whether any of it was right. She probably ended up, beneath the mask of makeup, looking more like she'd looked in 1957 than 1987, since that's the way I always pictured her in my mind when I was far from home. I didn't go to see the coffin. I didn't want to see what bad choices I'd made or how awkwardly the undertaker had applied the Max Factor makeup I gave him. I also gave him, for her, a pair of the finest silk stockings money could buy.

Some things, I don't want to tell, not even to myself. But what's the point of lying? "Nothing that happens hasn't happened before and won't happen again." That's one of the few things my father said that I can still remember. What happened was, I used to touch myself with my mother's nylons when I first started doing that kind of thing. Sometime in those years, probably after Starkweather, I retrieved a couple of ruined ones from the trash and used them that way. I hid them in my room along with a ragged *Swank* magazine I found in a box of books my father left in the basement. To me, their soft touch was like the smooth skin of all the women in the magazine, all the women I imagined my father had known, all the women I believed I would someday come to love.

I envied my friends in the neighborhood who were Catholic. During their confessions on Saturday afternoons, as early as fourth grade, the Father at Our Lady of Lourdes started asking them about touching themselves. They would laugh about it later, or bitch about it, making fun of the priest's euphemisms and admonishments, but I thought they were lucky. To have somebody to talk with about it, to have somebody let them know what they were doing wasn't new at all, to be given such a clear, simple way to feel guilty about it.

I had to verify her signature on dozens of different papers. The will was notarized and fairly complete, but there were other forms, insurance and such, and the undertaker took me by surprise when he showed me the organ donor release forms she'd filled out shortly before she died. It was her signature, I was sure, always so neat and precise, a thing she took such simple pride in, but still, I stared at it so long that he asked me if something was wrong. I guess it fit the kind of person she was, but she'd never mentioned the idea, ever, as far as I could recall, and it made me question how much I may have never known about her.

My signature is messy, flamboyant, hard to read—like my father's. I still have a ham radio license from '55 that has his signature scrawled across the back. I've often wondered how it is we ever come by an actual signature, something so recognizable and confidently repeatable. I've also wondered if he's still a ham operator, if he's living somewhere, broadcasting late-nights to people in trouble or to other faraway, lonely hobbyists. I try to guess what his call letters might be.

Thirty years is a long time until you remember something vital. Then it can get closer than what you ate for breakfast two hours ago. Whether it's true or not, I remember Starkweather and his girlfriend were still killing people in Nebraska in the week before Halloween. After the girl's family were murdered, everybody had assumed the couple would take off and go as far and fast as they could. But one week later, a family in Lincoln, along with their maid, were found dead. The whole state panicked. People armed with shotguns and deer rifles picked up their children at school. Schools closed. Halloween was canceled—not in so many words, but all up and down our block, everybody quit talking about it, acted as if it were already over. My mother gave me some of the candy she'd bought for trick-or-treaters. She said I could have part of it early since she didn't want me to count on going out this year. That night I started eating those little bite-size candy bars right after dinner.

I had no idea how afraid she was. When a TV bulletin said there were no new leads in the Starkweather case, she said, "At least I'm glad your father's name is still listed in the phone book. I'm glad I left it on the mailbox," but I didn't really understand that. I think that's when I got the idea of scaring her, though—when she mentioned Father. He'd always been a joker around the house, jumping out from behind doors or pretending to fall dead in front of Mother or me or sometimes both of us. We'd laugh about how he always fell on the couch or the bed. I recalled the one time he'd scared my mother by pulling a nylon over his face and making strange noises, on a night when they'd both been drinking some. When I thought of that, Mother was in the bathroom and one of her nylons had fallen on the hallway

9

floor. I pulled it over my head. I turned the living room light off. When I turned the TV down, she called out from the bathroom. I began to realize this probably wasn't going to be funny, not with Starkweather and all, but I'd already begun. I didn't answer her.

I stood in the hall, waiting. She opened the door and began to step toward me and I raised my hands. She jumped back and screamed with a watery sound in her voice. I saw right away I was wrong to have done it—her face went as white as the bathtub behind her. She slammed the door in my face. All she screamed was "Ralph," my father's name, and mine, although until the day I left home I was always Ralphie to her. She screamed it three times, each one less loud than the one before, the last two from behind the closed door. I stood there in my nylon mask, afraid of the way she'd looked, of what she'd said. The house seemed darker than it had before. My mother was silent in the bathroom. I called to her, apologized the way a boy will. "Mother, I'm sorry, it was just a joke, are you OK? I'm sorry." I said this several times, I'm sure. I could think of nothing else. I knocked on the door. I wondered if she'd had a heart attack, if she was crying. I suddenly felt pity for her, maybe the first time I'd ever felt pity like that, pity that somehow included myself. Pity because her husband had run out on her and because even the neighborhood didn't seem safe and because her son was a stupid kid with no sense. I started to work the nylon off.

The light under the bathroom door went out. I dropped my hands from my face as the door opened slowly. She stepped out at me. Her face was squashed and rumpled and bloated beneath the brown nylon. I screamed and ran for my bedroom, feeling my own tears wetting the tight nylon mesh around my eyes. She followed me, making no sound. The small duplex seemed like a maze. Nothing was familiar. I lunged onto the bed face down as I heard her steps coming toward me. She switched on the bedroom light, and I rolled over to face whatever it was she had become, whatever I had made her into. The silent, misshapen head above my mother's nightgown floated across the room and towered over me. In the light, I forced myself to look at her. I knew it was her eyes—I knew they were still the same clear blue even behind the dirty gauze of nylon. I stared at them, shivering, my teeth chattering. "Stop, stop," I cried. She wouldn't. She leaned over and put her face on mine. Inside, I felt as ugly and deformed as our faces. She made a loud smacking sound as she kissed me on the mouth through the two layers of nylon. "Starkweather," I raved at her as I pushed her away, "Starkweather."

She pulled the nylons off, first from my head and then hers. She turned every light in the house on and turned the TV up loud. But she didn't come back in my room that night. I kept expecting she would comfort me, somehow, but what could she have done? I fell asleep alone. The next week, on a Tuesday morning, two Wyoming highway patrolmen caught Starkweather and his girlfriend just across the Nebraska state line. The papers said they took them without a struggle.

When I sit and think about it, I believe I can force it to be simple: I love my mother and I cried when she died. I fear Starkweather and was glad when they killed him. I hate my father and don't care if he's dead or not. It could all be as easy as that. And if I say it that way, maybe more than once, maybe it can be, perhaps it will begin to be. Because so much is possible in the imagination.

The day after her funeral, before we flew out of Omaha, while my wife and daughter recuperated at the Sheraton, I went back to the old neighborhood. I walked past the duplex where we'd lived the year my father left and Starkweather reigned, the place where I'd learned about fear. I roamed over to Hanscom Park, only a couple of blocks away—so much looked the same. I thought of picnics with my mother in the summers after

Starkweather. She and I'd come over to the park after she got home from work and cook hot dogs or eat cold cuts with iced tea. Even then she'd wear her nylons with summer sandals, and sometimes a lone man would give her a long look, the kind I was yearning to understand.

As I walked through the park, I imagined my father's fine suede jacket for the first time in years, the one my mother had splurged to buy for him, the one with the soft, velvety nap I'd loved to write my initials in. I strolled out into the old baseball field, reliving those great and silly summer games I'd played there. Tall, dark clouds were banking up off to the east, promising relief from the humid April afternoon. I made straight for the very center of center field, as far from a tree or building as I could get, watching those clouds arrange and rearrange themselves beneath my gaze.

Seven

THE LAKE SHORE LIMITED was two hours behind schedule, lurching through the mirror-dark landscape of western New York, halfway between Syracuse and Rochester. Madeline Kross braced her knee against the rough fabric of the fold-down couch in the small roomette and paused, a lipstick tube poised an inch from her lips, until the train settled down again into a rhythm she could predict. Her shade of choice was Berry Passion, strawberry with just a hint of purple.

Madeline and Mitchell, her husband of six and a half years, had gone to the coast for a late September getaway, and they'd spent half the week's vacation at Fenway Park watching a White Sox/Red Sox four-game series. She'd accused him of planning the trip around the series, but he swore it wasn't so. The trip had been pretty much a failure, and Madeline was beginning to feel the same about the marriage in general, her third. The only time Mitchell had gotten even remotely passionate was in the back

13

seat of a Checker taxi, returning to the hotel after the second game of a doubleheader, the only game the White Sox won all week, a 3-2 cliff-hanger that Mitchell kept calling an old-fashioned pitchers' duel.

Poetic justice, she said to herself, thinking about the marriage, poetic justice in action. She'd married Mitchell for his money—he owned a pizza franchise in Chicago—and he'd proceeded to slowly but steadily lose it through a sequence of bad business moves in competition with the national chains—each loss compounding the ones before it. Like a bullheaded poker player who wouldn't push back from the table, he'd lost hand after hand until his franchise was whittled down to only two stores, one of which he had to manage himself, twelve hours a day, six days a week. But Madeline took some comfort in the fact that at least she'd been honest—she'd made no bones about the fact that she married Mitchell because of his money. She'd told him as much: that she liked him but wasn't in love, that she wanted security and luxury more than anything else. Mitchell, on the other hand, hadn't been honest.

He'd never said that he married Madeline for her breasts, but within months of the wedding he'd made it abundantly clear. He'd told her he'd been obsessed with them, that they were the most beautiful he'd ever seen, that he knew from the start that he had to possess them. The nicest thing he ever said about her breasts was on their wedding night—he'd cupped his hands under them from behind and whispered that he felt he was riding the back of a beautiful bird: he said her smooth curves made him feel as free as the wind.

The meanest thing he ever said was one night about a year later when he was drunk and they were arguing about money. He said he would've married the wicked witch of the west if she'd had tits like Madeline's.

Well, now they were gone, too, just like Mitchell's money. Victims of the surgeon's knife, Madeline said to herself, feeling cynical in a bittersweet way. She closed her eyes, and for just a

moment she pictured her breasts buried in a green shady graveyard marked by two white granite stones streaked with moss.
The image startled her—its originality made her leery of the
depths within her. And yet intrigued: what else might she un-
cover there? She let herself imagine more: an entire graveyard
just for body parts—arms and legs, stomachs and spleens, hands
and hearts. Why not? They had them for pets, for Christ's sake.
And her breasts were a damn sight more important than any
cocker spaniel.

Life. Isn't. Fair. Madeline.

She spoke it aloud with her mother's unfailing intonation, an
ominous down-sliding sound that always ended on Madeline's
own name, as if she and the name that stood for her were all the
proof needed for such a depressing proposition. No, but some
of us can at least tell when it's ironic, she thought, answering her
mother in her mind as she never had in person. She eased the
eyeliner across her lower eyelid in one careful swirl, twisting the
brush at the end of the stroke.

Someone knocked on the metal roomette door, four loud
hollow clicks—an insistent, imperial sound. For a second,
Madeline hoped it wouldn't be Mitchell. But she knew it was.
Who else could it be?

In the lounge car, they sat at a table with two brothers from
Chicago, Arthur and Lee Trescent, who were returning from
their half-sister's funeral in Albany. They looked to be the only
people in the car of an age with Mitchell and Madeline, and
Mitchell seemed happy to talk to hometown people, until the
point in the conversation when both brothers denied ever hearing of his pizza stores, something Mitchell didn't seem willing to
believe.

Madeline was pretty sure Lee was making eyes at her while
they smoked and drank. He was broad-shouldered, and he acted
confident in spite of a strange round reddish scar—about the size
of a quarter—on his left cheek. She watched him from behind

15

as he went to the lounge bar. He didn't carry anything in his back pockets.

By midnight a large collection of tiny empty bourbon bottles spread out from the center of the table, nearly half of which had been Mitchell's. When Arthur tried to explain how perfect the light, thin rain had seemed to him during the service in Albany, they all began to tell funeral stories, round robin, one after another. After each story they'd drink a toast with their plastic glasses raised: to the living, to the dead, to the people whose names you could remember, to the ones whose names you'd forgotten. It seemed to Madeline that the stories supposed to be funny turned out sad, and the ones meant to be sad got the biggest laughs. Mitchell told about his great aunt's funeral in Detroit when the body had been put face down in the coffin and the viewers saw only the back of her head. That was one of the funny ones that turned out sad—Mitchell almost cried talking about an aunt Madeline had never even heard of. Madeline's turn caught her thinking about her mother, about the awful months after she'd refused the same kind of operation Madeline had later survived, about her funeral on a clear sunny day in April, a day so beautiful it was hard to mourn or pretend to mourn, about the small sparrows that flitted among the nearby gravestones, chirping over the minister's drone. But instead she told about the group services for four of her high school classmates who died in a convertible on graduation night in June of '65, in Topeka, Kansas. They'd arranged the four coffins in the school gym in the shape of a cross and held the funeral for all of them together. Madeline remembered how utterly useless the glass backboards and fragile nets had looked to her, drifting above all the black suits and dresses.

After his sixth bourbon, when it had become obvious to everybody at the table that Lee had an eye for Madeline, Mitchell asked Lee what happened to his face.

Lee laughed. He laughed too long, long enough to make everyone uncomfortable. It was the end of the funeral stories.

. . .

"Cigarette lighter," he said finally.

"You're shitting me," Mitchell said.

"He could be, but he's not," Arthur said.

Madeline stared at Lee. She decided it was his knee she felt pressing lightly against hers under the small table. Not Mitchell's.

"Car accident," Lee said. "One weekend when I was up to Milwaukee visiting an old girlfriend. I was lighting my cigarette, and some eighteen-year-old fuckup—pardon my French, Madeline—some young kid broadsided us at a four-way stop. The lighter burned into my cheek."

"That's horrible," Madeline said, trying to imagine the pain. For just a second she wanted to tell about her operation, about what she'd been through in the two years since, tell everything: how she sometimes felt that she'd had to have her mother's operation, literally. As if her mother's refusal had consigned it to Madeline, unavoidably, no matter the number of years intervening. Mitchell never wanted to talk about the operation. Whenever the subject got close, he'd say the same rehearsed thing: "It's a terrible weight to bear, but what's done is done." As if Madeline intended to ask him to fix her somehow, make her whole again. Yet to give him his due, he'd also told her he'd stay right by her side, that he wouldn't abandon her just because of what she'd lost. She believed he was scared to death by what had happened to her—and her mother—even though it could never happen to him.

"Not so horrible," Lee said. "Not so much. I was lucky. No broken bones, nothing except a brand on my cheek. Circle O. Marlboro country." He laughed again, and the burn mark almost disappeared in the crease of his cheek.

"The girlfriend died," Arthur said.

"Could you zip your mouth for once, Art," Lee said.

Madeline poised to jab Mitchell in the ribs if he asked anything else, but he let it go. He went to the bar. She watched him. He was weaving a little. He carried a fat handkerchief and a thick wallet in his back pockets.

Instead of returning to their table, he sat down at a table nearer to the bar with three college kids who were playing some sort of trivia game with cards and who sounded, from where Madeline sat, as drunk as Mitchell. She turned to the window. She saw the silhouette of a lone tractor. It was parked in the middle of a huge plowed field as if it had been abandoned in a hurry. Then it disappeared.

"You know what Alicia believed," Arthur said. The two brothers were arguing. Madeline hadn't been listening.

"Our recently departed half-sister," Lee said to Madeline.

"Alicia said God never gives anybody more that they can bear at one time." Arthur looked sincere; it was clear he agreed with Alicia, that her truth was one that comforted him. Madeline saw how unalike the two brothers were.

"Alicia, rest her soul, was full of baloney sauce," Lee said. "That's what people with cancer always say. What do you expect? I never did buy that line. Suppose there is a God—why would he waste his time giving and taking to us little people fuming around down here, weighing and balancing the good and the bad like a butcher at the meat market. No, all the giving and taking is left up to us. From one person to the next." He put his drink down slowly.

"What do you think, Mrs. Kross?" Arthur asked.

"I think there is a God," Madeline said, sounding less emphatic than she'd wanted to. "I don't want to believe we waste his time."

"There," Arthur said, spreading his fingers on the table. "You would have liked Alicia. Right up to the end she had her faith. She said we don't always deserve what we get, but we get what we deserve."

"Now that," Madeline said, "I'm not so sure I do understand." She looked at Lee's scar. He was staring at her chest. Before, she'd always liked it when men looked her over—it had

18

made her feel proud and powerful—but since the operation it unnerved her. She felt Lee could look right through her blouse and see the polystyrene pouches nestled in her bra.

"But I'm sure she was a good person. I'm sorry for both of you."

"Thank you," Arthur said.

"People take what they deserve, Mrs. Kross," Lee said, mimicking his brother's formality. He was still staring at her. Madeline thought of her second husband, the boyish gleam in his eye that he never could hide. He would be what now?—fifty?—wherever he was. Would she still recognize that gleam? Could it have survived this long?

Mitchell started yelling, two tables away. "What number was Mickey Mantle?" He turned around toward the other end of the car and yelled the same question. "These young peckers don't know Mantle's number." He turned back to the kids. "You all ought to go back to school."

Everyone in the lounge car turned to look. Mitchell's face was red, and he was waving his arm around. His cigarette had an inch-long ash on it that wouldn't drop off.

"I'll give a ten-dollar bill to the man who can tell me what number Mickey Mantle was. I can't believe this bullshit." The teenagers all laughed. He pulled his wallet out.

"So who's Mickey Mantle?" one of the kids yelled.

"Minnie Mantle's husband," another answered.

Mitchell looked like he was going to have a stroke. If Madeline knew nothing about him, she knew that baseball was the most sacred thing in his life. He'd told her that some mornings when he read the paper, he wouldn't be able to tell he was in the same damn country he'd grown up in, if it wasn't for baseball. It was all we had left, he said.

"Mickey Mantle," Mitchell said, addressing the whole car like a drunken preacher, "Mickey Mantle just happened to be the best all-around man who ever played the great American game of baseball." He licked his lips, his eyes racing from face to face. Madeline tried to catch his attention but saw he needed something she couldn't give him. She was ashamed of him, for him, and yet at the same time she felt a kind of love for him pulling at something inside her, insistent as a riptide. Everything important was beyond explanation.

"Mitchell," she said, "let's get back to our room."

"You go back," he yelled, "I'm not moving until somebody can tell me what number Mickey Mantle was. Is this America or not here? I'm asking you, is this train in goddamn Siberia?"

"If you know his number, why don't you tell us," said another of the kids whose card game Mitchell had crashed.

"You bet your sweet hope I know," Mitchell said, swinging around. "I know his number, his career stats, his birth date—"

"Three thousand." A guy from a different table joined in. "Number three thousand. Remember? They had to give him that extra-wide hat to get it all on."

"You people really don't know, do you," Mitchell said, in a lower tone, "you really don't remember Mickey Mantle at all."

"Yaz is Number Eight," said a guy with a Boston accent.

Mitchell sat down on the floor as if it had just dawned on him that he was the butt of the joke.

"Here, take my seat, partner," Arthur said, helping Mitchell back to the table. "I'm done in, anyway."

"Can I walk you back to your car, Madeline?" Lee said, standing up. "Looks like your husband's going to have to wait for a true sports fan to show up." He winked, and she was positive that he remembered Mickey Mantle perfectly well.

She didn't answer him. He and Arthur went up the stairs.

Mitchell put his head down on the table, the money still in his fist. When Madeline tried to move him, he pulled his hand in, as if she'd been trying to grab the money.

"Tell me," he said, his whisper hoarse, angry.

"Mitch, c'mon, you're making a fool of both of us."

"You don't know from fools," he said. "Leave me alone."

She waited a minute or two until conversation picked up at the other tables and then went back toward the roomette alone.

Two coaches down, Lee stood in the vestibule between cars.

"No Mitchell?" he asked.

"He wanted to stay."

"This is my favorite place on the train," he said.

"Oh?"

"Aren't you going to ask me why?"

"It's just ironic—it's my least favorite place."

"Well then, let me ask you why." He smiled. "Why?"

Madeline saw something like Arthur's politeness in his face.

"All right," she said. "Number one—it's the noisiest."

"You're right there, but it's not noise to me, it's music."

"And number two—it's the most dangerous."

"How so? You believe those warning signs? Bah, they just want people inside where they can count their noses after every stop."

"If there were a wreck or derailment, a person could get crushed out here. The cars would press right together."

"Never thought of it. Anything else I should worry about?"

"And what if they disconnected? The ground would go right out under our feet."

"Like one of those big round barrel rides at the carnival, huh? I used to take my girlfriend on those rides. Know what I did whenever she got scared?"

"No."

Lee moved to her quickly and put his hands behind her waist. He brought his head down to hers and his scar went out of focus. Madeline kissed him back. He lowered his hands and pulled her tight against him. She let herself go, just for a little longer she told herself, just for a minute. She felt his wallet in his jacket coat against her chest. She let one of her hands slide down behind him, too. With his hand on her leg, he hooked a thumb under her skirt and started to raise it up. They were in the dark corner of the vestibule. Madeline held his hand back. He put the other hand on her chest, softly rotating his palm. Madeline panicked, sure he would notice, but his breath got thicker and heavier. Mitchell would never touch her there, but then, Mitchell knew the truth. She felt herself excited by the fact that this strange man was aroused by nothing more than his own expectations. When he took her top blouse button between his thumb and index finger, Madeline pushed herself away, enforced a space between them. Then an arm's length.

"What's the matter?"

"Everything. I don't know you. I don't like it here. Mitch could come by any minute. Or a conductor." In the back of her mind she was imagining the possibility of letting this man have her, somewhere on the train. Maybe, if they kept their clothes on, he'd never notice. And she'd never see him again. But she wasn't sure who he was. Not a name—that never told you anything—but the kind of man he was.

"You're not a prick-tease, are you, Mrs. Kross?"

She took another step back. "I hate that term."

"If the shoe fits."

She stepped toward the door. He put an arm up on the metal wall on both sides of her, backing her into the corner.

"Hey, it doesn't take a genius to know when a woman wants something, and just what it might be. You've got too beautiful a body to let it go to waste. You know about train love, sweetheart?"

She didn't speak. She felt threatened and tried to decide how not to make a bad situation any worse.

"Well then, let me tell you. You snuggle up under a blanket in a big double seat like a couple of teenagers in heat and just let the train rock and roll you all the way to heaven. Why go back to Chicago empty-handed?"

"I'm going back to Chicago with my husband, who is probably headed this way right this minute."

"Like I said. Empty-handed."

"You're a very rude man."

He backed away from her.

"I don't ever force a woman."

Madeline stepped toward the door. "How reassuring."

"You really love that guy?"

"I didn't say that. In our own way. We do. I do."

"So why not give him a little present?"

"And what would that be?" She stood at the door, her hand on the press button, ready for another vulgar comment.

Lee smiled again, the polite, friendly look back on his face.

"Mantle's number."

"You knew the whole time, didn't you?"

"Any man Mitchell's and my age would know. I grew up thinking Mickey Mantle was some kind of god."

"So tell me."

He leaned closer again, and Madeline knew something else about him. "That accident was your fault, wasn't it?" She nodded toward his scar.

"Aren't we all shrewd tonight? I told you, I was broadsided. You want the number to make Mister Baseball happy or not?"

She did want it. It was a small thing that had gotten big, had become vital the way only small things can.

"Yes."

Lee whispered in her ear, a wet sound. "Let us have a little first." He touched his finger to her skin right above the top button of her blouse. "Do it for drunk old Mitchell. Let it be his fault."

She stared at him through ice, disgusted, wondering what kind of weak women he could have ever been involved with. And how badly he must have hurt them.

"You tell me first."

Lee grinned. His vanity was shining from his eyes, blind but visible. He bent and whispered the number. She disappeared into the next coach without looking back.

• • •

Behind the locked roomette door, Madeline waited. When she looked out the window, she saw faces swelling up from the black landscape. She closed the curtains. After thirty minutes, Mitchell hadn't returned.

She went back to the lounge, hurrying across each dark vestibule, but she didn't see Lee again.

Mitchell wasn't where she'd left him.

She watched until she saw people come out of both lounge bathrooms. Then she went to the next car, checking the empty coach seats. She went downstairs and knocked on the bathroom doors, calling his name.

He was sprawled on the floor in the oversize bathroom, the one equipped for the handicapped, gripping the fat stainless steel railing next to the toilet.

"Madeline? That you? I lost my wallet, honey."

"What? How?"

"I don't remember. Somebody took it. Or it's down there."

He pointed down the stool next to him. Madeline looked. It was empty. She pushed the flush button with her foot and heard the train's loud rhythm on the rails, as if she'd opened a door on the naked sound of the world's machinery.

"Mitch, we've got to get you back to the room. How much money?"

"I dunno. Lots. Maybe three hundred. More. I dunno."

"Traveler's checks, dammit. I've asked you so often. Nobody carries cash anymore."

"*He* would've. A real man keeps his money with him."

"Who? Lee?"

"Mickey Mantle. The man nobody goddamn remembers. It's like he never even lived. Like I never lived. Am I alive, Madeline?"

She looked down at the top of his head, full of pity and terror at what we become, how quickly the mask slips off in the dead of the night.

"You're alive, Mitchell. You're on a train with your wife going home to Chicago. Let me help you."

Mitchell leaned against the wall outside the roomette while Madeline made down the bed. She pushed him inside onto the bed and undressed him. He was right. His wallet was gone. She opened her traveler's checks. She had one fifty left.

Right before he rolled over to sleep, his eyes cleared. He stared straight at Madeline, kneeling next to him with her clothes on.

"He played every day of his life in constant pain."

"Mantle? Why, what was the matter with him?"

"Right from day one. Pain, and more pain. He had class, Madeline. Like you."

She kissed his ear, her touch light, reassuring—a mother's kiss, she was sure, although she'd never been one. She whispered the number Lee had told her.

Mitchell closed his eyes and smiled. He rolled toward the window.

She pulled the curtains back. She didn't feel afraid anymore.

"In heaven," Mitchell mumbled, as Madeline stepped into the hall and closed the door. "In heaven."

The coach car was almost dark—only one small reading light on in the middle and a running light at either end. Arthur slept about a third of the way back, his face in his hands. She scanned the sleeping passengers around him, readying herself for Lee. He'd seemed just malicious enough to have taken Mitchell's money, whether he needed it or not: He hadn't stopped the scene in the lounge car when he could have—he'd tried to seduce another man's wife. Maybe that was all she'd been in his eyes the whole evening, an easy trophy in an endless war of male humiliation. Well, you've handled drunken bozos like this before, she told herself. It was the vestibule that had frightened her so much, that had made her so confused and vulnerable earlier. Not the man.

25

He was asleep alone in the last seat, a blanket wrapped around him from just under his arms to just below his knees. His shoes were off, and he had a hole in the toe of one sock. Madeline stood over him, her feet set wide against the swaying of the train. She stared at him, trying to wake him with will alone— she didn't want to touch him. So this was the fabulous seat of ecstasy he'd promised her: a tired-looking man with a strange scar and bad memories, wrapped in a cheap blanket—with nothing but dreams for comfort. It was no wonder people were desperate to take tiny moments of pleasure wherever they could.

His sport coat was folded beside him. She picked it up and patted the pockets. Mitchell's wallet wasn't there—only Lee's. But Mitch's money might be in it. How would she know? She pulled it out.

"You're getting a little ahead of the game, aren't you?" Lee's eyes opened, but he didn't move. He watched Madeline holding his coat, his wallet. "If you want to play that part, you left out one big step."

"Somebody stole Mitchell's wallet tonight."

"Not me. Jesus. What do you take me for?"

Madeline dropped the coat and wallet back onto the seat. "I'm not what you think I am," she said, letting her arms fall to her side. The movement drew his eyes to her chest again. "Not at all."

"So that makes us even. All right? But you're here, for whatever reason. Maybe that means something." He reached his hand toward her, his palm upturned, the question still in his eyes.

Pantomime, she thought, charades—anything except the unending procession of words that never seemed to get two people any closer to the truth between them. What could he understand? A vision faded as fast as it arose: she saw herself handing him her pads, unbuttoning and filling his open hand with them before he could possibly imagine what she was do-

26

ing. Would he see them as payment of some kind, a strange twist in the down-to-earth, one-on-one taking and giving he'd been so willing to defend? Could he arrange them into the barstool stories of his life, like the Milwaukee girlfriend, the circular scar?

Lee dropped his hand and turned his face to the window. She stared at his reflection. They knew as much about each other at this moment as they would ever know. And that was fine. That happened all the time.

She walked away down the aisle, her hands grazing the seatbacks on either side of her as if she were blessing each sleeping passenger, as if she had that much power, generosity. She was thinking that she wasn't really the same woman who'd boarded the train in Boston, nothing like the one who'd let her mother belittle her out of the house into the first of a string of unlucky marriages. Nothing like that.

Madeline lay awake in the dark, working the buttons of her blouse slowly, feeling the tips of her nails and her fingers as they delicately worked against each other, unbuttoning as carefully as if she were taking apart an elaborate and fragile puzzle someone had sent her from far away. She scooped a pad from each side of her bra and held them in her hands, as limp and helpless as baby rabbits. She put them on the bed between her and Mitchell and understood for the first time in two years—at least for a moment: there was only one loss per lifetime. And all the ones that seemed so separate flowed together within it, like an ocean with its bays and sounds. She turned to the window and gazed across Mitchell's back into the sliding night.

She saw a movement she at first wouldn't recognize.

Three snow geese settled into a vee next to and just above the window, so close that Madeline felt that if the window were open she could almost touch them. Too close, she thought, to the hard speeding steel of the train. But they seemed unconcerned, flapping their strong wings in a steady, synchronized

rhythm, keeping easy pace with the train. From the distant lo-
comotive, the train's whistle rippled backward to her, as if all
the unfair irony in the world had been condensed into one ele-
gant, muted sound.

She clutched her hands to her chest, frightened, but not for
herself, for Mitchell, for Mitchell and the geese, alone and asleep
in the darkness on separate sides of the glass. She closed her eyes
and looked inside. It was the only way to make them never
disappear.

Babyman

AT THE POCKET INN on Detroit's North Side, the crowd thins out after midnight. Carroll Spark carries a five-month-old baby girl, his unnamed daughter, across the icy parking lot. She's wrapped in a little pink parka he scored at the Goodwill. The girl sleeps, a bottle nestled in the parka next to her. But if she wakes up, so much the better. The game is better if the baby cries.

It's smoky inside the Pocket. Carroll edges up to the bar, stands next to a platinum blonde in black jeans and high-heeled boots. He orders a screwdriver. When Carroll sets the baby on the counter, the blonde turns around to face him. Too small. He looks away.

He eyes two gals across the room. A brunette with a big nose and chest and a pretty redhead with hoop earrings. He walks around the bar as if he's looking intently for someone, holding the baby in front of him like a shield or a badge.

Ignoring the women, he stations himself close enough for them not to be able to ignore him. He reaches into the parka, pinches the baby's bottom. Several people look over when she cries.

Carroll fidgets as if trying to calm the baby. Inside the parka he pinches her again.

It's the brunette who bites first. Carroll plays the bars like a fisherman working a stream.

"What a little sweetheart," she says. "What's the matter with you, honey?"

As the brunette reaches out, Carroll hands her the baby, as if that's what they both had intended. He catches the woman's eye and shows her a bland, even smile. Not even a hint of a threat.

Carroll knows his features are even, his brown hair full and fine. Even the deep lines across his forehead are smooth and symmetrical. But he worries that his ears and his lips are too big and too red.

The baby stops crying. The woman smiles. Carroll grins back, as if this sudden three-way happiness is a little trophy he's earned. Something to take home and keep.

The redhead goes home alone. Carroll and Joleen leave the Pocket in Carroll's van. Tonight he calls the baby Dianne.

Carroll stops at the Nite Owl Package Drive-Thru for a pint of vodka, a quart of orange juice, and a quart of whole milk. He gets on the Morton Expressway even though it's just for a mile. He likes to get above the city and see the rooftops and lights spread out in the distance. In the van, on the road, the city can play tricks with your mind. Get close enough, down on the streets, it looks like a huge, silent wrestling match, all grimaces and tears. Back way off, up on the freeway, it's like a cold stone tableau, like one of those friezes on the old buildings downtown, all finished up and dignified. He exits on Eisenbach and drives to the double garage he rents off the alley behind Gannal

Street. He drives down the alley for the last six blocks, easing the van over rough spots, steering around open dumpsters and abandoned cars.

Joleen doesn't seem to notice the freeway or the alley. She stares at the baby on her lap and talks about her job—factory work at Campbell's, the Banquet division. She runs a machine that plops peas and potatoes into trays from three to eleven, five days a week. She plays with the baby, saying "peas and potatoes, peas and potatoes," as she touches the little face. Carroll can already tell she's never had a kid. But wanted to.

The way Carroll tells it to Joleen, the baby's mother is a real scumbag. He's trying to get her back, he says, but she's strung out, and he only sees her by luck in the bars. He's waiting for her to come to her senses, come back to him and baby Dianne. It's almost beautiful what a crock of shit most people are dying to believe in. Almost beautiful.

In the garage, Carroll opens all the van's doors. He puts Eddie Money's first album in the van's cassette player, his only sound system. The room smells stale, like something dirty's been burning. Carroll twists open the round orange air freshener stuck on the refrigerator door. Joleen sits on the couch against the far wall while Carroll mixes screwdrivers for both of them.

"Healthiest drink there is. Plenty of C. And no beer breath. Even baby Dianne likes 'em." He laughs like he's teasing. A sip or two really does quiet the kid down at night though.

"You're terrible. And she's such a cutie pie." Joleen juggles her screwdriver in an oversize plastic Dixie cup while she holds the baby's bottle. "You're raising her all by yourself? Here?"

She looks around the garage. In one corner stands a big oil-drum wood stove, with concrete blocks stacked up all around it that can hold the heat a long time. Carroll burns garbage from up and down the alley. He could buy firewood—he's got a decent job—but he likes to scavenge. He's a security guard downtown, same place for years. Routine's good for a person. And

Carroll lives cheap. Some of his money he sends to southern California where his first child lives with his first and last ex-wife. The kid's in high school now. Damn expensive—that age, that place. Cars, clothes, CDs, drugs. Not like when they're babies. Milk and diapers are all they really need, as long as they're healthy. The garage is well insulated, not too cold in winter, not too hot in summer.

"I don't know what else to do. I'm so in debt from the drug clinic where I sent her mama." He points at the baby, still in Joleen's arms. "They want a small fortune for treatment. And she was in there all day every day for thirty days. It's like a god-damn taxi meter clicking, that's what treatment is. I went to twelve-step meetings with her till I saw those twelve steps in my dreams. I really felt we had it licked. Now look at me." Carroll waves an open palm slowly around the room.

A carpet covers the half of the garage floor where the van doesn't park. It's rolled across the floor and then right up the wall behind them and nailed down near the ceiling. In one corner, there's a crib. Above it hangs a delicate mobile, little pastel balls so light they move when someone walks by. Carroll conjures a tear. Joleen kisses it.

Carroll pulls away from Joleen and rolls over in the bed. He starts to move toward the crib. Joleen hugs him to her.

"Hope I didn't wake Dianne up with my hollering," she says with a new tone of intimacy to her voice. "Haven't you finished yet? Is there something wrong?"

"No, nothing wrong, baby, just something missing. You want to satisfy me, don't you?" He nuzzles his head between her breasts. The right one seems slightly smaller.

"Sure, Carroll, I'm just tired. You gotta give a gal some breathin' room. That's all. You need some special TLC from Joleen?"

"I need the baby." He moves to the crib in the half-dark room. "Feed us, honey," he says as he gets back in bed. "Feed us both." He nudges the baby's head toward Joleen's ample left nipple. The baby's mouth slides around her breast. Carroll squeezes out milk from a plastic bottle all around the baby's mouth. Some babies fall for it, some don't. Carroll takes his chances.

"I don't have what she needs," Joleen says as she starts to pull away from them. "Really, Carroll, I don't."

"It don't matter," he mutters as he kisses at her other breast and pushes the bottle into her hand. "It don't matter. You both got what I need."

Eddie Money begins Side Two for the third time. Carroll watches the baby's lips work on Joleen like a fish mouth, feeding, trembling, at the bottom of a pool of clear water. He hopes Joleen doesn't say anything, doesn't wreck it with words, doesn't argue, or laugh. All of his own words slide out of his head until it's just him, him and the baby, alone together with a woman.

Then he hears Joleen. She does what most people would call crying, what Carroll would call crying at any other time and place. She does it quietly, holds two heads close to her, opens her legs again.

People do things. Things you'd never expect. That's what makes it interesting. Like a torture chamber. Like a symphony orchestra.

Carroll can get a woman pregnant, as long as certain conditions are met. Conditions like in the garage, the first night with Joleen, with the baby. And that's what he does—gets her pregnant. Women are like jackpots, he figures. You play 'em. There's skill and there's luck.

Skill was getting her home, getting her bedded. Luck was getting her pregnant. More luck was that she's pro-life. One hundred percent. Pregnant and pro-life. Bingo.

Skill will be getting the baby.

"Ever since I told you I'm PG you been actin' different to me," says Joleen. "I never shoulda been mixed up with you and

Dianne. If I hadn't been dog-tired that night and seen that sweet kid—you're cuckoo—they'll take that kid away from you, Carroll. They will. Less you marry me." She says it like she's trying to be mean and sweet at the same time, like she's trying to match the way she thinks Carroll is.

Carroll laughs. What she doesn't know. He's traded babies since '81. Leon, a friend on the city police, has connections. Bought and sold and traded. Out of downtown, into the suburbs. Out of the suburbs, over to the coast. Leon likes it, Carroll likes it, people uptown like it, people on the coast like it. Even the babies like it. Dianne, this little girl, wasn't a trade though. But she sure could be.

"The day Reagan was shot," Carroll says.

"What the hell you talking about. I'm serious, damn you."

"So am I. That was the first one I bought. My grubstake. Little boy. Blue-eyed."

"I don't want to hear this crap. Where's Dianne's mother?"

"It ain't no Dianne, and there ain't no mother. Except maybe you." In spite of himself, he smirks at her like a boy who's played a clever trick. "Maybe I just called her that 'cause you said you had a niece named Dianne that night down at the Pocket, remember?"

"Carroll, listen to me, dammit. Don't tease me. I'm pregnant, grade-A pregnant, no ifs, ands, or buts—I was at the clinic. We could make out together—I just know we could. Between the both of us, we got two jobs and a van. And Dianne."

Carroll has started polishing the leather pistol holster he wears at work. He whistles low. "Two Tickets to Paradise." Eddie Money.

"I said listen you mother, I loved you and that little kid just how you wanted even if it is damn near sick the way you . . . the way you do things."

Carroll points the empty holster at her. His ears are bright red. He licks his lips. He still doesn't answer.

"Look, it's common sense. I can't raise no kid on my pay.

Half my check'd go for day care. And you're gonna need help with Dianne before long."

Carroll puts his fat finger through the holster hole. Rubs it back and forth.

"Truth is," he says, pointing at her belly, "truth is, you're the one who's sick."

Watching a woman get desperate is its very own brand of fun. Like the old flicks with the villain who always has a railroad track handy and knows all the train schedules by heart. As long as you know you'll be there to untie the ropes before the train chugs through. To Carroll the trick is to be both the villain and the hero. Be your own damn movie. Hire your own actors.

Like Joleen.

She's over six months into it when baby Dianne disappears.

When she finds out, she throws a fit.

Dianne was getting too big to keep anyway, and Leon called in an IOU from a trade last year. That's what friends are for— especially downtown. Carroll knows in advance Joleen will freak. But without the baby, it means no real sex anyway. Carroll can go a long time between drinks of water. There'll always be another woman, as long as there's another baby. And vice versa. The game goes on and on.

At midnight he slips Dianne through the window of Leon's cruiser along with a little bag he's packed with some diapers and milk. Leon sets her carefully down on the passenger seat next to an upright double-barreled shotgun. He gives Carroll a thumbs-up and disappears down the alley.

Carroll waits till he's done missing baby Dianne himself before he sees Joleen again. Almost a month. Nobody should ever think Carroll don't care about the babies, too. He cares in the way they all just have to come and go, in the way there's so many of 'em and they're all so much alike. Almost a month. That's what makes him the babyman, deep down.

• • •

"Her mama took her back," Carroll says when Joleen asks about Dianne. "She moved to New York, they got better clinics there, she's gonna be a drug counselor while she keeps up with her own treatment. The drowning saving the drowning. That's the way things are, Joleen. The blind find the blind. Like you and me, honey, like you and me." He reaches toward her swollen belly. "Let me feel it kick again."

"Don't touch me or it. You told me so many stories I can't tell what to believe anymore. All I know is I can't stand up all day in that line much longer."

Carroll plays advocate for the devil.

"Is it too late for an operation, Joleen? I know you said you don't approve and all."

"It was too late one minute after you gave me this thing. I don't want it and you don't want it, but I sure as hell ain't gonna kill it. God moves in mysterious ways, Carroll."

"Damn if he don't. I gotta say I admire you there, Joleen, truly I do. Jesus, you're gorgeous."

It takes him almost an hour to calm her down enough to touch her.

They lie in bed. He rubs her feet where they're sore.

"Honey Joleen, my baby. I didn't know this would happen. You working so hard every day. Damn that factory—no maternity leave until after three years. What a bitch."

He watches her. He waits till her face relaxes.

"We just gotta make a plan, baby. I'm gonna say it slow one time so you know I ain't kidding. I'm not gonna marry you, sweetheart."

Joleen listens to the truth and the lies, all mixed up. Her eyes blur. Carroll sees she's learning. There's no good way to sort it out. You believe everything and get your heart broke time and again, or you believe nothing and your heart gets numb and sandy like a foot that's gone asleep. Carroll's proud of all he's figured for himself.

"I'm not marrying nobody, not ever again after the first time.

I got a boy in high school I ain't seen for five years. Carroll Jr."

Carroll traces a finger around the hollows of his earlobe. He can't remember if he's ever told Joleen about Carroll Jr.

"So that's that. But I respect that you got to be true to your feelings and have this baby, that's all there is to it. But then you get to start over." He pauses to let those words sink in.

"I'm past startin' over. I'm here in my niche. You know about niches?"

He waits for her to look in his eyes. "This city's got a million niches, and I'm in mine for the long haul. You just need a niche for yourself. You got plenty of chances left. Look, here's what we'll do. You take leave without pay, and I pay the bills for the next month, including the hospital. And then we go our own separate ways, simple as that, two people, two ways. OK?"

Joleen is doing it again, what she's learned so well at Carroll's place, that unnamed kind of crying. She'd have learned it somewhere anyway, Carroll figures. Just a way of being voiceless in the dark, a way of praying and cursing all at once, a way of making do with it.

"And the kid? What about the kid, Carroll."

"Baby'll be OK. I promise. I'll take the baby."

Carroll stays in the slow lane on the expressway. The van's out of alignment—it pulls off to the right. He thinks about Joleen in labor. He dropped her off at St. Luke's this afternoon. This is the worst part of the game even though it's the best part.

She was on the verge of screaming in the van, sweat on her forehead as thick as honey. A baby's on the way for sure. Carroll wonders where it will end up. Maybe in a plush living room in a house by the lakes, learning to walk on carpet as deep and thick as pelt. Two parents hovering around, loving it even more than usual because they had to buy it. That's real love.

He checks the gas gauge when he realizes he's on his third loop around the city. People are switching their headlights on.

On his way home Carroll drives by St. Luke's again. He remembers how mad his wife had been in West Covina when Carroll Jr. was coming and he'd taken off for two weeks. He double-parks in the hospital lot. He counts by heart the floors—one, two, three, four, five—fifth floor maternity. Room after room filled with women and babies, women with babies inside them, babies on top of them, girl babies who will have babies inside of them someday—Carroll thinks of those nesting egg toys that you just keep taking apart, one inside the other, each tinier than the one before.

And boy babies too—boys like Carroll Jr. and Carroll's little brother, the first baby he'd ever seen. When Carroll's father had brought him home from the hospital, the little red head poking out from the blanket, all wrinkled and indistinct, Carroll had thought it was a joke, as if somebody'd squeezed out the simplest features of a face in one of his dad's huge fists.

Somebody honks at Carroll and he looks away from the fifth floor windows. He puts the van in gear and says a private "so long" to Joleen, although he knows he'll see her at least one more time to get the baby.

On his police-band CB, he hears his friend Leon turn in a robbery call at a pharmacy a few blocks away. Carroll stops in his alley and collects some cardboard boxes out of a dumpster. Cardboard burns really hot.

Carroll goes to the passenger side of the van and lifts the baby boy he calls Joey out. It's a muggy summer night on the South Side. He gets a bottle of formula from the glove compartment and heads into Marcie's, a small tavern near the Midtown Glover Plant. His son cries all the time. It gets on Carroll's nerves.

He sets his face to look like a brand-new father—worried, distraught. What he doesn't know is that the expressions he tries for, ones he copies from TV shows, aren't ever quite the ones he gets. What shows now is a boyish kind of fear, a desperate look, mostly around his pale eyes.

The bar's pretty empty. He sits in a corner and sips a screwdriver beneath a neon electric guitar that says BUD. He gives Joey a bottle and waits for the swing-shift traffic.

A woman with no purse walks in, and Carroll hears her ask the bartender if that little prick Mickey has been in. The bartender says no and gives her a can of 7-Up before she asks. She's tall with thin, long legs and arms and neck, fine-boned, but with a bust like in the old days. She's got a light mustache or some sweat on her upper lip, but she looks like she doesn't care which or who wonders. She looks over at Carroll and his kid in the corner. Joey starts to fuss. As Carroll dabs at his face and picks him up, the woman comes over to them. It's sweat.

Her breasts are full and large beneath her cotton dress. Carroll shakes the hand she pokes in his face as she takes the baby. Her name is Dora Mattsen. Everybody just calls her Matty. Carroll tells her his name.

"Poor little kid, so hungry." Matty sniffs the bottle Carroll's been using and wrinkles her nose.

"You trying to kill the kid? Forget this sour stuff." She sets the plastic bottle on the table. "We know what this little fella needs, don't we." She bares a swollen, golden nipple and pulls Joey down to it. "Same as all of them need, young or old, eh?" She winks at Carroll. He sits back down, flushed.

When they leave, Matty carries Joey, still attached to her, and Carroll follows.

Matty directs Carroll to her place, a run-down fourplex on Mc-Nain that she manages in return for half her rent. They park in the driveway between two bikes and an oversize skateboard as big as a small sled. As they go in, Carroll sees a hand-lettered sign in the window. BLOCK HOME.

"What's the block home business, Matty?" Carroll makes small talk. He can't get an angle on how to sweet-talk her.

"What? Oh, kids can come in here. I'm always at home in the daytime—I run a little day care, the Johnson twins upstairs in number four and a couple of others. I got a sign up over at the Grimebuster Laundry. You'd be surprised—I have to turn people away."

"Yeah, I know, before Joey's mother ran out on us, she was having trouble even finding babysitters." He tries to look as if he's not really wanting sympathy.

"See if you can get a good picture," Matty says as she hands Carroll the remote control for the TV. "You may have to fiddle with it. Are you any good with your hands?" She disappears down the hallway with Joey.

Carroll looks at the TV. The VHF knob is broken off, and a piece of coat hanger is wired onto the rabbit ears. He goes to look for Matty. He didn't come here to play fix-it man.

He sneaks up behind her in the dark bedroom. He plans to show her just how good he is with his hands—that line was a come-on if he ever heard one. Just as he gets to her, she turns around, naked to the waist. Joey's on the bed behind her. She puts her arms around Carroll and kisses him and then pulls away and returns to Joey all in one continuous motion, all without a word. He watches her half-naked silhouette as she changes the baby's diaper and begins to nurse. But when Carroll shows her his hard-on, Matty tells him what he can do with it—for all she cares, she says—take it to the bathroom.

Matty makes it sound simple. She says she loves babies, loves kids, but doesn't have much use anymore for men—and even less for sex. She's got four kids already. Her youngest, Dean, is fourteen months. She lets Carroll watch her nurse Joey and Dean as much as he wants, but whenever he asks for more, she just says "tough" to him. She says it a lot, that word. "Tough."

"You got a thing about tough, don't you, Matty." Carroll tries to bait her. "How'd you get these kids in the first place? Musta not been so tough somewhere along the line. Somebody opened the oven door sometime, didn't they?"

"How I got them is my business, Carroll. I don't ask you

about Joey. What's the use of us telling each other a pack of lies? Tell me that. It's not questions that make this world go round."

The van is perfect for what Matty calls "outings." Matty drives it like a bus while Carroll reads city maps and the little brochures about local attractions that Matty's collected from the Detroit Tourist Bureau. She likes to take her family all over town, from the downtown to the suburbs. And back. Every weekend.

She tells Carroll you don't have to go a long way to have a good time—she says they could go someplace different every weekend of their lives and never get outside the Greater Detroit Area. When he tells her where he's from, California, she says she's never gone west of Iowa City, Iowa. And doesn't really care to.

Carroll keeps the garage and his job and his van, but his party money, his game money and baby money, all goes to Matty and the kids. He rolls the carpet up and tacks it down in Matty's TV room so the kids will be warmer. Mostly Carroll uses the garage to work on the van. He puts new brake shoes on and turns the drums. He puts a new clutch in. Matty rides the clutch real bad.

But she's a great cook and smart as a whip. That's what it really boils down to—smart. The way she don't even wait for Carroll to tell her a lie, the way she marches right on around the parts of life Carroll struggles to hide and explain away—she's smarter than Carroll. And he's just smart enough to figure that out. They say grace before every meal.

"You're always telling me about your friends on the force," Matty says. "So go for it. God knows the City pays better than your rinky-dink company."

"Yeah, I've got just enough friends on the force to know better. Money's not everything. I like my job. I'm used to it."

"So you can get used to being a policeman. You can get used to anything, give it enough time. Here, I'll call for you." She dials the number in the City's newspaper ad for recruits and makes Carroll an appointment for next week.

Carroll slams down his pop and it fizzes over on the end table. "I'm too old anyway. I'll just be wasting my time."

Matty wipes up his spill and slides a cardboard coaster under his pop can as she talks. "Too old? What's with you and too old? You're as old as you think you are." She flashes him a wide smile. "Look here, there's ways and there's ways. You're not the only one with friends. You think there's nobody in this town don't owe me a favor or two?"

"Maybe everybody owes you a favor, Matty, but maybe not me, maybe it's time for me to go my own separate way here. You're getting too far into my shit, way too far." He rises from the vinyl recliner. It squeaks as it folds up behind him.

Matty pushes Carroll back into his chair with the tips of her long, fine fingers, as if her movement were the shadow of a real gesture, as if he weighed nothing, as if she couldn't even imagine resistance from him. "Stay put, you're not gonna go anywhere, Carroll. I've got your number. I got it the first night I met you." She heads down the hall to the bedroom. "They'll be proud," she says, "a policeman right in the house. It'll be safer for everybody." She comes out with the babies, Joey and Dean. She calls the other kids out of the TV room.

Carroll sits still as they assemble around him like silent little animals, their unflinching eyes on him, gazes as warm as sunlight, small hands all over his knees. Matty watches him like he's already safe behind bars. She gives him Joey to hold as she nurses Dean.

"Hold Joey while I feed baby Dean."

"Goddamn, his name ain't even Joey. That's just what I call him because his mother's name was Joleen. None of this is me, this ain't my niche. It's not my niche here at all."

"So we'll make it your niche. Hell, how does anybody get a name? How'd you get yours—was your mother's name Carol? Was it?"

Carroll winces. His ears go red.

"See, it goes right on, it might as well be here. I'll take care of you and your baby and you take care of us. We'll keep calling him Joey—we'll keep calling you Carroll. There's nothing wrong with those names, nothing at all."

Carroll wonders what the night patrol shift will be like. He wonders if he could get Leon as a partner somehow. It'd be just like one of those old TV shows. He closes his eyes as he hears the baby sucking on Matty. It's like the wet, thick ticking of a moist, living clock across the room. He squeezes little Joey so tight up into his face he can't tell at all where he begins and the baby leaves off. One of them is crying.

Walt and Dixie

IT WAS AFTER midnight. I stood on Interstate 80 in northern Indiana, heading toward New York City, hitchhiking. I had my summer savings from construction jobs, twelve twenty-dollar bills, under the innersole of my left shoe, just like in the movies. I was nineteen.

I'd had four rides since leaving Grand Island at dawn. The last, a Michigan salesman sipping from a tequila bottle, had let me off when he'd turned north toward home. I stood next to a light pole at the end of an entrance ramp, with my green canvas duffel bag at my feet and a sharp cone of light spread around me as if I'd stepped onstage somewhere. It was September, and cool, but with no breeze I felt fine in a short-sleeved shirt. The stars were out. Michigan lay within the horizon to the north. I imagined it stretching away from me like the mitten I'd seen on the map.

It was my second hitchhiking trip, and I felt as alone and free

45

as I'd ever felt in my life. Yet the two separate feelings seemed to occupy the same space inside me, or maybe it was just two words pointing to the same exact thing, like those people from the South with two first names, Jim Bob or Joe Ray. In the air was the raw scent of cut hay mixed with the lingering oily smell of the pavement in front of me, still warm from the day. I sat down with my thumb out, my neck craned back, counting stars.

A shiny white Cadillac with giant fins and bullet taillights, a '59 or '60, I thought, but restored to perfect condition, rolled by slowly, and then stopped and honked. I grabbed my duffel and walked toward it. I didn't see another vehicle in either direction. The Caddy backed up slowly, its brake lights blinking like double red winks. I opened the front door.

"Hilo there, my friend. Need a lift?"

"I'm headed to New York City."

"El perfecto. That's where me and Dixie-Queen are bound." He stuck his hand out toward me, his palm up. "I'm Walt."

He wore an old man's ribbed sleeveless undershirt, and the white hairs on his chest matched the white stubble on his cheeks and chin. He looked older than my father. A black suit-coat lay folded across the seat-back next to him. His arms were as thin as I'd ever seen, twisted off-white ropes with large calloused hands at the end. His collarbones disappeared like struts under his shirt. I shook with him, our hands horizontal. He didn't let go for several long seconds, just kept smiling, looking into my eyes in the dim light from the dome.

"Rob," I said. "Thanks for stopping."

"You can stow your bag in the back with her," he said. "Welcome aboard the Lost Angels–Madhatter Express." He laughed, then stopped and spread his hand out as if he was inviting me into his living room. "Coast to coast comfort."

His eyes were gray, and when I looked at them I had trouble looking away until after he did. I didn't see anybody in the back seat.

"We're your last chance for tonight, I reckon," he said. "I

know how it goes. I've spent many a night on the side of the road." He pushed a button on the panel in his door and the lock on the back door popped up. "Many a night." He slapped the seat-back. "Dixie-Queen, wake up, we got company. This here's Bob."

It was a frequent mistake. There wasn't really that much difference. Once I'd worked for two weeks on a summer roofing job, and the foreman called me Bob the whole time.

I opened the back door and looked in. A little girl straightened up in the seat. Her short legs rested on an open cardboard box on the floor. But she had nylons and high-heeled shoes on. She wore eyeshadow and lipstick.

"Just call me Dixie," she said, wiping at her eyes. "Isn't nobody but Walter calls me that other."

Her voice was a woman's, and as I looked closer I saw she was. Her face was like a miniature, painted on a doll. Twenty-five, maybe thirty years old. I hoisted my bag up, brushed off the bottom, and put it on the seat.

"Will that bother you?" I asked. "I could keep it up front."

"It's fine," she said, "there's more room than enough. That's why Walter got this car. Isn't she just beautiful?"

I slammed the back door and sat down in the front seat. Walter stuck out his hand again. I felt just a little uneasy, as if maybe I should've waited for another ride. But I shook his hand again.

"Bob's got his own pair of eyes, DQ." He laughed. "He can see same as me that you're the beauty here. They don't make an automobile that compares to my Dixie-Queen." He let go my hand. I was tired. I closed my door. Walt pushed the lock buttons for all four doors, and the sound of their snapping sounded final. I put my elbow out the window.

"Walter, you're the sweetest man there ever was," she said.

Walt steered the Cadillac back onto the highway. I watched the speedometer needle creep up to forty-five and hover there. You could hardly hear the engine.

Walt looked out his window at the farmland brushing by in

the dark. "My friend, it's a gorgeous night here in creation. Just look at it, slipping away in every direction like black satin."

I looked out the window. My head tipped to the side and the breeze of us blowing through the night felt like somebody was washing my face.

"How tall are you, Bob?" Dixie asked from behind me.

I turned half around. I couldn't see her well.

"You look like over six foot," she said.

"Five-eleven," I said.

"You look taller," she said. "I'm four-foot-one because I had a condition when I grew up. Walter's six foot even."

"Sock-footed," Walt said. They both laughed like kids who just thought a certain word sounded funny.

When they stopped, the silence felt like a hole I had to fill up. "So you've come all the way from Los Angeles?" I asked.

"Every mile," Walt said. He scrunched toward the instrument panel and squinted at it over the steering wheel. "Twenty-one hundred, sixty-two and four-tenths." He slapped his hand on the wheel. "Started out day before yesterday. Haven't stopped but to fill up the Caddy's tank. Or drain ours."

"Walter," Dixie said. "Your language."

"When do you sleep?" I asked.

He winked at me. "I carry some truckers' aspirin with me." He patted the jacket next to him. "I take two every state line we cross."

"Show him our pictures," Dixie said.

Walt reached over and opened the glove compartment. He pulled out a stack of Polaroids and clicked on the dome light. I thumbed through them. Pictures of the two of them standing by state-line signs: Arizona, New Mexico, Texas, Oklahoma, Missouri, Illinois, Indiana. The top of her head came to just above his belt. In each of them his big hand rested on her shoulder, and she had her arm folded up across her chest and her hand on top of his. They grinned like two retirees on the trip of a lifetime.

I put the photos back. "Those are great," I said.

"I got sleep tablets, too," he said. "If you need them."

"Don't take those, Bob," Dixie said. "I took one the first night of our trip, and I couldn't get my eyes open the next time we stopped for pictures. Which one was that, Walter?"

"Texas," Walt said. "I just thought Bob might have trouble sleeping. It happens on the road. A man gets all vibrated up or something."

"Do you want a milk ball?" Dixie asked. She shoved an open box of malted milk balls over my shoulder.

"No thanks," I said. "Boy, you two have a little of everything."

"I love milk balls," Dixie said.

"I buy 'em by the case," Walt said, smiling at me. "It's her weakness."

"You like screen magazines?" Dixie asked. She held up a *Photoplay* with Elizabeth Taylor on the front. "I like the old ones best," she said. "The pictures look better when they yellow out."

"She's got two more cartons in the trunk," Walt said. "I scour them up for her at beauty parlors."

For the first time, I think I gave him an odd look then. I must have let my thoughts show through.

"You think there's something kinda funny with reading old movie magazines, eh Bob?" He was still smiling just the same. He kept moving his head around, looking at the countryside, at me, at Dixie. About every fourth look was at the road ahead. The speedometer still read forty-five.

"No. No. My mother subscribed to *Silver Screen* once. She bought it from one of the kids selling magazines to go through college."

"Something's on your mind, though. I saw it. I'll tell you the truth, Bob. I'm forty-six years old, and I can't read much more than road maps, street signs, and menus. I can't write much more than my own name. But I can read people. Oh Lordy, how I can read people."

"Walter has a sixth sense," Dixie said.

I looked back out the window. Clusters of farmhouses and outbuildings were scattered across every knoll. A dog barked from a long way off.

"Well, the truth is, you two just aren't much like other people I've met, I guess. That's all." I tried to put it as mildly as I could.

"There you go. Good for you. Listen, friend, the world's full of folks all the same as one another, like racks of summer clothes on the sidewalk. Nosir, not for me. Be an In-da-Wid-U-ul— right, Dixie-Queen?"

"An In-da-Wid-U-ul," Dixie said. She laughed, tipping her head back and opening her mouth real wide. Walt laughed, too. Their laughter was so good-natured and unforced that this time it caught me up in it. When I got my breath back, I said "sock-footed." We laughed in little waves then, one of us stopping and then hearing the others and starting up again.

"Whew-eee," Walt said, wiping his eyes on his jacket sleeve when we finally stopped. "Not too many things in this life bone-free," he said. "But laughing's one. DQ and me like the free ones."

I felt the little lump of bills inside my shoe, or thought I did. "The best things in life, they say," I said.

"Yeah, but they don't believe it," Walt said. "Do they? Only time you have a chance for believing it is when you've just got no choice. You have some money, don't you?"

I didn't say anything.

"I have eight dollars," Dixie said. "You can have it if you need it."

"You don't have to answer," Walt said. "It's fine you do. Now me—I got this car and my helper pills and a trunkful of secondhand stuff. Dixie's got her magazines and her milk balls and her eight dollars. I thought you spent a dollar at that rock shop, Dixie."

"Seven dollars," Dixie said.

"How're you making it all this way?" I asked.

"You have me, Walter," Dixie said.

"And I thank the Lord for that," he said, craning around and smiling at her. "Of a night and of a day." He turned back to me. "Let me tell you about us making it." He pointed out the window with the flat of his hand. It came to me then how his voice didn't fit him. It was deep and strong, like dark wood with fine grain, but he looked unhealthy, like he hadn't eaten much and hadn't been out in the sun for a long time.

"I look out at the world, and I just see a big old ship," he said. "With a full head of steam—making progress all the time. And folks like me and Dixie, we're what the ship throws off when it falls behind schedule or hits bad weather. You know, to lighten the load up and ride higher. To make better time." He pointed his long index finger at the clock on the dash. It was broken, all three of its hands stuck on six. "And we see it, sailing on without us. What could we do for it, anyway?" He laughed, as if an answer had come to him that struck him funny.

"So here we are, Bob, some kind of junk, cast-off in deep water. Now there's only two ways to go in that kind of deal. You sink and drown, fast or slow, but still going down, down, down, just the same all the time." He punched his finger toward the floor of the car each time he said "down."

"Or you swim?" I said. I felt like I'd heard this advice before.

"That seems right, doesn't it? Sink or swim, sure. But think on it a minute. Where exactly to? In the middle of the ocean, swimming's just another kind of sinking. Nosir, you dance."

"Dance?" I was so tired it was hard to follow him, but I couldn't quit listening. In the back of my mind, I kept thinking: This is Indiana. It's Thursday. You have two hundred and forty dollars cash.

"You said it same as I did," he said. "The good black book says the son of God walked on water, are you still with me? Well, dance, too. You look up at the sky and forget that you're junk and dance. That's what this trip is—Dixie and me love each other and that's a dance that keeps us on top of the water. It's no more account where the ship is or what the folks on board might say." He paused, his palm up, as if he could almost hear a crowd in the distance.

"I'm just saying what I know here, son, and it's sparse enough, if you tally up the years I put in finding it. I'm just telling you so you'll know what's up with Dixie and me and won't think we're loony or feel sorry on us."

I remember hearing the pages of Dixie's magazine turning while he talked and the whistle from a train and then I was asleep. I had a restless, sitting-up car dream where I was on a tall boat, sailing over meadows and trees, parting them like water. I climbed up flight after flight of stairs to the wheelhouse. Walt was at the wheel, standing in his undershirt like a broken-down preacher, talking and talking to Dixie, who was nowhere to be seen.

I woke up only once after that before morning. The car swerved slightly, and I sat up straight.

"Leastways, that's the way I told them," Walt said. I heard Dixie giggle in the back seat, and then I slipped asleep again.

I woke up in Pennsylvania. I'd slept through two of their state-line photo stops, and they showed me the Polaroids to prove it. In the daylight Dixie looked even smaller and Walt looked more thin and washed-out, as if the sunlight had shrunk them both, although in different directions.

We stopped at a cafe for breakfast on the outskirts of a small town. Four big trucks were parked at odd angles in the lot.

"Can I come in this place, Walter?" Dixie asked as we got out.

"You know I don't mind ordering for you," Walt said. "Not one whit. You just read your magazines and we'll be right back, sweetie."

On the way in I asked him if Dixie always stayed in the car.

"I don't have to tell you Dixie's a looker, Bob," Walt said. "But you'd have no way of knowing how innocent and trustful she is. She don't understand men and what it is they're always needing to get at. I have to protect her from the wolves of this world."

"She sounds to me like she loves you and only you, Walt," I said. We walked into a small glass foyer with a newspaper stand and a phone in it.

Walt beamed a big wrinkled grin at me as I held the door open.

"Thank you," he said. "That's very kind of you to say that. I just have a need to be vigilant," he said. "Anyway, truth is, she don't really like to go in places much."

We ordered three cinnamon rolls and two black coffees and a milk to go. I said I'd eat in the car with them. While we waited, Walt circulated among the tables, selling ballpoint pens for a quarter apiece. His inside suitcoat pockets were full of brand-new pens with company names and slogans on them. He sold enough in just a few minutes to pay for half of the tab.

As we stepped back out into the parking lot, Walt continued talking about Dixie right where he'd left off on the way in.

"I don't mind telling you that's one reason I looked you over so careful, Bob. Last night."

"What do you mean?" I asked. I thought I'd been the careful one.

He shook his head and patted me on the shoulder. "It could be you're too young to know," he said. "But there's just such all kinds of people footloose in the country anymore," he said. "I can take care of myself, but Dixie's different altogether. There's times she's just too pure for our world. It's my faith I was put down here on the ground to care for her."

I smiled because I didn't know what else to do.

"Well, it looks like you're doing just fine by her," I said. We were almost back to the car. He stopped again and pointed at the Cadillac and Dixie in the back seat, reading.

"She's the first woman has ever really loved me," he said. "You know, all the way down deep." He pressed his hand flat against his chest.

Dixie poked her head out the open window.

"Those rolls look real good, Walter," she said.

At a gas stop later, near the middle of the state, we pulled over by a water spigot, and they washed the Cadillac with rags and sponges they kept in a bucket in the trunk. Dixie did the low parts, cleaning the California license plates and the bumpers and the fender skirts, and Walt stretched his long arms across the top and the wide hood and back deck. I offered to help, but Dixie told me they enjoyed doing it. She kept flipping water on Walt when his back was turned, and he'd look up at the cloudless sky and act amazed. She laughed like a kid with her dad.

At another stop that afternoon, in a crowded station near a large interchange, Walt confessed he was flat out of money, something I'd already figured. I offered to pay for one tank of gas. He said he might take me up on it yet, but he still had a card or two up his sleeve. He opened the trunk and pulled out three sets of jumper cables that looked brand-new and a used set of expensive-looking walkie-talkies. He went around to the people gassing up at the pumps and coming out of the restaurant, talking and gesturing like an auctioneer.

While we waited on Walt, I sat on the edge of the back seat with the back door open, talking to Dixie. She showed me pictures from her magazines. She knew exactly how tall every movie star was, male and female, and she got me to admit that I was surprised at a lot of them. She said they used every kind of trick to fool you on the stars' heights in the movies. She said Walter told her she had the face of a movie queen.

I asked her if she'd like me to sit in back for a while so she could sit up front with Walt.

"I can't drive," she said. "My legs won't reach the pedals."

She pulled her skirt up to show me, and I saw her white panties before the skirt settled back on her hips. I looked away.

"Walt's a good driver," I said. "Steady and safe."

"He used to make his living that way," she said. "But that's not why I've rode the whole way in the back. Can you keep a secret, Bob?"

"What do you mean?"

"You know. Something you whisper and promise not to tell around. Friends tell them back and forth. Can't you keep one?"

"I suppose I can. Sure."

She leaned over close to my ear. "There's a special word for what I am. Walt told it to me."

I didn't want to be hearing her secrets, especially about whatever her condition might be. I didn't know how our talking had come to that point. I looked around and saw Walt heading for the car, counting the cash in his hand.

"Virgin," she said. She giggled. "It rhymes with urgin'. Walt says it's best for me to stay in the back seat. He says I make him feel too frisky otherwise. For this whole last year we've been saving me until Walter's got a proper job and we're married."

I stood up beside the car. Dixie's skirt was still pulled up high on her hips. Her expression turned thoughtful. She picked at the upholstery.

"Bob, would you tell me something?"

"If I can." I saw my shadow broken across the top of the car and the open back door. Dixie squinted up at me.

"Walter says those other times, the ones who made me do it, don't really count. He's not just saying that, is he? They don't count, do they?"

I stared at her and realized she'd had a whole life, one much longer and harder than mine, one I'd never be able to even guess at. Walt was coming closer. I leaned my head into the car, whispering, without really meaning to.

"No. Not at all. Walter's telling the truth."

"So what's going on, Bob?" I turned around. Walt stood next

to me. Before I could answer he leaned into the car. "Pull that down, DQ. It doesn't look right."

"Dixie's telling me all about the movie stars," I said. He was staring right into my eyes again. "And how you take such good care of her."

Dixie slid over in the seat and put her small hand on Walt's thin wrist.

"He's a perfect gentleman, Walter. He's our friend."

Walt smiled a little. "Is that true, Bob?"

"You bet," I said. "Of course it is."

"I just knew that," he said. "I just knew I wasn't wrong on you." He slapped me on the back again, the way a father would.

"Well, over there isn't coming any closer sitting over here," he said, pointing down the highway. He closed Dixie's door and walked around the car. I climbed back into the front seat. I felt like I'd been with them too long.

"How'd you make out with the sales?" I asked, wanting to talk about anything besides them or me.

"We're doing fine," he said. "Except I feel kind of shoddy, a little."

"What'd you do, Walter?" Dixie asked.

"Those walkie-talkies is broke," he said. "But I didn't say so. I sold them like they wasn't."

"It's all right," Dixie said. "You did it for our trip. We'll remember it and make it up to somebody we meet down there in New York."

At the New Jersey line, near sundown, I took a photo of them, and then we took one with me, too, using the rickety remote device Walt had rigged up with a coat hanger threaded through a piece of plastic tubing and the camera propped on the hood of the Cadillac. Dixie stood between us, with her arms reaching upward to hold one of each of our hands. They gave me the picture and I put it in my back pocket. If you only ever saw that one photo, you'd swear it was of two men, a teenager and a middle-aged man, with a little girl between them, a younger sister or a niece.

After the photo stop, I felt sleepy again, and I drifted in and out, mostly out, but I did hear Walt say he'd driven a cab in Manhattan for almost ten years and was planning on supporting both of them doing that again. He'd bummed around the country for years after that, looking for something but not knowing what it was until he'd found Dixie in Los Angeles about a year ago. She was living in a halfway home for the retarded, he said, and I'd never heard a word said with more bitter regret than the way Walt said "retarded."

"Walter knew I wasn't that other," Dixie said. "I'm just short."

"The best things in the smallest packages," Walt said, and they were off again, laughing and cooing at each other like newlyweds in old movies.

They weren't married, but Walt said they were going to get that way once they arrived in Manhattan and he found a job. On top of the Empire State Building, Dixie said. They invited me to come. I kidded them and told them I'd watch the newspapers for their pictures and announcements. A cool wind blew up and the sky went dark as we crossed New Jersey.

We stopped at a diner, the Go-By Inn, near an exit in Teaneck, just a few miles from the George Washington bridge into Manhattan. Dixie couldn't stop laughing about the name of the town. Walt went in to get some sandwiches with the last of what he called his swap-meet money. It was dark and he parked the Cadillac near the highway at the edge of the parking lot. I wanted to go in and use the restroom and wash up. Dixie stayed in the back seat, munching on milk balls and starting on a new box of old magazines. Walt locked the car.

Walt ordered, and I heard him asking the waitress if she wanted to buy a ballpoint as I went into the bathroom. I'd pulled a washrag from my duffel, and I washed my face and hands and neck until I felt wider awake than I had all day—ready for my first look at New York City. I pulled a twenty from my shoe. I paid for the three roast beef sandwiches and root beers Walt had ordered. We headed back for the car, juggling the food. Walt promised me a cabbie's tour of Manhattan when we crossed the bridge.

But when we got to the Cadillac, I didn't see Dixie. Then I looked in from the passenger side and saw her lying on the floor of the back seat. I yelled at Walt. He dropped his food and unlocked the car. I went around to his side as he turned her over and lifted her up on the seat. It seemed like she only reached halfway across it. Her face was somewhere between blue and red, and yet not purple, something different from purple. Her eyes were wide open, and both the white and the black of them was way too bright—glary, shiny—like she'd seen the true source of everyone's worst fear and hadn't looked away. Saliva streaked all around her mouth, and little brown flakes plastered her chin. In her small white fist the candy box was smashed, and the wax-paper liner squeezed out at both ends. I stood there like a mannequin, a roast beef sandwich and two root beers in my hands, and I wanted to be anywhere but there in Teaneck, New Jersey, with Walt and Dixie.

I asked if she was dead, even though I knew she was. He didn't answer me. He kept shaking her and kissing her forehead and cleaning her face with a napkin. But when I headed toward the diner for help, he stopped me, and the next thing I knew, we'd paid a toll and were on a bridge over the Hudson River with a Welcome to New York sign sliding out of sight at the top of the windshield.

I wanted to get away from them, and yet I didn't want to abandon Walt. I wondered if the police would believe she'd choked to death, and I was afraid I'd be blamed for something, anything. I wanted to call my father.

As we turned onto the Henry Hudson Parkway, I looked up

into the bright thrum of New York City. I heard Walt talking for the first time since we'd gotten back in the car.

"She ain't that far ahead of me." His hands were winding around on the wheel like it was something he could wring out.

"Do you know where there's a hospital?" I asked.

"She's still in this car," he said. "I know she is." He seemed to be driving without seeing anything. For the first time since they'd picked me up, our speed was changing all the time. He'd run it up to sixty and then drop back to thirty.

"It's not your fault, Walt," I said.

"It's not your fault, Dixie," he said, as he pulled the Cadillac off the expressway, and then we were suddenly at street level in Manhattan.

I didn't know where we were or where we were going. Walt drove like he knew, though, and at every red light, I thought about getting out. My bag was upright behind me, but I didn't want to look at it because I never wanted to see that blue face again.

We parked on a narrow dark street. Walt turned the car off.

"Where is this?" I asked.

"Can I have that?" Walt said, pointing at the root beer I still held. I handed it to him. He reached in a pocket of his suit-coat and pulled out a little Bayer aspirin bottle with the label half torn off. He set them both on the dash in front of him. "I did you a favor, stopping for you back there, right, Bob?"

"Of course, sure. Sure you did."

"So you can pay me back now. You're the only one who can do this for me. You owe me."

"Anything. I've got some money. I'll help you."

He reached in his coat and pulled out one of the new pens. He opened the glove compartment and grabbed the top photo: he and Dixie and the New Jersey sign. He turned it over and handed it and the pen to me. He had my eyes locked up with his, and it felt like he could do that whenever he wanted.

59

"I don't need money now. If I ever needed it, I don't have no more use for it now. You can write, can't you?"

"What?"

"Just write what I tell you," he said, pointing at the pen and photo in my hand. I hesitated. "They got to know her name," he yelled. It was the first time he'd raised his voice in the twenty-some hours I'd known him. He lowered it again. "Please," he said. I put the pen against the paper.

"To whatever people who cares," he said. I wrote it. I felt like I'd stumbled into someone else's life, and at exactly the wrong moment. It had nothing to do with anything I could remember before this one day. I just wrote what he said.

"This little lady is Dixie Margaret Ann Logan. She's thirty-two years old and she choked on a milk ball and I couldn't save her. I spent half my life looking for her and I'm not going to let her get away now. The best thing if someone can do it would be to put us to rest side-by-side."

He pulled the photo and pen from my hand. I thought I was going to be sick. I watched him sign his name at the bottom of it.

"Walt, you can't do that," I said. "Come on. No."

"I really appreciate it," he said. "Now you go on. Just keep walking that way," he pointed behind us. "When you come to 8th Avenue, turn left. Go a few miles. There's plenty of cheap hotels."

"Walt. You're not thinking straight."

"I'd let you have this car but for two things," he said. "It's not really mine, title-wise," he looked away, as if ashamed. "And we need it."

"I can't leave you like this," I said.

"You're going to," he said. He reached for the root beer and the pill bottle. "Get your bag and go. This ain't nothing about you. Dignified comes in every different flavor, my friend. This one's mine. You understand?"

"Yes," I said. I didn't move.

He got out and went around and opened both doors on my side. He set my bag on the sidewalk and got in beside Dixie. He set the photo on his lap and opened the pill bottle. I still didn't move.

"You have no right not to let me go with her," he said. "You promise me you won't call anybody to stop me. Promise me."

I stood up and slammed the front door, staring right at him. "I promise."

"Then thank you," he said. He let go of my eyes for the last time. "So long." He closed the door.

I swear I could see that bright white Cadillac from one block, two, three, four blocks away. Almost as if it were glowing, a small moon with four whitewall tires parked on a side street in Manhattan in the night. Finally, when I looked back, I'd lost it.

I walked for hours. I tore and retore the photo of Walt and Dixie and me into confetti and threw the pieces into three different trash barrels. When I couldn't walk another step, I stumbled into the Key Hotel for Men, shoved a few dollars at a cashier behind worn brass bars, took a freight elevator up to a room on the fourth floor, went in and lay down on a metal bed with a two-inch mattress. I kept my hand on my bag next to me. I didn't undress or take my shoes off, and I didn't exactly sleep, but I got through the night.

In the daylight the next morning, it turned out I was only about six blocks from the Empire State Building, but I never went up there or looked for work or did anything else I'd had in my mind. I took a bus from New York to Boston the same day. I had a high school friend in college there.

As the Greyhound drove me away from Manhattan, I counted my money and put it in my wallet. I still had almost two hundred dollars. It was Friday. I was still nineteen. I didn't know at all what I was feeling, except that I didn't feel alone anymore. Or free. I watched the ships, pushing down the Hudson, silver lines of froth slanting across their hulls, and then the rows of dark waves racing away. I stared at the surface of the water for a long time before I closed my eyes and finally slept. Only sunlight danced upon it.

Insolence

DWIGHT SHAW thought he might be lost. He'd been caught in the Exit Only lane—a red Buick had cut him off— peace on earth, good will to you too, pal. Three days after Christmas and the race was in full swing again.

Shaw looked through a haze of light snow at a part of the city he'd never seen before. Grainy snow leaned and drifted against the old buildings as if it had been there first, as if the city had erupted through it from below. At roof level, charred timbers jutted out at awkward angles like broken bones. He pictured his townhome in Hidden Hills. 1444 Cedar Way. Where he should be now.

Something dark ran in front of the car. Shaw tapped the brakes, skidded, tapped them again. He heard a bump and then a rough screech like a needle skating on a record. He double-parked the Accord next to a Chrysler with no tires and every window broken out. Inside it, snow drifted above the back of the seats.

The cat was all black except for a diamond-shaped white spot between the eyes. Its back legs and tail were crushed, froth oozing from its mouth. Shaw watched the eyes move in two orbits, distinct from each other and from the slow circling of the head—as if death could happen one eye at a time, one sense at a time, organ by organ.

Something moved on the sidewalk. Shaw took a step toward his car door, then steadied himself on the fender. It was only a man, a single person, beneath a small tent of wet plastic. Shaw had heard of such.

"Can you help me?"

"I doubt it," said a voice under the plastic.

The man stood up, the plastic gathered around him like a poncho or a shroud. He wore a hooded sweatshirt and shredded cotton gloves that reminded Shaw of the gloves the rock singers on MTV wore. The bizarre ones his twelve-year-old boy Devin liked. Heavy metal. The man's wiry beard surrounded thin chapped lips. Shaw watched them instead of the man's eyes.

"I hit a cat."

"I saw."

"It's not dead."

The lips didn't move.

"I think I should kill it."

"So do I."

"I'm not sure how."

"Well, lessee." The man reached out and lifted the end of Shaw's tie, laughing. "You could always throttle it with your twenty-dollar tie."

Shaw saw the man's rough red fingertips against his smooth gray tie that had cost closer to fifty. He backed up two steps. The tie dropped.

"I'll pay you," Shaw said.

"For what?"

"For helping me. We'll help each other. You live around here?"

"Me? I live where I am. Forty years to figure the simple—a slow learner, huh? Right now I live here. With you."

"Just take a look at the cat. By all rights, it should be dead. God, I hate this. You can understand that, can't you."

"Sure." The man folded the plastic sheet double and then double again, creasing it with the edge of his hand, and wedged it between the bars of a grate where he'd been sitting. Slow. As if it weren't cold out at all, as if the cat had plenty of time to die in.

"Is that a heating grate?" Shaw peered into a darkness that smelled like coffee mixed with wet iron.

"Not like you mean. But it won't freeze over. Heat rises, huh?"

They moved toward Shaw's car, idling in front of the cat.

"I didn't mean to disregard you. On the contrary. What's your name? I'm Dwight Shaw." He put his hand out without looking at the man. He felt disoriented, the way he'd felt all the time in Europe, two summers before.

The man put his hands beneath his sweatshirt, up under his arms.

"Morrison," he said.

The cat's head and eyes still moved in feeble orbits. Shaw thought of his daughter Milan, a month shy of five. She hadn't spoken a word yet. He and Laura had to watch her all the time. Shaw realized he was sick of it, although he'd never said so, never even admitted it in his mind before. She could even cry without making a sound.

"Step on its neck," Morrison said. He rotated his shoulders.

The Accord's exhaust had melted a gray spot in the snow. Both men stared at their shoes. Shaw wore cordovan moccasins with dark rubber soles. Morrison's were faded blue deck shoes. Shaw couldn't speak.

"You got a tire iron?" Morrison asked.

"No," Shaw lied. "My boy borrowed it. For his car."

"You don't look old enough to have a driving boy."

"Listen, I'll pay you to give me a hand. Just guide me and I'll back over it." He looked again at the cat's swaying head. "No, you—you do it, I'll guide. Twenty dollars cash."

"Twenty bucks to drive over a cat?"

"Yes. OK," Shaw said, as if Morrison had proposed it.

"Lessee the twenty."

Shaw reached for his wallet. He turned and bent to the tail-light. The money looked strange in the red glare, fake. Six twenties, five tens.

"Look." He turned back around with two tens folded lengthwise, pale green blades between his gloved fingers.

"How do you move the seat?" Morrison asked as he got behind the wheel. The car looked alien to Shaw with Morrison in it. A VW rolled by, wipers going, the first car. Shaw thought of hailing it but he didn't.

Shaw pulled the lever on the side of the seat. Morrison slid forward. He closed the door and looked through the open window. His eyes were light blue, crinkly like cellophane, not unlike Shaw's. He looked bewildered.

"You can drive, can't you?" Shaw asked.

"I can drive good enough to take my brother everywhere he ever needed to go, can't I? Right up to the day he died, I could drive that good. I drove him everywhere but the last place, Dwight Shaw."

Shaw tried not to let his face go slack. Was this one of the crazy people the news talked about, loose on the streets in droves?

"I didn't know your brother."

"Did I say you did? You ask can I drive. My brother'd tell you. Listen mister," he motioned Shaw closer. Shaw felt everything was out of control now. "My brother loved me just like you love this cat."

Shaw backed away. Morrison laughed again.

"What's this mean?" Morrison asked, pointing to the stenciled warning on the outside mirror.

"Nothing. They all have them. Watch me through the back window."

Shaw stood behind the cat and gave Morrison hand signals as the car backed up an inch at a time. Just as the cat's head disappeared under the tire, Shaw clamped his eyes down tight. He balled his fists up. He felt like the boy he'd been once, somewhere, in a playground or a classroom, or after dinner in the kitchen—where had it been? Somewhere the boy was struggling not to cry and not to run. Hadn't there been any other choices?

When he opened his eyes, he knew he'd already heard Morrison shift into first gear. Shaw watched the car's lights disappear over a hill as he heard Morrison find second and then third. He swore at himself. His hands felt like small cold boxes at the end of his arms.

He started to walk away, but turned back. From the hood of the parked car he scooped snow and covered the cat and the bloody tire-track until there was only one more mound of white amid the snow. He pulled Morrison's plastic from between the bars of the grate, wedging it under his arm like a newspaper. He still had the wet tens stuck between his fingers. He let them drop, one at a time, into the dark.

"Services rendered, you goddamn thief," he said, as if Morrison himself lurked out of sight below the grate. He heard a faint echo, a wet metallic hiss.

The police took him all the way home while they filed the stolen car report. "It's Christmas week, what the hell," Sgt. Twine said.

"1444 Cedar Way," Shaw said when they asked him where in Hidden Hills he lived, his voice subdued, hesitant. Yes, he worked downtown in Twin Towers—a systems analyst for Booke & Smith. He explained how he'd gotten sidetracked in the traffic. No, he hadn't been drinking.

Twine wanted descriptions. The car was easier. There was

nothing out of the ordinary about Morrison—blue eyes, brown hair, dark sweatshirt.

"Just your basic no-frills dumpster diver, eh?" Twine said. Shaw couldn't tell if he was supposed to laugh. He didn't.

Between the questions, Shaw thought of two things: Milan's silence that no one, not even the pediatric neurologists at Lanier Clinic, could explain to him. And Morrison. He wondered if Morrison really had a brother and if he was dead or alive. People will say anything.

When the police turned onto Cedar Way and Shaw sighted his townhome, he thought for a second that Morrison had been someone in disguise, someone who knew him and had played a joke on him—he thought he saw the Accord pulling into the driveway. But only for a second. Then he saw it was only Laura in her car, also an Accord but older, a '91, and darker blue. Both the kids were with her. As the police pulled around the cul-de-sac and stopped, he was glad the red light on top of the squad car wasn't whirling around, wasn't casting its quick, eerie shadows on his family and across his neighbors' cars and homes.

"Smooth move, Dwight honey," Laura said after dinner when he told how the car had been stolen. Everyone had been silent over the dinner Laura had kept warm for an extra hour. Shaw wondered if Milan even noticed.

"You let a total stranger, a street person, get in your brand-new twenty-two-thousand-dollar automobile and take it for a test drive?"

"I told you. The guy seemed too out of it to even care about the car. And that awful, squashed cat. Have you ever seen anything like that?"

"I make it a point not to. What are we going to do on Monday? We can't make it on one car during the week."

"That's two whole days. Maybe they'll recover it by then. Maybe the guy'll bring it back. He was just crazy enough."

Shaw realized his address was in the car. "Or we'll rent one. Insurance will cover it."

"Even when they find out you virtually gave the car away?"

"I didn't give the car away." Shaw didn't mention the twenty dollars, and Laura hadn't noticed the plastic he'd carried into the house. He wanted to talk about Morrison and what he'd said about his brother, but now wasn't the time. Laura always badgered him when things like this went wrong, not to be mean, he was sure, but to be reassured by the security she could glean from his steady responses.

"How's she been today?" Shaw asked, motioning toward Milan.

"Silent."

Shaw glared at her.

"Sorry—she's fine. I took her to Dr. Elden and then to the mall. She loves being in the car. We got our hair cut, didn't we, sweetheart?" Laura bent forward and smoothed Milan's bangs as she rattled red wrapping paper on the floor.

Milan had ignored most of her Christmas presents in favor of her brother's gift—wrapping paper, her favorite toy. At her last birthday party she'd left the table and fished wrapping paper from the kitchen trash, smoothing out the wrinkles, draping it around her like a little dress. Laura had thought Devin's gift was a sweet idea, but it irritated Shaw, partly because he didn't like to encourage anything in Milan that seemed obsessive and, too, because she hardly played with the expensive set of talking books Shaw had given her.

"Speaking of insurance," Shaw said, thinking of Dr. Elden.

"I know. I know. But what do you suggest?"

"Maybe not the highest-priced psychologist in west County."

"But what if her problem's different, Dwight? They can't find anything wrong with her hearing. And they think she's bright. I'm beginning to think it's not physical at all."

"I hope, for her sake and ours, it is. If it's not, it's not covered. This testing alone is like a whole other mortgage payment every month, and for what?—nobody's making her speak."

"You don't *make* somebody speak. Did anybody make you?"

"How do I know? I just wish the problem was something visible. Visible you can fix, for Christ's sake." His voice got louder. "If she's miserable, I want to know why, dammit, I want her to tell me."

Devin turned around from the set where MTV was on without the sound.

"Dad? Can I turn it back up?"

"No. In fact—" Shaw looked at the flickering images of women pulling on nylons alternating with leather-gloved hands picking strings on plastic guitars. "Turn it off, Dev, it's junk." He saw Morrison's hands on his tie again. Insolence.

"Can I watch it in my room?"

"No. Talk to us. What'd you do today?"

"He didn't do laundry like I asked him," Laura said.

"No cash, no work, that was the deal, Mom."

"I had to go to the bank machine, I told you."

Shaw looked at Laura. This arrangement was news to him. Milan rolled silver wrapping paper around her legs.

"Know what Rudd says, Dad?"

Rudd Micklin was the friend of Devin's that Shaw most disliked, a bright, bratty kid who lived across the cul-de-sac in a townhome identical to Shaw's. Maybe he didn't want to talk after all.

"He says you can freeze goldfish and then thaw 'em out."

"And?"

Devin had an aquarium in his room. Milan spent hours in front of it, slowly rotating her head, following the fish as if she were hypnotized.

"And nothing. So it's sly. So we could try it."

"Not in my freezer," Laura said. Shaw didn't laugh.

"Know what else? Rudd says he put his painted turtle in their trash compactor just to see how strong its shell was."

Milan pulled a sheet of wrapping paper with little white angels up over her eyes. She blew it away from her face and let it fall.

"Drop it, Devin. Don't you have any other friends? Laura, take that away from her face, it makes me nervous."

"He's my best bro."

"Terrific. My kid's best friend is an animal torturer."

"No, Dad. That's the point. The turtle was OK, it was sly. Rudd pried the bundle open and the turtle was fine. He'd put him in a wad of newspaper. He was just experimenting."

"So were the Nazis."

"The what?"

"Never mind. Maybe you should watch TV. I'm going to bed."

Devin went to his room. Shaw stared at a photo of himself on the wall and imagined a wall with photos of Morrison and his brother. He saw them as identical twins, two Morrisons, arms around each other's shoulders.

"Probably only at the post office," he said, looking over at a hinged triptych of Milan and Devin and Laura.

"What?"

"Nothing. I'm going to bed."

"I heard you before." Laura leafed through a catalog on her lap, studying the sale prices on kitchen appliances.

"Good night, Milan."

At the sound of her name, she pulled the wrapping paper from her face and turned her dark eyes to him. Shaw bent down and kissed her ear.

Saturday morning Shaw woke from a dream about Milan. She was trapped in plastic, coughing for air, a second skin of cellophane pulling tighter and tighter around her face with each breath. He sat up. He remembered leaving Morrison's plastic in the downstairs bathroom when he'd taken a shower after the police dropped him off. It was construction plastic, surely too stiff to suffocate anyone—it wasn't like a dry-cleaning bag. But he couldn't shake the fear, his fear, not Milan's, because when he closed his eyes again and saw the nightmare, she was suffocating in silence, with no sign of emotion, the way she seemed to do everything else.

He hurried downstairs. The plastic sheet wasn't there.

"Laura," he shouted. He didn't know where anybody was. "Laura."

"I'm in here."

Shaw went toward the family room. She was reading a paper.

"Where's Milan?"

"In Dev's room, I think."

"Where's that plastic sheet I left in the bathroom?"

"Dev took it to the trash. I thought it was something he'd drug in. Next you're gonna tell me you wanted to save it?"

"Of course not. I'm not even sure why I brought it home. Listen, that man, last night, the one that stole the car, he really got to me—you sure it's gone?"

"I'm sure. We've been up for hours, Dwight. I paid our little entrepreneur two dollars to shovel the front walks and a dollar more to take the leftover Christmas trash out, including that dirty plastic. Today's pickup day. What's the matter with you anyway? You want some breakfast?"

"Not now. That plastic sheet was that guy's house, his home, his everything. And it's nothing but a piece of garbage."

"His everything includes our car now," Laura said. "And that reminds me, Dwight, we have to take the tree down today, it's shedding like crazy."

It was a beautiful arrangement. Shaw stepped out on the back deck and looked out over the yard and beyond into the wooded commons. Four townhomes on each circle and four circles sharing the commons and a service access with a row of rustic mailboxes and two cedar-fence enclosures. One for firewood, delivered weekly in the winter, and the other to screen the garbage haulaways from view.

He heard Devin's high laugh. Shaw shaded his eyes with his hand. Devin and Rudd were sledding at the far edge of the yard on Morrison's sheet of plastic. Shaw called Laura out on the porch.

"Looks like fun, doesn't it? Leave it to kids to find the best use for anything. I feel better already."

"Good," she said. "It's great out—let's go, too. You used to love to toboggan."

"That's hardly a toboggan, honey."

"But it looks big enough. C'mon."

"What about Milan?" he asked.

"Get her, too. I'll put on some boots."

Shaw found Milan at Devin's aquarium. She wouldn't move. She looked right at him when he asked her to come out, but as soon as he quit talking she turned back to the tank. Laura stuck her head in the room.

"She doesn't want to come with us."

"You go on ahead with the boys, Dwight. I'll watch her."

"I'm tired of arranging everything in our lives around her. We'll be right at the edge of the yard. She'll be fine. If she gets lonely enough, maybe she'll come out."

"I don't know, Dwight."

"I told her where we'd be if she needs us. I know she understands."

They both watched Milan tip her head from side to side as the fish circled in the tank.

"Hell, Laura, that aquarium's a better babysitter than TV."

"Just for a few minutes," Laura said.

"We'll try it this once," Shaw said.

"What are you guys doing?" Devin asked.

"Same thing you are—sledding," Shaw said. "It's a free country, at least on Saturday. Anyway, whose sled is it?" He punched Devin on the shoulder.

"Yeah, elderly folks like to have fun, too," Rudd said.

Laura threw a snowball at Rudd, and Shaw grabbed the plastic. They threw snowballs all the way up the hill. At the top everybody got on.

Shaw laughed all the way down, forgetting everything he couldn't understand: the dead brother he wasn't even sure was real or dead and the cat he'd been unable to kill, Morrison grinning at the wheel of his car and Milan transfixed by stupid fish. He was home, safe in his neighborhood, and for a few minutes even his daughter's stubborn illness was out of his sight and his mind. The four of them each held a corner of the plastic up—like sledding inside a glass bubble. Near the bottom Shaw let his corner go and rolled into the snow. Lying in a drift, grinning at the sky, Shaw heard the mail jeep honk, and he watched the Metro trash truck pull down the service alley and upend the dumpsters one by one. After one more ride, they headed back to check on Milan. The plastic had started to rip anyway.

Milan wasn't in Devin's room. They looked for her calmly, sure she was around—they often had to find her. It was usual for her not to come when they called for her. Shaw told Devin to look in the basement and the garage while Laura and he searched the house. When they met back in the kitchen, Shaw remembered Morrison. He sent Devin to look outside.

"It's Morrison," Shaw said when Devin was out of earshot. "He had my address, he came while we were sledding, and she answered the door."

"Calm down, Dwight, she's here, I know it. Maybe she's hiding. We'll search the house again, from top to bottom. Why would that man come here?"

"Because he hated me. I knew it. He hated me more than just stealing my car. My little girl. Jesus. I'll call the police."

"Let's look again. If you call the police and say your daughter's been missing ten minutes, they'll laugh at you. I'll check the basement."

"Devin already checked there," Shaw said.

"Yeah, and I know how well Devin looks for things."

Shaw went to the front door, looking for footprints on the porch, Morrison's footprints. But the walks had been shoveled. He dialed the police. The Missing Persons dispatcher told him to check with neighbors and her playmates and to call back in an hour. Shaw didn't want to say his daughter had no playmates but fish. Shaw explained about his stolen car, and kept saying Morrison's name and telling how Morrison had grabbed his tie. The policewoman told him he wasn't coherent. Finally she said they'd send someone out in a few minutes. Shaw sat on the couch and tried to relax. The police were on their way.

He picked up a crumpled wad of wrapping paper on the floor and squeezed it into a hard red ball. Then it came to him. He remembered the grinding rumble as the Metro trucks retreated down the service lane. He threw the wrapping-paper ball across the room and ran for the door.

At the corner of the fence, he collided with Devin and knocked him backward into the snow.

"Take it easy, Dad." Devin stood up, brushing the snow off his pants.

"Is she here? Did they empty all of them? What are you doing?"

"I tossed the plastic. I haven't seen her anywhere. She must be in the house."

Shaw looked at the open gate to the trash area.

"You left it open."

"Oh. I'll get it."

"You left it open before, didn't you?" He shook Devin's shoulders.

"I don't think so. What's the matter? You're hurting me."

Shaw stared at his hands, pinching his son's shoulders. The boy put his hands in his pockets and stared at the ground between Shaw's feet.

"Just go back to the house," Shaw said. "It's my fault."

"I don't know what you're talking about," Devin said. He walked away.

Shaw pulled himself up on the edge of each of the haulaway bins. They smelled like wet newspapers and bananas and coffee. Only the last one had anything in it—two grocery sacks filled with trash and the piece of plastic they'd been sledding on. He hung there, sure she'd come for the wrapping paper. He could picture her seeing the boxes and paper on top of the dumpster and climbing up on the crossboards in the cedar fence and crawling in. While he was having fun in the snow like some damned kid. Shaw pushed himself off the lip of the last haulaway and landed flat-footed, his mouth wide open, the air rushing from his lungs all at once.

Shaw tipped his head back, looking above the cedar boards of the fence. You spend every minute, he thought, every minute trying not to make a wrong turn. He was trembling all over, and the voice inside him rose and fell in short jerks as if a huge hand pounded his back. Every minute, and the worst thing still happens. His eyes were wet and cold. The worst thing. He stared so hard at the sky it seemed to separate from itself. Its pale blue color hung above him like a shell of paint, but a transparent dome collapsed around him, wrinkling and matting to fit him, making it impossible to breathe or speak. It was his dome, only his, and on the other side he thought he saw dim upright shapes, growing smaller, moving away from him while the sky shrunk around him as tight as his own skin. He tried to scream, tearing a hole in it, but he heard nothing except the sound of air, whistling in and out of his mouth like wind.

He shuffled back to the house, eyes level, staring off to the north as if he could see miles away to where he'd met Morrison the night before. He pushed a button on the side of the house. The garage door lifted in a series of short jerks. He would take the car somewhere far from Hidden Hills, far away from his life. He didn't want to face Laura or Devin.

The doors to Laura's car were locked, and it came to Shaw

that he didn't have the keys anyway. When he looked in the back seat, he saw Milan huddled on the floor in her coat and snow boots, looking up at him, as if she were waiting to go somewhere.

He patted his empty pockets and tapped on the window. Milan didn't move. He circled to the other side, breathing deeply, panting, knocking on the glass until his knuckles hurt. She followed him with her eyes.

"Let me in, Milan. Push the button." He pointed down below the window at the lock button, squashing his face against the glass. "I couldn't find you. Push the button. I know you know how to do it."

She smiled, as if she understood, but didn't budge. He circled the car again, her smile infuriating him. He looked on the wall behind him where his tools and a bag of golf clubs and his tennis racket hung on hooks in pegboard. He grabbed a tire iron from a hook.

"Answer me, Milan," he mouthed at her. He shook the tire iron at her. "I can make you speak."

Milan seemed to smirk at Shaw, and he believed then that she would never speak to him. He felt trapped between his anger and his fear, and it dawned on him that he, too, had little, perhaps nothing, to say to her.

But that would not prevent his love.

He wouldn't stand for it. Nothing would prevent his love from reaching her, from reaching everyone. He raised the tire iron above his head. He stared at her behind the glass.

What Hurts the Fish

I LOVE EVELYN, but I'm afraid of her shoe. It's brown and thick as if two or three shoes have been put together—as if the machine that made the shoe got stuck and just kept building it up and up. I call it her sick shoe. Evelyn needs it because she's crippled. She was dropped when she was a baby. Almost thirty years ago—on New Year's Day of 1930—that's what she told my mom. She said she still doesn't like that one holiday, New Year's Day.

Whenever Evelyn walks without her shoes, she seems much smaller, and her head bobs up and down in a little half-circle. But with her sick shoe on she walks OK except her hip swings out on one side. Evelyn is a pretty lady with a soft face that smiles a lot even though she was dropped. She left her shoe under the sink next to the toilet where I'm hiding. It lies on its side next to her regular one with the flatter heel, which is sitting upright as if she just stepped away from it.

• • •

I shot Jamie in the eye with a BB gun. He said not to tell anybody. I'm sick. I'm sick with fear and shame. I haven't looked Evelyn in the eye since I got home. I tried sitting on the big purple couch in the front room and reading Superboy comics, like always, but she kept looking me over as she did her ironing in front of the TV. I never come home from the park alone in the summertime for no reason. We spend whole days there at Hanscom Park, Evelyn's boys and me, hours and hours at the baseball field or fishing in the lagoon or by the recreation shack or with our bikes on Devil's Hill. Unless it's time for lunch or it's raining or I'm sick, I never come home like this.

She knows something is wrong. So I came up to the bathroom. Whenever I remember the blood on his eye, I flush the toilet. The loud whoosh of the water on its way down to wherever it goes makes my memory stop. But then it starts up again. I turn the faucet on.

I've never touched Evelyn's shoe before. But I've wanted to. It's heavy. It's as heavy as both my shoes put together. The leather is scuffed and frayed on the side. The inside of the sole has small soft depressions, little hollows like the sides of my Grandma's cheeks when I kiss them. I put the shoe back on its side like it was.

I will pray about Jamie and his eye. It will be different than talking to myself. I close my eyes to concentrate.

The shoe's still there. Should I pray for Evelyn too? Or should I stick to one thing at a time? Evelyn's accident was a long time ago. Nearer than that is my father's accident. Just the spring before last, my father died in his car accident in Iowa. That's across the Missouri River from here.

My mother told me once about Dad locking himself in the bathroom when he was in third grade. He'd been spanked by a nun in front of the class. He said he wouldn't come out until his folks agreed to let him go to public school, that he'd never go back to the class where he'd been spanked. But his father talked him out of it, or maybe he got hungry, I'm not sure how it ended. Most of my father's stories I hear secondhand from my mom. I wonder if this is *my* bathroom story. Except I'm finished with third grade, and I'd come out any time if I could just be sure Jamie's OK.

The phone rings downstairs, and I hear Evelyn move to answer it. I hold my breath, but I can't hear her voice. Then she moves again. I flush the toilet so she can hear it—I want her to believe I'm sick. You can get sick from fear. It's not always germs or bad food.

"Lucas," she hollers up the steps for me, "come out of the bathroom. Jamie White's father just called. You need to come down here and talk to me right this minute."

Evelyn can make me do anything. She never really gets mad even when she is mad. And it's got something to do with her shoe. I look at it again lying on its side like a little brown animal someone shot right here in the bathroom.

Downstairs, Evelyn and I sit on the purple couch. She turns off "Queen for a Day." It's a show for women, I think, but I like it too. I like the little applause meters and the way the women cry when they get crowned into queens. I pick at the doily on the armrest.

Evelyn waits. I blurt it out. "I shot Jamie. I didn't mean to. I just went to shoot his BB gun. He rents it out for a quarter an hour. All the kids do it. I saved my pop bottle money."

"What kids do it?"

"Everybody. Jimmy and Joe." I shouldn't have said it. Those are her boys. Her eyes widen. "And the Zakursky brothers, and Mike Johnson. You can set up tin cans and practice your aim. But his eye got so red so quick and it dripped on his T-shirt. I didn't mean it. I didn't mean to hurt him."

"Easy, Lucas, just tell me what happened. I know you didn't mean to hurt anyone." She puts her arm around me.

"I don't know." I keep seeing it in my head, but the words are way below it. I can't circle it in with words fast enough. I can't rise up to the picture at the top of my head. "I was holding the gun at my waist and the next minute Jamie was screaming. He was coming out on the back porch and telling me not to shoot toward the greenhouses. I remember thinking how dumb that would be—to shoot at a greenhouse. I was gonna yell something at him, but the gun went off. I wasn't even aiming it. He was bleeding and I was so scared."

"But why didn't you tell anybody? Why didn't you tell me?"

"Jamie said not to. I tried to look at his eye, but the blood was all over—in his eyebrows and his hair. Both of us were crying. He said he'd get Marcia, his big sister, to fix it for him. He said his dad would kill him if he found out about the BB gun. So I left."

Evelyn strokes my shoulder. She looks at the gray TV screen for what feels like a long time. I stare at it too.

"It's wrong not to tell anybody. Accidents happen, but you can't just come home and hide away. Jamie's at the hospital now. Lucas—"

I hear my name but it sounds different today, not matched up to the voice inside me—it could be anybody's name.

"Lucas, are you listening?" I turn to Evelyn. Her eyes seem brighter than the rest of the room, with the curtains closed to keep the heat of the August afternoon out. Evelyn made the curtains.

"I think so."

"I know what you should do now."

"What?"

"Think about it for a minute. I think you know too."

"Pray? But I did. I already did. In the bathroom."

"That's good. But I'll pray now. I'll say a private prayer for Jamie's eyesight while you're gone."

"Gone where?"

• • •

Evelyn tells me about the man who dropped her. One day when she was thirteen, the man who dropped her when she was a baby came to her mother's house and talked to her. He told her his name. He had been a friend of her father years before her father left her mother. He said it was an accident, that she had slipped out of his big hands onto the kitchen floor in a way he had never been able to understand his whole life, in the way something that could never happen just does. He'd been sorry for it every day of his life, he told Evelyn. She said that seeing the man and hearing his name had helped her grow up. His name was Randall Mazur. He had large hands that he kept in his lap. He was wearing a uniform. She said he was dead now. That he died somewhere in the South Pacific only a year or two after that.

"I didn't hate him," Evelyn said. "I didn't hate him in person the way I had inside my mind. He came and took his responsibility, Lucas. And I didn't hate my leg after that either."

"You hated your leg?"

"Everybody has their own responsibility, and sooner or later, they have to own up to it. This is yours, Lucas. The longer you let it go, the more you'll hurt in your heart, and the more Jamie and his family will hurt, too."

"Why your leg? Will Jamie hate his eye if he loses it?"

"You know where the Whites live. I'll be waiting right here for you. I'll call your mom at work and tell her." She kisses the top of my head.

I stand up because I'm sure I'm supposed to.

"Someday, a long time from now, you'll think back to this day. You'll remember me. You'll realize I've told you the truth."

Jamie's house isn't far. Down at the end of the block there's a shortcut where you squeeze through a broken spot in the board fence underneath the billboard that faces Johnson Boulevard.

The billboard has a blonde lady with real red lips and long hair and her mouth open. She's looking at a man in a suit pulling a cigarette from his Old Gold pack, and her balloon says, "It's a lighter, finer smoke." I've seen it a hundred times. Me and the Zakursky brothers meet here. You can usually find some pop bottles lying around under the billboard. They're good for two cents each down at Sylvia's Market on 23rd Street. I cut over to Layton Avenue. Now it's only one more block.

I slow down my walk. I picture Evelyn's word—responsibility. It's a long word, but I can spell it, and I've seen it and read it in books and magazines. But that's a word I rush over. I like to read, but I can read the things I read without being sure about it, like a long foreign name that's hard to pronounce. But when Evelyn said it, it was different. It welled up right out of the center of her story, of her life.

I'd never heard Evelyn talk about her leg or Randall Mazur before. Usually she just jokes about it now and then. She'll say, "I don't know why we bought this old house with an upstairs bathroom with me and my gimpy leg. I musta been dropped on my head, too." And then she laughs real fast and high. Or she'll say, "It's hard for a crippled lady like me to keep up with you wild Indians," sometimes when we all go somewhere and she falls behind. She winks and laughs then, too. But we never laugh when she says those things. It's as if those are her own jokes, just for herself. They make me a little nervous, though, like when I first came to stay with her and Mr. Sattley and the boys in the days. I had been upset about Evelyn's leg and shoe, but Mom said to treat her like any other adult and do what she asked, just like her own boys.

My mom works downtown. She has to leave early in the morning to catch her ride at the corner. Sometimes I stand on the Sattleys' front screen porch and watch her waiting on the corner. She looks much smaller down there than at night when we're home together.

• • •

I see the big black wrought-iron "W" on the front of the Whites' house near the door. It's usually funny that the "W" is black and stands for "White," but not today. I figure they're richer than me and my mom and the Sattleys. That's why they have a big "W" and a greenhouse and those empty lots to play in. At the door, I try not to think about Jamie's blood. I worry sometimes that when I cut myself it will just keep bleeding until all my blood is gone, but it never does. There are some people like that though. People who have to wear bracelets or necklaces so everyone will be real careful of them. I suddenly wonder if Jamie is one of those. There's so much to worry about once you start thinking. I ring the bell.

Jamie's dad is real nice to me. I guess he can see I'm truly sorry when I admit it was me who shot Jamie. I tell him my name twice. He's in a good mood because his wife called from the hospital and said Jamie's OK. They removed the BB from the side of his nose right next to his eye. "We're all very lucky," Mr. White says. "Boys will be boys," he says. He explains Jamie was in the wrong, too, for renting the guns, and that maybe we've all learned our lesson. "I'm very pleased you came over and took responsibility for the accident," he says, using Evelyn's word as if it were his own. He can't talk long because the new baby is crying in the other room. He shakes my hand. I don't know how long to hold on. He lets go first.

I walk back a different way. It's late. Mr. Sattley will be home soon. And then my mom, too. Adults make sense of everything so quickly. Evelyn and Jamie's dad and Mr. Sattley and my mom. They know the right words.

My mom acts mad at me at first, but I can tell it's because she's worried about me. I go to bed early. She says I'm getting to "that age," and she sighs as if that's something she's been afraid of for a long time.

"I hid in the bathroom, Mom. I touched Evelyn's sick shoe."

"Don't call it that, honey. You were just upset. It's over."

"Why didn't Dad ever tell me his bathroom story? Why didn't he tell me any of the stories you tell me about him?"

"Maybe he would have, Lukie. Maybe he was waiting to." She turns the light out and then stands near me. A streetlight on Shirley Street shines through the screen like a little moon on a stick.

"Your father had a hard childhood. He didn't tell anybody much, except me. But maybe he would have."

"Am I having a hard childhood? How do you tell?"

"I don't think so. What do you think?"

I look through the window. "No." I wonder if I'll ever get married when I grow up. Would I tell her about my childhood?

"Your daddy was a sensitive man. Things hurt him very easily."

Mom always says this, but I already know it because I saw him crying several times, usually late at night, when he never knew I was looking. I've never seen Mr. Sattley cry. He's a Catholic too. But maybe he never got spanked in front of the class and locked himself in the bathroom.

I wonder if I'm sensitive. I like the sound of it on my tongue. It feels better in my mouth than "responsibility." As I fall asleep, I hear my mom in the kitchen washing dishes.

I walk on my hands, like a circus clown, Evelyn's big shoe strapped on my left hand. The neighborhood is hot, like summer, but there's no leaves on any trees. Evelyn's shoe pinches my fingers, my arm shrivels up. I hear Jimmy and Joe in the backyard, hollering and playing, but their yells sound slowed down and wavy like they're making noises underwater. Evelyn comes to the door. I look up at my feet and a thin layer of white clouds flattens out across the sky as if they're floating just above the houses. She's barefoot. Her leg is OK—it's the right size. But she's frowning. She's got a bright red eye-patch pasted on her face, like a mad lady pirate. She says a man is looking for me. He wants to know what

I've done with the big steel letter I stole. My mother comes up behind me. She has a nun's dress on, but it's way too big—it pools around her feet like black water.

It's six-thirty A.M.—time to get ready to go to the Sattleys'. The corner streetlight is still on. Mom's only been up a little while, but she looks tired already. While I dress, she talks from the bathroom like she'd rehearsed what she says.

"Lucas, you have to promise me never to shoot any kind of a gun without my permission and knowledge. I just cannot work all day long worrying about things like that. Do you understand?"

"Sure, I promise, Mom. But listen, I had a dream, a nightmare, just now. It was so real. I had Evelyn's shoe—"

"Evelyn's shoe is the last thing you need to worry about. You need to worry about being safe, about using your head. Accidents happen all the time. Jamie could've lost an eye—so could you. Think about your father."

"He wasn't in the dream. But you were, in a nun's dress, and I couldn't get the shoe off. The whole neighborhood was different, too, like I didn't belong anymore."

"Luke, listen. I want you to concentrate on your promise. Dreams aren't real. Today is what's real—from here on out until bedtime tonight. That's what we have to think about—how to get through the real day. Dreams just help us get leftover things from the daytime out of our systems. They wash us out at night and leave us clean and ready for a new day. That's all there is to it."

"I promise." It's overcast outside. But the streetlight blinks out.

The grass and sidewalks are still wet from a night rain. I kiss my mom in front of the Sattleys'. I watch her walk to the corner. When she's gone, I go in through the front porch. Evelyn is ironing while the twins watch Tom Terrific cartoons. Joe's in the kitchen opening a can of corn.

"What are you doing?"

"Goin' fishing at the lagoon. Perfect day. Dad said so. Wanna come with?"

I look at Evelyn. She's barefoot at the ironing board. She winks at me. "OK by me—stick together and be home by noon."

At the park lagoon I get out the old rod and reel Mr. Sattley found for me on a shelf in the basement. Joe is already casting out. We like fishing because you can be quiet and sit still like the men do. As long as you have your line in next to you, nobody can say you aren't doing anything. But you can daydream all you want and really be just loafing. I like to loaf at the edge of the lagoon and look at the still water. You can see the reflection of clouds and trees and everything, and when the ripples roll across the water you look up quickly to see if the real world ripples in the same way.

And there's a third world, too, the one down below in the deep green water. Nobody's sure how deep it is down there, although some of the high school boys say they dived down to the bottom one time late at night.

None of *us* ever swim in the lagoon though.

We say it's because the lagoon's just for fishing, but really a lot of it is because of the story of the boy who drowned a long time ago. Sometimes I think it was just made up to scare us kids from swimming, but one time on a Sunday when Joe reeled in a mossy, bloated-up old shoe, Mr. Sattley said it must have belonged to the drowned boy.

Everybody around the park seems to have heard about him. And in every story I've heard, the little boy's friends have to go for help and leave him alone. And in every story, by the time they get back with the adults, the water is quiet, and the boy is gone.

But there would have been some adults around. There's always somebody at the lagoon in summertime—people fishing and having picnics or walking. It doesn't make sense. They could have thrown him something to hang onto—even a fishing pole or line. Maybe they could have pulled him back to shore with a line somehow. But that doesn't make sense either. The idea of a boy on the end of a line sounds crazy, and it reminds me of my dream.

That's the trouble with what mom says about dreams—they happen in the daytime too. Sometimes in the park or the neighborhood the whole day seems like a dream.

The clouds are lower now, they're just above Evelyn's head. I'm sitting on my hands, hoping nobody sees the shoe. My mother and Evelyn move closer. As they bend over me, the clouds come down with them. I have to get the shoe off before the clouds drown us all. I swing my shriveled arm. The shoe flies off and lands between them.

My line moves in the water, but it's just the breeze. I won't think about dreams. I will concentrate on other people, real people who are far away from me now. I imagine my mom downtown in the office at the desk I saw one Saturday. Evelyn is watching "Beat the Clock" and ironing. Or maybe in the kitchen making onion soup for lunch. Mr. Sattley is at the wheel of the forklift he always talks about. I wonder if Jamie is home today. I had such a close call yesterday, and I learned something about Evelyn's word—"responsibility." Now I can see it in my own head. It's about not hiding in the bathroom, and about saying your name, and then I realize my mom knows about it too, she knows it's about not paying so much attention to dreams. It's such an important word to the grownups—I'm going to learn all about it.

I turn the reel handle until it clicks, and the line slices the water like a razor. I secretly hope I don't catch anything. That's the part I don't like. I have my own set of ideas about the fish and what hurts them. I sometimes picture the hook swimming through the calm water until it finds the fish, no matter where they hide. The fish wouldn't stand a chance. But I believe with all my heart that the fish don't hurt as long as they're in the water. It isn't the hook or the pull of the line or even the fighting that hurts them. It's breaking the surface.

At that instant, everything becomes crystal clear to them in their own fish sense. That they are helpless, that something big and powerful is dragging them away from the cool deep home that they love. It's the shock. It's the realization. It begins drying out their little watery souls the second they break into the air on the end of the line. It isn't the hook that hurts them. It isn't the hook at all.

And Quinn

"I'M LEAVING Maryville anyway," Neal says, as if it were a secret he'd saved for just the right moment.

Quinn thinks of the other time, her first pregnancy, in October, seven months before. She'd confirmed it a month after she first slept with Neal, and they calculated it was from their first weekend together, maybe even the first night—or time—and even came to laugh about that later. But this night she sees their whole time together as a joke, one that keeps being repeated, long after it receives its last laugh.

"Because I'm pregnant?" she asks. Quinn stares through Neal's window at the lights from other windows, signs, street-lamps. She believes that people only tell their secrets after dark, but she doesn't know why. She wonders if Neal, who has been her lover almost every night for eight months, is a man for whom even secrets are false clues, deflections, lies.

"Of course not," he says. "I said 'anyway.' As in the job is almost done, and Peters doesn't like me enough to put me on steady. I go where the work takes me. You know that. I've always told you that."

Neal is a bricklayer. He's been working on the new athletic building on the campus since last August. To Quinn, Neal's hardworked body and sun-rough face have been a sculpture whose curves and strengths she's been compelled to learn by heart. Skin, skim, surface. Yet Neal had driven her to the abortion clinic in St. Joseph, waited in the hot parking lot for two hours, and stayed with her, ordered pizza and paid, gone out for video after video as the weekend waned and Quinn's strength waxed. But they had not talked. Beneath the surface was only another. Peeling onions.

"When?" Quinn asks. She hears her own short questions— bit-part, straight-woman routines—angry at herself for the minor role she's playing in her own life.

"One week, two," Neal answers. "Depends on the weather. The inside work's done. All that's left is the steps in front and the entry piers. It's just real bad timing, Quinn. You know I'll take you to the clinic again."

Neal almost smiles, and Quinn knows he has said this before—was it to her?—sees that his itinerant life draws power from love stranded, senses the rearview mirror satisfaction it gives him. A roving itinerary of walls topped off, jobs winding down, foremen put in their place. Women as easy as postcards. Rotating wire racks that squeak in the stale air of drugstores with tile floors.

"Look, Q. You're fertile. And I'm potent." This last he completes with his winning smile, something he builds on his face one word at a time, like a wall. Quinn sees that to him there are no feelings, only conditions. Her pregnancy, bad timing, like a rash in hot weather.

He waits, unable to read her thoughts and, clearly, not wanting to, while Quinn has a premonition, unbidden, vivid: he falls from a high place, steps off a scaffold, walks off a wall. She sees it, a home movie in her head, badly shot. On his way down, will he see the faces of women?

She stands and zips her jeans that he had unzipped just before he heard her news. She slips her arms into her jacket as if she were cold, and she knows she will be. She walks across Neal's room and bends over his toolbag, wrapping her fingers around the wooden handle of his trowel. He is still sitting on the bed. She turns and throws the trowel over his head, into the mirror behind him. A wedge of silvered glass nicks out and falls on the bed like a jagged jewel. The trowel lands on the floor right side up. Neal's face has an expression Quinn has never seen before: surprise. He moves to pick up his trowel. While his back is turned, she walks out without closing the door.

Quinn comes to the first corner before she sees she's left her purple hightops behind. Barefoot and pregnant, she thinks, looking down at her feet and then over her head, imagining the cliché hovering above her like a garish neon sign. A breeze in the sycamore branches plays shadows on the pavement in the light from the streetlamp, and the sweet smell of lilac drapes the humid spring air like pink crepe. She won't go back for her shoes.

She steps off the curb but stops short in front of a parked pickup truck with a cabover camper. Out-of-state plates. She stands still, her feet cold street roots on rock. A semi pulls out of the Skagway loading docks two blocks south, and she listens to the rising bass roar of its engine, and the one, two, three times abating as its gears snap and grind back home like steel bones breaking. A harsh sweep of light washes the street, and as she feels the truck moving toward her, rattling the small-town night with its rough bellow, close enough now to scrape the low-hanging branches and overscent the gentle lilacs, Quinn imagines herself stepping into its path. She is more frightened than she has ever been.

· · ·

When she hears the swifts stitching across the black sky above her, and when the spring air settles back around her like a dark sheet floating down over a newmade bed, she finds her motion again. She shakes her head to test it, her loose brown hair tracing a ragged arc.

As she crosses the street, her bare feet force her to pay attention to each step, the cold pavement's raw sting on her skin. Dense boughs of maple shade her path, and the trees have buckled the sidewalk in several places, the concrete squares rising and splitting apart around swollen exposed roots. She thinks of sidewalk games, years before, and the Fontenelle Boulevard neighborhood where she played them in north Omaha. One hundred and twenty miles away. As the crow flies.

Running hopscotch. Grass-safe team-tag. Step on a crack.

Quinn pictures her destination from above, the way the birds might see it, her home: a one-bedroom trailer on the edge of Maryville, a small college town in the northwest corner of Missouri, twenty miles south of Iowa, twenty miles east of Nebraska. A month shy of her twenty-third birthday, Quinn has been in Maryville two years, one year in school, and one year since quitting. She has walked from Neal's downtown apartment to her trailer many times before, often at night. But never before barefoot. It is just over a mile.

After four blocks she passes the old house where Aaron, the van driver at the florist shop where she works, rents the first floor. They've worked together for almost a year, and Quinn considers him almost a friend. Yet as she stares at his house, she thinks of how little she knows about him. He is three years older than Quinn, he grew up somewhere in Iowa, and she has thought he might be gay, although they've never spoken of that. She knows he has to work in the morning—it is after midnight—and tomorrow is one of the busiest days of the year for him, the Saturday before Mother's Day, but through one of his windows, beyond the silhouetted spears of a tall standing houseplant, a yellow light shines.

• • •

At the door, Aaron says her name like a question, and she thinks it sounds best that way, rising, not finished.

She hesitates. "Hi. Can I borrow a pair of shoes? I thought I could make it home barefoot." She points over her shoulder to the square-block world of shadows beyond his gate. "The sidewalk's cold."

Inside, he says he can find a pair of shoes for her, but he doesn't look for them right away, which is better, what she wanted without knowing. As well as the cup of goldenseal tea he fixes her. And the talk—yet another fight with Neal, but the last one, she swears—telling half-truths, making light, almost joking. Broken up, she says, like the plays in her father's TV football games.

No, he's not in a hurry to go to bed. He's napped earlier—a habit of his, he says. Quinn is in no hurry, either, to go back to the empty trailer. As Aaron pours tea, she stands too close behind him, and then she feels herself leaning forward, a slow fall. It is not what she wants, this light warm press, only two T-shirts between her breasts and the lean of his back—it stands for something else that she cannot ask for, speak of.

"It's not right, Quinn," he says. From the other side of both their bodies, the spoon rings on the china like a bell.

"Tell me a secret," she says, moving away, embarrassed, and sorry, and saying half of it aloud. "I'm sorry." Her feet are warm in the socks he's given her. He hands her the tea.

"No need. Everybody runs scared one time or another." They sit in his living room. A cane rocker Aaron has repaired and a chrome and leather chair recycled from a barbershop waiting room via several Saturday swap-meets. Two cups between them on a round tile table.

"I run scared most of the time," he says and looks away. She follows his eyes and notices the dried flowers on the walls. Then she sees them everywhere, in vases, baskets on the floor, above the doors. And a line of flowers drying, upside-down clusters clothespinned to a wire running the length of the room by the windows.

"That's too general," Quinn says. But before he responds, she waves her hand toward a wreath on the wall near her. "Are all these from the shop? They're beautiful."

"Recycled," he says. "I sell them, too." He stands and reaches for a spray leaning against the wall, one with violet-crimson dried roses in eucalyptus on grapevine. "Would you like it?"

Quinn takes it, keeps it on her lap, sips tea. She is afraid to touch the roses, but can't keep her hands from them. They are tougher than they look, though, a delicate carmine leather.

He watches her fingers on the roses. "Too general, you said?"

"Like if I tell you that I almost didn't make it here tonight," she answers. "This far." She wonders if he heard the truck, pulling out of town under load. The roses rest in her lap. "Thank you," she says, lifting them. "I hate seeing how many flowers they waste." She remembers the florist shop's full garbage cans each day when she leaves at five.

"I'm gay," he says. "Is that specific enough?"

She realizes that must have been what she'd expected to hear, but she can't think of anything to say. She sips her tea. The silence settles in, yet the room relaxes her. Her foolishness in the kitchen comes back to her, and she wishes the night were over, had never happened, would not end.

"I had an abortion," she says. "Last fall. With Neal."

"I'm sorry," he says.

"No," she says. "I don't regret it. Just that I went ahead. I saw all the signs, right at the start. And I went on."

"Isn't it often like that?" he asks.

"It?"

"Love," he says.

"Sex is," she says. "For me, I guess."

"I'm waiting for the right person, the right time," he says. "I'm not letting it be easy enough, I guess."

"I make it too easy," Quinn says. "The difficulty comes later."

"With me, that's first," he says. "It's here inside." He puts his hand on his chest where people think their hearts are.

Quinn sees pain in his eyes, honest, unfeigned, something she's not used to seeing but recognizes anyway. She touches his forearm.

"Aaron, I like you. I don't really know why I came here. I had a moment on the street corner when I was close to the worst. The absolute worst."

"You can tell me about it if you want," he says, even as she realizes she doesn't. She shakes her head. "Do you want to stay tonight?" he asks. "I've got an extra bedroom."

"Maybe." She looks around. It's a huge apartment for one person, twice the floor space of her trailer, she thinks. "No. Just the shoes. And the talk. You're very kind to me."

"Want to hear a story?" he asks. "I'll get the shoes." He goes into his bedroom and brings back a pair of white canvas shoes. Quinn puts them on. They aren't that much bigger than her own. She can lace them tight.

"Ever watch the softball games over at Play Square Park?" he asks.

"I don't like softball," she says. "Baseball." She's not sure what the difference is. Her game is tennis. "I've almost never played."

"I quit when I was eight or ten," Aaron says. "But the first summer when I moved here from Clarinda, I was so lonely I'd go out and watch."

"Clarinda?"

"Forty miles northeast. You've never been there?"

"I've heard it on the weather, I think. It's a pretty name. I always drive the Interstate."

"Actually," he says, smiling, "I'm a farm boy."

Quinn thinks of the only place she's seen him work: at the florist shop, intent, careful, poised. She can't picture him walking behind a baler, riding a tractor.

"So I got this crazy idea," he says. "Something I wanted to do so badly, and yet was so afraid of, that I told myself if I didn't do it I'd kill myself. Like a bet with myself. But I wouldn't have."

"How crazy?" Quinn asks.

"This one team," he says, "I saw them play so often I felt I knew them. And the last game of the season, at the end of the game—which they lost—but have you ever seen the way they shake hands at the end of a softball game? Both teams line up. The whole teams. It was my favorite moment. And it was my last chance. I ran down at the final out and got in line."

"With the players?"

"As if I were one," he says, not shifting his eyes from hers.

Neal's face, or the thought of Neal's face, appears in Quinn's head, and she thinks: I let him lie to me. I lied, too.

"I don't think anybody noticed," Aaron says. "The benches cleared and everyone was so, I don't know, jovial and well-meaning, and I shook every hand and looked them each in the face. In that line I felt connected."

Quinn thinks of the baby beginning inside her and the loneliness kids grow into, in Clarinda or Omaha or Maryville, and must wear or wear out like Little League baseball suits or tights and toe shoes. She sees Neal as a boy, playing baseball, holding himself back from his teammates and friends, the hurts trailing behind him like a collection he owns but never sees.

"I just never liked baseball," she says. "I'm glad you didn't kill yourself, Aaron."

"Likewise, Quinn," he says, standing. Their tea is gone. The dried flower arrangement slips to the floor when she stands. One of the rose petals powders, after all, a thin smudge on Aaron's shoe like dry red clay. She hands the flowers back to him.

"Can I get this later? I'm walking."

"I don't have a car," he says. "You sure about not staying?"

Quinn feels her legs trembling, as if she'd run four miles instead of walked four blocks. Her eyes feel sandy, washed-out. The scene with Neal seems months ago.

"No. I mean I'm not sure. Would it be all right?"

Aaron puts the flowers on the table next to the teapot and shows her the extra bedroom. She lies down on top of the comforter. She feels him fold it over her, feels wrapped and warm. Her feet hang over the bottom of the bed. Aaron takes off the shoes. She pulls the comforter up around her face.

She hears him lock the front door and go to bed. The light Quinn saw from the street, behind the tall Dracaena in the window, stays on all night.

Quinn had planned on leaving early Saturday morning for her parents' house in Omaha to spend Mother's Day weekend. She had thought, if she could let it happen spontaneously, that Neal might come with her. But then the real Saturday morning is there, and so different: her light, restless sleep and Aaron's alarm and a half-painted dream gone like a swirl of fog. And as she dresses, the unfamiliar sounds of Aaron in the kitchen, and the idea in her head, an adventure, a cure, a lark.

Aaron agrees when she asks, and she goes with him on his deliveries, riding shotgun in the florist van, running the flowers up to the doors. They load the van by eight, empty it by eleven, and eat lunch on the brick benches by the campus sundial. They load up again and finish for the day by four. Aaron says it would have taken him till at least seven by himself. On the way home, Quinn offers him a ride to Clarinda. At first he says he'd planned on a quiet Sunday alone, just a phone call to his mom, but when she mentions it again, he accepts.

Near the horizon, the setting sun swells, and around it the sky streaks away in feathered gold-orange stripes like a clouded watercolor flag. Quinn and Aaron ride in silence in her '63 pink Plymouth Valiant north on Highway 71, following the easy brown curves of the Nodaway River. In the west, dark thunderheads cantilever toward them. Quinn notices a slight smell of rain, still far in the distance, then turns her head and smells the last two bouquets in the back seat, one for Aaron's mother and one for her own.

The clipboard list from the day lies face up on the dash: each line a woman's name and address. Quinn looks at the forty-seven entries on the lined sheet and thinks she can almost remember the smiles that went with each one. She smiles now, feeling the unexpected grace of the day.

She looks at Aaron, but he's not smiling. She senses unease in him, his body tensing, his jaw tightening.

"Hey," she speaks for the first time since they left Maryville. "Why weren't you planning to go home for the holiday?"

"We don't get along," Aaron says. "They don't know me."

"Let me guess," she says. "You haven't told them the baseball story?"

"Have you told your folks about the abortion?" he asks.

"No," she says. "They wouldn't want to know."

"I didn't say all the truth last night," Aaron says. "I'm a virgin."

"You said gay," she says, her eyes on the highway. They've crossed into Iowa, the land still rolling like a movie of mild seas, stop-actioned, freshly sown to green.

Aaron laughs. "It's not either-or," he says. "It's both."

"How can you be sure?" she asks.

He looks out the window. "I'm just sure. Weren't you sure before your first time? So far I'm only gay in my head. First things first, right?"

"Will you tell them?"

"Someday. Sure."

"Have you told anybody?"

"You."

"Jesus," Quinn says, "it must be . . ." She pauses, but she can't think of an easier word. "Lonely."

"Difficult," he says. "I'm growing up. Not the way they planned, or I planned. But I'm getting there." He points to the sign just now readable ahead of them as they round a bend:

Clarinda—20. "In a beat-up Valiant. With a woman who—"

"Is pregnant," Quinn interrupts.

"I was going to say, who can't keep track of her shoes." They pass the mileage marker. "And Neal doesn't care?"

"He cares. He offered to take me to the clinic in St. Joseph again."

"Is that why you wanted to come with me today?"

"I don't know," she says. "Partly I didn't want to give myself a chance to stop by Neal's as I left town."

"Partly?"

Quinn remembers Mrs. Selin then, an old woman who only a few hours earlier had hugged her in the doorway of her nursing home, holding her flowers behind Quinn's back for a moment, her dim eyes wet with joy.

"It was like the last out," Quinn says, offering her hand to Aaron as if they'd just been introduced. He shakes her hand.

"Good game," he says.

They ride quietly again for a few miles. The grain elevators at Clarinda loom closer. And the water tower. Quinn reads the name in red across it, whispering it. She wonders what kind of woman the town was named for.

"So what will you do?" Aaron asks.

"I don't know. Not tell my mother on Mother's Day for starters."

"Is it expensive?" Aaron asks, as she slows at the edge of town, looking for the turnoff he's told her to take.

"It's not cheap."

"If you need money," he says. "Or a place to stay. You saw all the extra space at my house. I've got some savings."

Quinn takes the turn and stops on gravel, for a moment unable to drive or answer. The little town is three blocks deep from the highway on this side. The farm is only half a mile farther.

"I just mean, whatever I can do," he says.

"Thanks," she says. She takes her foot off the brake and the Plymouth idles forward.

"So what time will you pick me up tomorrow night?" he asks.

"Six-ish," she says. "Can I meet the folks then?"

"If you want to," he answers. "They'll be surprised. My mom will jump to conclusions. And that'll make her happy."

"One day a year," Quinn says, and they both laugh. She squeezes his hand one more time before they turn into the farm lane.

After she turns east at Lyman, as she's alone and nearing home, it is twilight. Rain clouds blow toward her from Nebraska, and the squall line passes above her like a dark forearm, raindrops the size of quarters spattering the windshield.

She leans over and rolls the far window up, then hers, as she feels the temperature dropping. She puts her wipers on, the lights, and still she must slow down as the storm erupts around her. The wind pushes the Plymouth toward the shoulder of the road. Quinn steers with both hands. Lightning flashes in the distance, high, and then near, a trident spike to the ground much closer. Thunder claps around her, sheets of rain descending like slanted wet walls. And Quinn, still slowing, waiting for the storm to abate, and for the lights of Omaha to appear, thinks, as the gray-black belly of the clouds lowers down and down, that the sky itself is about to give birth.

The Emptyheart Boy

IT WAS THE WINTER after my first divorce. The old apartment building on the edge of downtown Springfield, The Florence, was brick, that maroon rough-cut brick from the twenties or thirties, Dutch running bond with a row of headers every six courses, like it should be. A white frame porch with a balcony above it floated in front, probably added later. I lived on the second story.

Old Bill Scott lived directly below me. That December he still stood tall and walked straight and had a voice like old strong leather. Until he got so sick later in the winter, he traded and sold cars all the time, skimming a small downtown living off some nearby car dealers, old friends of his, parking a different shiny, freshly washed used car, always American, a Riviera or Cutlass or LTD, in front of the building every couple of weeks.

His daughter-in-law lived with him off and on—I never saw his son. The only time I ever heard him talk about either of them was one sunny day that fall when I ran into him out in front of the place.

"Hey, Michael, how's the old pickup running?" Bill always asked after my truck before me. I think he got a kick out of getting me defensive about it.

"Like a top, Bill. If the tappets didn't knock just a little, I wouldn't be able to tell it was idling when I stop at the traffic lights."

"Is that tappets I been hearing all the way from Kimbrough Avenue? You best let me find you a quiet vehicle, a luxury model."

"No way. I've had that truck longer than anything else I have."

It was true. I'd pretty much chased off my wife after we'd moved back to town, and the land on the river had been sold at a small profit, and the Whole Earth Catalog was just another coffee table book for me now, but I'd had the truck for over twelve years.

"And it's dependable," I said, "like an old friend. You think you'll have that Cougar ten years from now?"

"No, and I wouldn't be wanting to. I get a strong pleasure in my vehicles, how they look, how they shape up, and then I get a strong pleasure in trading them away. You know how many vehicles I've had the title on in my time?"

Bill slammed the trunk carefully. He'd told me this before. "Sixty-seven. Three more and I'll catch up to my age."

I didn't know whether to believe him about either one.

"Next you're gonna tell me you slept with a hundred women."

He grinned but didn't answer. I knew Bill just well enough to know that such talk made him shy in a charming kind of way. He caressed a nick on the fender of his car, sizing it up.

"I just don't see the good in a old has-been truck for a professor fellow, is all," he said, changing the subject. "The college been treating you OK?"

He always called it that even though it had twenty thousand students, and he always called me a professor fellow although I'd explained over and over I wasn't. He couldn't fathom me, a bricklayer, being a thirty-five-year-old sophomore. Sometimes neither could I.

"About the same, Bill. Anyway, the only thing I'm professor of is brick. Professor Brickwork. I can't drive one of your deluxe sedans—I've got brick jobs in the summer to think about. Could I haul five hundred pounds of sand in the trunk of that shiny Cougar?"

"Sounds to me like you need two vehicles. One for the day, one for the night." He raised one palm after the other. "One for the bricks and one for the ladies. How you gonna wine and dine them co-eds out of that rusty old truck?"

"I guess I'll just send them to see my friend downstairs."

"Don't do that, now." He laughed again. "No, don't you do that. Renee wouldn't take to that. She don't like excitements."

"Renee?"

"My boy's wife. She's down on her luck these last years. Ever since that emptyheart boy of mine run out on her. She don't drive. I take her on errands, and I told her she can stay here whenever she needs to. Somebody's got to stand good to my boy's word."

I almost asked if he knew where his son was, but he started moving toward the house, as if he'd already said too much. We walked together to the mailboxes on the front porch. I liked talking to him, even if the conversations were usually street-side and superficial, and I think he liked me, partly because of the very things he pretended not to understand—that I kept the old truck, and that I went to college.

I'd gone back after fifteen years.

With just a twist or two different, I probably could have been in some other kind of institution, but I'd been lucky or cautious or timid, and it was only the local university, three days a week, and the rest of the time on my own recognizance, so to speak.

Damn, though, sometimes that's the scariest of all, your own recognizance.

The only time Gary from the upstairs apartment in the back was friendly was when he was so high he couldn't see straight. I'd run into him in the hall like that, and he'd tell me to come by his place anytime for a toke. One time earlier that fall I'd started to take him up on his offer, one cold, sunny afternoon when I was sick of reading and I heard Side Two of the second Airplane album coming from his place. I walked down the hall toward the music. His door stood open. I inhaled and held my breath.

Gary was asleep on the living room floor. Two hundred-dollar bills lay on the couch next to a box of baggies and an unopened six-pack. The music played on. I stared through the window behind his couch at stark trees with a few brown leaves. Summer looked a long time gone.

It was the age of cocaine, but Gary was the kind of guy you'd figure to be always dealing one drug behind the times. He worked nights over at Mid-West Towel and Linen Service, three blocks away, and a chest-high stack of Mid-West towels stood in one corner. The rubber hall-runner was loose and curled up in front of his door as if someone had kicked it on the way out. I straightened it and tiptoed away from his door. I ran my index fingers down the dusty walls on either side of me.

In that December before old Bill Scott got so sick, I think Gary was screwing around with Lanelle, the woman who'd moved in downstairs across from Bill right after Thanksgiving.

Lanelle always wore short skirts, even in winter. Her eyes were small and almost colorless, and her hair looked worn out from being twisted into so many different perms and curls. She was tiny and flat as a board, but her legs were long and shapely.

Her old man, Kevin, worked for Redlight Wreckers down on Trafficway, and a lot of times he took Lanelle with him on calls in his tow truck. Other times Lanelle would stay home when he left. Maybe some of her friends knew Gary or bought dope from Gary, I had no idea. But I know I heard her platform shoes on the steep stairway more and more often.

I met Lanelle for the first time on the front porch. She was stringing a strand of Christmas lights around their window. She asked me to help. That was the first year ever I hadn't had a tree. She seemed friendly that afternoon while I helped her arrange the bulbs so that every other one was red, then green.

"I've never had outside lights before. Gary, upstairs, do you know him? I'm Lanelle, by the way."

"I'm Michael. Not very much."

"Oh, well, it was Gary that loaned me and Kevin these. He's sweet. You been here long? What's the scoop on the old dude and the young gal in number one?" She traded me a red bulb for a green one.

"Old Bill? He's retired, sort of. A mechanic." I could tell that wasn't what she wanted to know. "I stay pretty much to myself," I added.

"What for? I'd go crazy if I did that."

"I'm a student at the U. I have lots of reading to keep me busy."

"You don't look like a student. What do you have to read?"

"Literature, mostly."

"Literature." She repeated it slowly as she unscrewed bulbs that were out of sequence, as slowly as if it were some romantic foreign word from a movie like *Casbah* or *Arrivederci*. When she stretched up to arrange a bulb above her, I caught myself looking at her nylons where they changed to a darker brown shade, high on her thigh.

"Sounds different. You wanta get high sometime? You could come with me up to Gary's. He's got some great stash."

I lied quickly. "I'm studying for finals, thanks anyway." I knew I didn't want to get anywhere between her and her old man and Gary. Anyway, I already had a girlfriend.

I grabbed my mail and headed up to my place. People like

Lanelle downstairs and Gary upstairs reminded me why I'd liked living half a mile from my neighbors all those years in Shannon County, half-hidden from the world, way back on the Missouri side of the Jacks Fork River.

The girlfriend, Kathryn, was five years older than me. When I met her, right before I left my wife, I thought she was the best thing that'd ever happened to me, a sign that I was on the right track. I believed you had to go with your hunches.

Kathryn was a graduate student in music—she played clarinet. She had two kids, both in high school, both living with her ex and his second wife. She'd let go of everything once already in her life—house, kids, car, church, husband, even her memory—everything, finally, after a whiskey and valium overdose that threw her into a week-long coma, everything but her breath.

She'd had to relearn how to tie her shoes, make her bed, comb her hair, recognize the faces in family photo albums.

I figured she had a lot she could teach me.

She had jet black hair and the darkest eyes I'd ever seen up close. She'd played clarinet all through junior high, and after her last OD she said the one thing she could remember without any effort was how to play the clarinet.

That was eight years earlier.

She'd gotten Voc Rehab money and GSL loans to go to State and study music. She went to her meetings every day. She took six years to graduate, and she was borrowing money to work on a master's even though she was already over ten thousand bucks into the government, but when she'd play that clarinet or when she'd talk about the nuts and bolts of real-life resurrection, none of that seemed to matter.

The guy who lived across the hall from me was named Guy. Or nicknamed, maybe, I never found out which. Sometimes Kathryn called him Guy the Beatnik because he had a little goatee and no furniture. He was a paramedic who'd built a two-room house out by Joplin and only used the Florence apartment about three days a week when he was on call with St. John's. He had one of those gravity boot inverters in his living room, and whenever he was home in the afternoon, he'd hang upside down for an hour.

Guy was intrigued with me coming back from the land. He started kidding me, calling me one of those back-from-back-to-the-land-ers.

So I kidded him, too. I called him the Organic Space Man because in the summer he'd sit on the balcony after he'd hung upside down, wearing his foam-padded gravity boots and silk underwear, with his eyes dilated and his forehead scarlet, eating carrots and tomatoes from Joplin and tofu from the Whole Food Deli at school.

Actually, I'd caught myself thinking how handy it was to have Guy around. Since I'd moved there, I'd been having sharp heartburn in the middle of the night a lot. I'd wake up, imagining an early heart attack, one of those quick fatal ones they always call massive.

Here I used to live four miles down a gravel road, at least two hours' drive from a hospital, but I found myself worrying about a massive heart attack, banking on the paramedic across the hall. That's how people change—from night to day. It's lucky we at least keep the same names and faces. Or then again, maybe not.

Two days before Christmas, the eve of Christmas Eve, late, Kathyrn and I were in bed, lying still after love. The Florence creaked in the cold wind like the ominous sound of icy branches straining against each other. I was letting my mind roll back to Shannon County, wondering about the Scotch pine seedlings I'd planted on the flat by the creek, wondering how tall they would be and if they were past the danger of winter-burn.

I heard a door slam downstairs.

"Fine, that's fine, fucking fine with me!" Lanelle yelled, her voice high, trembling. Her shoes counted off the stairs, eighteen, and then clicked down the hall toward Gary's.

The door downstairs opened again, and Kevin yelled after her.

"You take one step in Gary's apartment an' you just may well move all your shit up there, Lanny, you hear me?"

"Threaten me, promise me," Lanelle answered.

"And don't even think about taking the Maverick anywhere. I'm getting about anxious to do some hunting on you. One of these times I'm gonna get my deer rifle and hunt your ass down, I am now."

The door slammed again. With every loud noise the apartment building seemed to get quieter, smaller, closer. Lanelle knocked on Gary's door. It opened. She went in. It closed. Gary's phone started ringing. Nobody answered. It rang a long time.

I fell asleep, curled around Kathryn, wishing I could take her to Shannon County and show her my neat rows of Scotch pine windbreak.

When I woke again, Kathryn wasn't in bed. A woman cried in the hallway. Kathryn's cigarette glowed red from the wicker chair across the room. I didn't move.

I heard voices I couldn't recognize, men's voices.

"Good show, Lana. Hot and sticky is this boy's favorite combo. I even order my pizzas that way." Someone leaned on the hall wall and then slid down it. I thought of the thick dust on those walls.

"Her name's Lanette, dickhead. C'mon, let's go, d'ya get the shit from Gary? What a deal, get loaded and laid in one stop."

The first voice got louder. "Yeah, good show, Gary. I like your neighborhood, I do. Merry Xmas, neighbors, free pussy in the hall." They clumped down the steps.

Lanelle's voice chased them. "You assholes, both of you put together aren't big enough to satisfy a woman."

Somebody yelled back. "One size fits all." The storm door snapped open against the building in the wind.

Gary came out of his apartment. "Those yahoos are so stoned they can't even close the damn door. It must be below zero out there. Run down and close it, Lanelle. And then we'll have a drink. No sense crying in the hallway—it's Christmas, remember."

"You creep. When I tell Kevin, he'll kill your ass."

"No he won't. He'll just be pissed I didn't invite him up for the party favors." The crunch of a beer can interrupted his words. "You're the one came running to me, so don't pull the high-and-mighty-bitch act on me now. Nobody forced you to do anything. Lighten up, you won't die from too much lovin'."

"Love. Shit. You used me to make your two-bit deal. Those guys didn't even want your headache weed till they got hard over me." She screamed. "You pimp-ass mother, you laundry boy."

"Shut your foul mouth, Lanelle."

"Bring me a clean towel, laundry boy."

"I'll bring you a towel, you tired-ass bitch. I'll bring you a towel on your bare butt."

Kathryn put out her cigarette. The windows over the bed distorted the streetlight as they flexed in the wind. She came over and shook me. I didn't know why I'd been pretending not to be awake, but it was too late to admit my pretense. I tossed my head and yawned.

"Michael, something sick's going on, we have to do something. They're liable to kill each other."

I looked at her as if I hadn't heard anything in the hall.

"Try this," I heard Gary yell. "Laundry boy'll show you." Sharp slaps echoed in the hall, like somebody snapping a throw rug or cracking a whip.

I wished I were somewhere far away. I was afraid of Gary and Kevin and Lanelle because I thought they were desperate without knowing it. Down deep I was afraid of people, period. I saw

111

myself clear for a second, goaded by fears and by the fear of revealing my fears. But I couldn't tell Kathryn that. She wasn't afraid of people. All she was afraid of was alcohol, and I realized then how lethal, and yet at the same time how comfortable, it might be to have such a sharp focus for my fears.

"Easy, K, they'll calm down, you can't go charging out there everytime people get drunk or loaded up. Don't you read the news? People don't like getting interfered with."

I stroked her hair in the dark. Everything was quiet for a long moment. I hoped she wouldn't ask me what I was thinking about because the truth was, all of a sudden I couldn't get the image of my wife out of my head. After our breakup she'd visited me only once at the Florence, the spring before. When she went out, she sat for an hour in her car before she pulled away, but it had never dawned on me until right then that it had been the real parting between us, the final one, that hour when she sat in the car at the curb and I watched her through the venetian blinds.

I lowered my head to Kathryn's breasts, expecting comfort without asking or explaining what for. Instead, she stood and dressed. I knew she thought I was wrong, or worse, thought I didn't give a damn, and that my fear and loss were invisible to her. It was as if we'd staked out positions that weren't necessarily real, around an issue that wasn't necessarily real either, but we were in opposing positions, and that's what we'd both been waiting for.

"It'll blow right over. You go out there, you'll just make it worse." Then I said something I shouldn't have, I took advantage. "This isn't a twelve-step call, K."

"Don't joke with AA," Kathryn said, pulling on her narrow boots. "It saves lives."

"Sorry, so sorry. But you can't save people from themselves. Sometimes you've got to be more Buddhist about things. Everything passes." It was the kind of wisdom I'd relied on out in my place in the country, years before, but right then it sounded lame and secondhand to me even as I said the words.

"Everything passes." Kathryn mimicked my emotionless intonation. I think she knew I wouldn't want to hear my own advice back.

"I'll scratch your eyes out," Lanelle yelled in the hall.

Gary yelled back. "You Christmas bitch. Stay out here then." He slammed his door.

Something thudded against his door. "I hate you, laundry boy. I hate every man who ever lived and ever will live." Another thud. She went downstairs without shoes, a heavy-footed sound. The storm door slammed.

I coaxed Kathryn into the kitchen for some cinnamon toast. We drank milk without saying a word. I wondered if fighting was contagious, if the anger between us came from somewhere outside, in the hallway, or beyond, or if it'd been inside us all along.

Kathryn wouldn't drop it. "So you can just sit and eat when you hear people hurting each other, people in trouble? Is that more of your abandon-the-sinking-ship, head-for-the-hills bullshit?"

I realized then that I'd been letting her patronize me all along, partly because I'd distrusted my own past and partly because I'd been changing so fast since I met her that I hadn't had time for opinions.

"People are in trouble every minute of every day," I said. "Ships sink right and left. There's no point in saving anybody else if you drown yourself in the swim."

Kathryn turned the light on and sat back down and looked at me as if I were someone in trouble myself. She rinsed her cup and upended it in the drying rack.

"Look, I'm already dressed and wide awake. I'm going to talk to that woman. And then I'm going home and practice. I'll see you tomorrow." She looked at her watch. "Today."

As she went, I did hear low voices at the bottom of the stairs, but only for a minute.

I was restless. I didn't like being so suddenly alone. I turned off all the lights. I got a warm beer and sipped it as I paced the length of the apartment. The building was fifty feet, front to back, not counting the porch. It's a habit of mine from estimating brick jobs, measuring with my step—three feet to my pace and I'm very accurate.

I heard Lanelle again, back at Gary's door, and even though I was sure I felt sorry for her, I was almost glad she was still wanting back in despite whatever Kathryn might have said, relieved somehow that Kathryn hadn't seemed to make any difference.

"Gary, let me in. It's cold in the hall, it's late. Let's forget the whole deal. Let me in, babe. I'm tired. I'll fix you breakfast in the morning. Gary. C'mon."

I stood there, a water in my eyes, not crying, just one-hundred-percent listening, voyeur to a world I couldn't believe in or reach toward. I wondered if she would try my door next. Or Guy's. I wondered if she was even dressed. Would I answer? And if I did answer, what then? Would Kevin stalk into my apartment with his deer rifle? I wondered if Kathryn was coming back. I began to believe the deal with love affairs was that it's only a matter of time until we get close enough to someone to see something we just can't look at, to find some flaw we won't forgive, and then we leave.

Then I heard her falling on the stairs. I went to my door. The sound of her thumping down the steps was flat and slow, a watermelon sound, the muffled, slapping sound a big sun-warmed melon makes when you start to cut it and it cracks open on its own, wet and dull and ripe all at once. But before I could step into the hall, I heard her again, heard every word as surely as if she were knocking on my door instead of Kevin's. Her voice was stuffy as if she had a terrible cold. She knocked as she spoke, but it wasn't a sharp knuckle knocking, it was a weak, steady pounding with the palm, and her words and her knocking got slower and slower.

"Kevin, open the door, please, I'll love you, forever, I promise, I give my promise word, I'm cold, I swear, I'm hurt, I lost my shoes, Kevin, open the door, I promise, I'll love you, forever, open the door, forever."

The door creaked open. Kevin's voice came deep and even, like the voice a novice actor might use in playing a judge.

"I got this one on tape, Lanelle, I got the whole thing taped with the Panasonic and the batteries are brand-fucking-new. You still want in? Yes or no is all I need."

"Yes."

Then I heard the sick sound of fist on flesh, bone driving to bone, that no matter when or where you've heard it, you don't forget, a sound that you're always flinching not to have to hear ever again.

"Now get in here."

The door slammed. I walked to the head of the stairs.

Lanelle's shoes rested in front of Gary's door, the heels pointing toward each other, beside a wet, twisted Mid-West Linen towel. Up and down the stairs were decorations, doves and santas and angels and bells, some of them stepped on, and a string of colored lights, every other bulb red and then green.

I saw a light under old Bill's door at the foot of the stairs. I knew he must be awake too, and I wished he would come out.

Even though my own door stood wide open, I saw the nightmare of it closing, of me pounding on Bill's door in panic, pleading for shelter like Lanelle. I pressed the bridge of my nose hard. And then for just a minute, under the thin sixty watts of light, looking down the stairs littered with Christmas trash, looking back and forth between the two ends of the hall with its cheap rubber runner, as if I could see all the limits my life would ever have, I forgot who I was.

All I could think for that minute was that one of the points to living must be exactly this brand of forgetting, like a moment of dangerous hypnosis, to go exactly through this hypnotic forgetting of who you were, to go through it and not get stuck in the middle of it, to not even move a muscle or blink because you might never surface from it, to stand still and go through it and get to another side of it, a remembering just slightly different from all the other rememberings before it, to do it exactly that way, stock-still, silent, from one side to the other, and to not go stark crazy in the middle of doing it.

I went back and got dressed. The Ford turned over hard and started slow, the feeble cab light dimming each time the starter cranked. I figured there were only two things that could really help me that I might be able to get, reasonably, soon, that same day, before the sun that was just about to rise into the blank December sky fell again.

One was to hear Kathryn play her clarinet, maybe all day, maybe right in my ear. The other was to see my old place again, to walk the fence lines and stand by the cold river.

The two seemed like each one would be the end of something and the beginning of something else and that doing either one meant never getting to do the other. I let the dimensions of the decision I was arranging for myself swell up bigger and bigger until it all felt important enough to convince me I was real.

I waited for the truck to warm up.

I got a hunch Kathryn and I were finishing up and we'd only just found it out tonight. I decided I liked the idea of her clarinet-playing more than the real sound of it. I hung one of the decorations I'd salvaged from the stairs, a chipped silver bell made from painted balsa wood, on my rearview mirror.

Three hours later I was graveling up the Jacks Fork canyon road. There was no snow on the road except some icy patches on the north slope past Tilward's Creek. I figured the new owners would be gone for the winter. If they were there, I decided I'd tell them I'd just come to remind them about leaving the heat lamp on in the well house and to wish them Happy Holidays, a plan that would probably have been awkward as hell if I'd had to use it. But they were gone.

I still had keys to the workshop shed. I started a fire in the same cookstove I'd strained my back moving out there years before, one of the things that went with the place when it sold, like the pallets of used brick and the cordwood in the shed.

After I got the coals banked in the stove, I took my fence line walk, like I'd wanted. I walked it all twice, once staring out and once staring in, slow because I knew I wouldn't be back there again. The river rolled right through as if I'd never left for a moment, one of those things you can count on, you can turn your back on.

I slept that night on a mattress in the shed near the cookstove. Once I woke up from the sound of the wind in the walnut trees, and for a second I thought I heard that tired, imploring voice of Lanelle outside, the one I'd driven away from, begging and promising like I'd never heard anybody do in my life.

I didn't come back to town until afternoon. The stairs and the hallway were cleaned up as if nothing had happened. I couldn't reach Kathryn.

"You ran out on me on Christmas," she said late the next day when she told me she'd gone for dinner at her mother's house. "On Christmas. Maybe you should figure out why, Michael."

Maybe I had, but I didn't see it that way then. And I didn't like being told what to figure out.

We didn't finish breaking off for almost another month, and by that time, Kevin and Lanelle were long gone. Their apartment sat empty for the rest of the winter. Bill got sick with influenza and went to the Vets hospital in Columbia, a hundred miles north, for most of January and part of February. When he came back, he was stick thin. His daughter-in-law Renee came up and introduced herself. She said sometimes Bill couldn't get out of the tub or bed.

She asked me for my phone number.

I said he could call me anytime he needed help. We talked awhile.

He called almost every day after that. But only once or twice for help. I think it embarrassed him to have me hoist him naked up out of the tub, especially when Renee was there. He'd mainly just call and talk. Mostly about cars, the cars he'd had through the years, he'd describe them down to the most minute details, the upholstery colors and the options and the prices and trade-ins he'd given and gotten. I got in the habit of putting his mail under the door, and he gave me his keys so I could start his car up every couple of days. He was worried about the battery and the engine block, even though he couldn't have driven anywhere.

The last day in February, a Thursday, Bill died. Guy came over and told me. Renee had found him and come running upstairs and beat on everybody's doors, but neither Gary or I was home. Guy had done CPR on him until the ambulance got there. But with no luck.

Friday, the first of March, was cold with a fine, light snow in the air. The only mail was a phone bill and a letter from my ex-wife in Santa Monica. We'd taken to writing each other these overly polite letters, newsy and inquisitive and old-fashioned, letters like I imagine people's grandparents writing years ago when correspondence still mattered. But I didn't want to read her letter then, or look at the phone bill that I knew would be too high.

I grabbed Bill's mail out of habit. I knocked and then pushed his door open when nobody answered. Renee had already started cleaning the place out. I wondered whether she'd be able to keep the apartment without Bill's social security checks. All the furniture was against one wall and some full cardboard boxes were stacked near the door next to a row of old grocery sacks filled with trash.

I set the mail in a conspicuous place on an armchair. On top of one of the sacks of trash, I saw the Christmas ornaments I'd seen on the stairs the night Lanelle had fallen.

I started to put Bill's ignition key with his mail.

But instead I went out and started up his Buick. I brushed the snow off the windows and the mirrors and the headlights as if I or he planned on going somewhere. With my mail in my hand, I sat in the car a long time, until it was warmed up and all the ice had melted off the corners of the back window.

Back inside the apartment house, I stamped the snow off my feet as the storm door blew closed behind me. I went into Bill's apartment and put his key on top of his mail and pushed his door shut.

Broken Promise Land

MILLER'S nickname was Storm because that's how he talked and acted. People usually thought he was on something because of his wild eyes, but he never even drank. Still, with the way he stroked his beard and talked fast like he was coming at you from all directions at once, well, the name could really fit him. I'd known him over a year—we played in a band together, Storm on drums and me on bass. It was just a weekend dance band, but we had fun with it. He was older than me and Mike, our guitarist and singer. Mike and I both went to college, first time around, at Missouri State in Springfield, but Storm was near forty. He was a character, a real sixties leftover, or holdover, or holdout, and yet he was still going strong.

Storm and I were headed to see Dylan and Tom Petty play in KC. He was asleep, his ticket pinned to his denim work shirt, and we were only an hour from Springfield. The early August weather was unbearable, over a hundred degrees—I kept waiting for the asphalt to melt and suck us in just like dinosaurs in the tar pits. Off to the north, dark thunderheads rose up like long gray horses and rumbled in the distance.

"Hey, good A.M. in the P.M.," Storm said, waking up as the thunder reverberated. "How far are we? Is the mobile geiger counter on?" He grinned and pointed at my radar detector under the dash. "Highway 13 runs up to Whiteman Air Force Base—one of the most radioactive roads in Turtle Island. If you see any Pantex trucks, let's slipstream them to heaven."

I laughed but didn't answer. I didn't want to get him wound up in that direction. He called North America "Turtle Island" because of some poetry book—he knew all kinds of obscure facts. He said it was no coincidence they made A-bomb triggers up in KC practically on the exact spot where bands of Osage Indians counciled. Or that almost all the bombs were made at Pantex near Amarillo where the Comanches fought the battle of Adobe Walls in 1874.

"How do you figure they'll play tonight?" I asked. "Together? Or back-to-back sets? I heard Dylan does an acoustic set alone some nights."

"In Long Beach in '66, he did the first set with just guitar and harmonica and didn't open his eyes once," Storm said. "It was like watching somebody invent their own private mass. I promised myself I'd see him again, sooner or later. Twenty years definitely feels like later."

I started to whistle "Yesterday" in my best syrupy McCartney style.

"Spare me, Davey, spare me," he said. "Or I might have to give you all three verses of 'Paint It Black.'"

I was thinking of a comeback when the Blazer missed, once, twice, and then stalled. Huge tractor-trailers wailed by and the Blazer shook as I pulled over and tried to start it again. The heat was vicious, and when I opened the hood, a wave of even hotter air hit me as if I'd opened an oversize oven. I felt sick with the trucks passing like someone tearing pages out of a gigantic book right in my ear and the sun hanging high and hot, a mad yellow eye in the sky.

Storm went for tools in the back of the Blazer and disconnected the gas line at the carb. "Turn it over one time while I watch this," he said.

The heat must have melted an old diaphragm in the pump—there was no gas getting to the carb. We started walking the mile or so back toward Collins. Storm swung his blue bandanna into a triangle and tied it behind his head. He walked with his thumb out, his back to traffic. Just when I was thinking he really had his head in the past, an old Ford with a homemade camper and a railroad-tie bumper stopped.

The guy and woman inside both had the same shade of light brown hair and looked to be around forty-five, somewhere near my folks' age I figured. They reminded me of something I didn't think often, that Storm was damn near old enough to be my father, but to me there couldn't have been two more different people in the world. My father had insisted I come to school in Springfield because of its safe, small-town reputation. It dawned on me that hanging with Storm, especially on a trip like this, was exactly the sort of thing my father had wanted to keep from happening to me. The couple's truck windows were down, the wind wings pushed wide open. The guy leaned toward us.

"Need a ride? Too hot to walk today."

"We broke down back there," Storm said, pointing behind us. "We're trying to make it to KC to see the Dylan concert tonight."

The couple's smiles went blank, but she opened the door and slid over. I wondered if it was possible they hadn't heard of Dylan—he was their age. But then I thought of my father again. Dylan wouldn't bring a blank look to his face, only a smirk. And he would never stop for a hitchhiker.

"C'mon, we'll run you into Collins," the man said.

We slowed down when they passed their home, and I could see the pride in the woman's eyes as she pointed out a little boxy building set way off Highway 13 with tall oaks on both sides and a hayfield behind. Neither of them was sweating a drop. A tiny Bible, smaller than any I'd ever seen—maybe three inches tall—was stuck on the dash with a magnet. We introduced ourselves. Maxine worked the floor shift while Roy clutched. I kept wanting to look at the little Bible to see if it was real inside or just something to hold keys or change. Storm and Roy were talking fuel pumps fast and furious as we pulled into the Apco station in Collins.

Five minutes later we headed back with a new fuel pump and a can of Coke for everyone, courtesy of Roy. "Chevy parts are everywhere," he said. He downed half of his Coke and belched like a foghorn. Storm laughed, and then me and Maxine. Roy stopped at their place for a tow chain so he could pull us into some shade to change the pump. I went in to use the bathroom.

It turned out Maxine and Roy had a hobby. They collected Coca-Cola paraphernalia. Coke trays and throw rugs and coasters. A big Coke pillow on the floor and a Coke-bottle clock on the TV. Coke postcards plastered on the fridge and a Coke cover tied over the toilet seat. I laughed to myself. These were the kind of people my parents made fun of, not to their faces, not even out in the open, but in little subtle ways you'd have to be part of the family to even pick up on.

"This is wild," Storm said. "Have you seen *The Gods Must Be Crazy?*"

"No," Maxine said, and her mouth tightened up a little, like for the first time she might be put off at us. "Is that blasphemous?"

I hoped he would keep quiet for once, and he did. He smiled and shook his head no. While we waited on Roy, I realized we were both looking for at least one thing that wasn't from Coca-Cola land, and there on the mantel, I saw it. The only picture in the place, it was in a small glass frame standing at a jaunty angle, like a picture of a family member, but it was that real familiar picture of Jesus, with chestnut hair and blue eyes the color of lakes on road maps, looking straight up—unnaturally, as if there's something up there only he can see, or like he's playing that old joke where you look up at the ceiling until somebody else does too. I stared at it, remembering the pictures on my great aunt's bureau and the way they'd vanished and never been spoken of after she died and my mother cleaned her room. I was still staring at it when Roy came from the garage, the tow chain rattling over his shoulder.

When we got the Blazer started again, we checked the map. Storm pointed out where the concert was, about halfway between Bonner Springs and Leavenworth, Kansas, just west of KC.

"Wanta cut over on 54?" he asked. "We could get a glimpse of the missile silos—see our tax dollars at work, like the signs say."

"I'd go out of my way to miss those," I answered. "I saw *The Day After*." It dawned on me how close we were to where that movie was set. I remembered Jason Robards' haggard expression at the end, as if all the regret in the world had been folded into the wrinkles of a single face. I'd watched the movie with my father. He'd called it Hollywood propaganda, simpleminded scare tactics.

When we hit the road again, Storm talked about the Osage arrow points he'd found on his place. He lived in an attic apartment in town, but he'd held on to twenty acres down in Travis County.

"Why'd you move back to the city?" I asked. "You never did tell me."

"My wife left. It was too lonely, even in all that beauty. She was from northern California—that's a hard place to stay away from for too long."

I got quiet, thinking about what was out there, ahead, waiting for me. I'd been in love twice, or at least that's what I would have said each time, but they'd both faded away without any deep feeling of loss, so much so that I wondered if they'd been the real thing. Storm kept talking.

"But it wasn't a lack of love between us, more like an excess of time. Ever watch a bird take off? Nobody asks what for. You just watch it fly."

I looked out the window, imagining birds, and then birds with the bodies of beautiful women. Sometimes I felt myself to be too suggestible around Storm. I kept trying to see into him, almost as if it would tell me something about myself. An old friend of his, McNace, had stopped in town the spring before and told me about Storm leaving UC San Diego in '68 in his last quarter and never coming back. When I'd asked McNace why, he said I'd have to find that out from Storm. I really wondered what made Storm tick. He wasn't from the Ozarks originally, but he loved the place as much as anybody I knew. He had a collection of photos he took of Ozark springs that were the most beautiful pictures I'd ever seen. He played with the band for fun, he did small stonework jobs for cash, and he wrote stories that he never tried to publish or anything, stories about an imaginary commune out in the Ozarks. I'd read a few of them, and they were like movies about some distant time, slow-moving, with not enough action for me.

Storm said the commune was perfect, and that it was all he wanted to write about because the one thing nobody could imagine was perfection—nobody could imagine what came next—but that he was training himself to imagine what came next by writing the stories. He said we were all so used to blood and pain and rancor and hiding our eyes that we couldn't even fathom what we'd do with perfection. He said his fictional commune was a place where people learned to fathom perfection. He could go on and on, and when he talked that way, I believed everything he said.

A huge inflatable beer bottle towered over the concessions at Sandstone Park, and beyond, thousands of bobbing heads stretched down a series of terraces toward the stage. Petty and the Heartbreakers were just finishing "You Don't Have to Live like a Refugee." We threaded into the crowd. The song faded out, and Dylan walked on and started a song I didn't know, but Storm sang along with it, a raspy, ironic ballad to somebody named Ramona. As an intro to one number, Dylan mumbled something about Leavenworth Prison, just down the road. He did an awkward dedication of the song to anyone unjustly imprisoned up there, he said. At that, Storm raised his arms, fists clenched, yelling, "Free Peltier. Sing the Spirit of Crazy Horse."

The song drowned Storm out. Leonard Peltier was one of Storm's main causes. He'd talked Mike and me into playing a benefit the spring before to raise money for one of Peltier's appeals, and he gave me a book about three inches thick on the whole deal—something to do with Crazy Horse, I remember— I never waded through it. Storm swore Peltier was innocent.

I missed most of the song, listening to Storm rave about how Crazy Horse was bayoneted in the back in Nebraska a century ago. I stood there thinking about how everything was connected whether you saw it or not. All those prisons and prisoners and songs written and forgotten and rewritten and resung and everybody's lives tied together across time, and dead people and living people always still affecting each other the way they did.

I was still halfway in that time-travel trance when I saw her, dancing by herself, barefoot. Storm danced right over to her. She was closer to my age than his, but beyond that it was hard to tell. Her hands moved in sweeping, fluid motions, and her long hair trailed behind her like it had a life of its own.

During a break, the three of us talked. Embroidered patterns in bright colors covered her jeans. Her eyes were a light blue, the color of sky on a clear winter afternoon. I had trouble believing she was alone.

Dylan began a new set with a song none of us knew. The melody was beautiful, but the words weren't coming through, as if they were rising straight up above us. I thought I could make out one line: "If we ever wake up in broken promise land," but then the guitar overpowered it again and I wasn't sure.

"Hey, this is our song," Storm said. "Everybody knows about that place—just like Heartbreak Hotel." He laughed, and when the chorus came up again, he made up lines that ended in rhymes—like sand and band—and the girl joined in with a line about stretching out your hands while she grabbed mine and Storm's. We danced then, holding hands, and sang our own words, and it was like our very own concert, just for a minute, but then the song was over. And after a couple of more songs and a short encore, the concert was over, too, and we headed for the big plastic bottle at the main gate. We were still holding hands. I heard the tired sounds of a crowd going home and hundreds of cars firing up in the distance. Somewhere in the crowd we stopped and told each other our names. Hers was Lily. Storm introduced himself as Miller. Lily said she had to meet her friends from KC for a ride back. People rolled by us on both sides, like a river dividing around a sandbar.

"I've got just two questions," Storm said. "Both important, OK?"

"Sure," she said, looking from him to me and back.

"One, can you let us give you a ride back into town? And two, will you have your picture taken with us in front of this crazy bottle?" Storm pointed at the old camera I carried. I'd been hoping for a close-up of Benmont Tench, the Heartbreakers' keyboardist, one of my favorites.

She laughed and smiled at me. I looked at my feet. It felt awkward. "Yes and yes," she said. Nothing more.

"I'll take you two together," I said, fiddling with the Polaroid.

"No way, Davey," Storm said. "We need one of the trio who sang their way to broken promise land and back." He stopped some guy and convinced him to snap two photos of us clowning there.

We were waiting for the pictures to darken when Lily's friends appeared, two guys and two girls. The guys looked pretty stoned—they scratched their heads like the thin guy in Laurel and Hardy. They talked while Storm and I backed off to one side. When they left, the three of us headed for the car. In the pictures it looked like we'd been friends, the three of us, for years, and we were all smiling.

Storm drove. When we saw a mile-long snarl of cars backed up on I-70 East, we decided to head north and cross back into Missouri at Leavenworth. "Did you hear Dylan mention Leavenworth?" Storm asked Lily. "Do you know about Peltier?"

"I did. I do. He got moved there from Marion this summer, right?" She said it like everyone should know. "Have you heard of Big Mountain in Arizona? I may be heading there. A friend of mine works with the Navajo."

"Maybe somebody's coal cars will haul it away," Storm said.

"Right," Lily said, "only now it's uranium and coal."

"Black trains and white trains," Storm said, like a line in a ballad.

"And every shade in between," Lily said, as if they were still making up lyrics, or talking in code. She said she'd graduated from Reed College in '83. They talked a lot about Portland and then a small town on the Oregon coast, Coos Bay. I was quiet because I'd never been to either. In a way I felt like I'd never been much of anywhere, not counting the vacations with my folks, which I didn't—they had a knack for planning trips that seemed identical, no matter what the cities were named.

"So is that home?" I asked her. "Coos Bay?"

"You mean like hometown?" she asked.

"Yeah, where you grew up. I grew up in St. Louis."

"On the river," she said. "I love Twain."

The air cooled where the road dipped down to cross a wash. Storm steered around two box turtles, but Lily asked him to stop. Before we could explain how common they were, she

129

hopped out and walked toward them. Storm wandered off into the trees with his back to us. I watched Lily rescue the two turtles in the moonlight. The pavement was still warm from the day. When we got back in the truck, she kissed me, a light and friendly kiss on my cheek, almost on my ear.

"Miller's lost," she said softly.

"No, he's just going to the bathroom," I started to explain, but she was looking right through me, and I knew that wasn't what she meant.

We stopped at a Leavenworth Git-n-Go for coffee and directions. Storm asked the clerk, a teenage girl with punk hair, about the federal prison.

"It's only a mile from here," she said, pointing up the highway. She popped her gum and wiped at the name-tag— Sherry—pinned to her orange employee vest. "There are four separate prison facilities in Leavenworth County," she said as if she'd memorized it. "There's a higher ratio of prisoners to citizens here than in any other county in America."

Storm told her about the Dylan concert at Bonner Springs.

"Oh, yeah, is he the guy playing with the Heartbreakers tonight?"

"That's the one," he said, "the same. So, doesn't a nice girl like you get afraid living around so many prisoners?"

"My folks live here," she said. "It's home. I'm used to it."

"Right," he said, looking around the store. "Do you have any spray paint for sale, Sherry?"

I'd been around Storm on and off for a while, so I sensed trouble coming, usually. I said I needed help with the coffee, but he headed off where Sherry pointed. He came back with three cans of black spray paint and three pairs of black cotton gloves. She rang it up like so much cola.

Four blocks down the road, Storm turned off the highway. Lily asked him where he was going. I thought I knew, but I was hoping against it.

"Shouldn't we leave a message of support for Peltier?" Storm asked.

She didn't answer, which he took as yes, like always, and we went down three cul-de-sacs in a row in silence. We were in a subdivision without any trees, houses set in cornfields. It reminded me of the suburb where I grew up—four or five models of large, shiny houses alternating along a maze of curving streets, every driveway its own little dead end. Seeing them I felt like a little kid, the last thing I wanted to feel like with Lily sitting next to me. I remembered myself as a kid, sitting on a brand-new bike between my dad's new car and the new washer and dryer, afraid to leave the new garage, feeling like everything, even the driveway and streets were fake, too clean and too alike. We turned off Leavenworth Court onto Leavenworth Way. Even the street signs, drifting above the corn tassels, looked recently painted, fresh from the factory. We rolled through an open gate in a long metal fence. The sign on the gate came up too fast to read. To our left stretched a long low white-block building with no windows or doors.

"Looks like the back side of a long row of garages," I said.

"Maybe the prisoners park here while they do their time," Lily said. She and I laughed. Every time she laughed, I felt a little closer to her.

But Storm started in on the history of Leavenworth—from the Indian chiefs to the Wobblies who'd died there—as he steered the Blazer across a rough-cut lawn straight for the building. Before I knew it, they were both out in the moonlight, waving the cans, spraying on the walls. Suddenly it felt like I was the one they'd met at the concert. I expected helicopters, or at least squad cars, any second, but I figured what the hell, and grabbed the third can and joined them. I watched Storm paint in small round sweeps and Lily spray wide block letters. I helped her finish FREE PELTIER. FREE CRAZY HORSE. We left the cans and gloves by the wall.

Going back through the gate, I read the sign we'd missed:

Northeast Kansas Minimum Security Facility—Grounds Closed 8 PM–8 AM. Storm shrugged, and Lily laughed, but I still expected sirens or floodlights. I didn't relax until we coasted over the river bridge into Missouri.

"That felt good," Storm said. "Swinging your arms, getting wild in the moonlight. Lily, you're great. You would've been great in the sixties."

Lily was quiet a second, and then she said back to Storm that he would be great in the eighties. Right away I wished I'd said it, and at the same time, I hoped his feelings weren't hurt. That's the way it was with Storm and me then. Sometimes I wanted to tell him to shut up or grow up or straighten up, but something real important to me would have been lost if he had.

Storm laughed at Lily's comeback and invited her to come visit the Ozarks before she headed west. He told her she could hang out on his twenty acres as long as she wanted. We all exchanged addresses and phone numbers in front of a tall white frame house on 44th Street in KC.

While we said goodbye, Lily pulled out a necklace from underneath her blouse, a gold chain with fine links and a small gold cross. I couldn't help staring as it hit me again how damn beautiful she was. Then she was out of the car, waving, and I said the only thing I could think of, the obvious thing—"Till we wake up in broken promise land"—and I waved. She put her pack down and twirled like when she was dancing and spun right up to the Blazer.

"Can you two crazy people wait about half an hour while I pack my stuff and get ready to head south?"

Storm beamed like a bright light had blinked on behind his eyes, and I heard myself thinking that I was going to remember this night a long time.

"So, Lily," Storm said, once we were heading south, "you want to see a silo? There's five counties of them buried between here and Springfield."

"No thanks," Lily said. "I just read in the *KC Star* about those priests and nuns who got ten years for tapping on the gates up around Whiteman with little ball peen hammers. The government doesn't fool around with those places—they're like some kind of holy shrine to them."

I got a funny picture in my head of all these intent, robed clerics lined up like penguins, tapping ceremoniously on the walls of the sacred military shrines. But I didn't feel like laughing. I realized how tired I was and how far we had to go.

When we saw a sign for the Schell-Osage Wildlife Area, Lily looked it up on the map. "Think there might be wild turkeys there?" she asked. "I've never seen one. People say they should be the national bird."

"Summer isn't the right time," Storm said. "Unless you get up at the crack of dawn. And you're lucky. And patient."

"Sounds like us," Lily said. "Let's camp there—it's after midnight."

We headed down the first gravel road on the refuge, and after a couple of dark, slow miles we crossed a low-water bridge. The Blazer lumbered up a steep road and into thick woods. We stopped in a field on higher ground.

Storm said that in the morning we could find a way out to the south of the refuge without backtracking. We took our bags and arranged ourselves like spokes in a wheel, our heads in the center, close together, talking.

Lily asked Storm about UC San Diego in the sixties. When she asked why he'd quit, he told about his friend David, his best friend then.

"He was a philosophy major. He kept pictures in his room of the Saigon monks on fire. He had beautiful long black hair. The first time either of us took LSD, we listened to *The Rite of Spring* twice and walked all night in the eucalyptus groves behind campus. We were really close, but then he started withdrawing from everybody, finally even me. He'd walk past me with his eyes

133

down, or he'd do an odd little bow like I was some important stranger.

"I pretty much lost track of him, and then one day in February '68, I saw a crowd at the edge of the quad by the woods. I heard someone screaming, and I started running. I heard a wild, sucking sound like a wind out of nowhere and a high shriek that stopped as soon as it started. Flames rose straight up into the eucalyptus branches. It got warm even back where I was. Two people in front fell on their knees and threw up on the grass, and then I saw him, burnt, burning, like a shrunken charcoal effigy of himself, all bent over and flaming. All I could smell was gasoline and burnt hair.

"A few days later I left—I headed north, north, and more north. When I got to the Monashee Mountains in British Columbia, I stopped for a few years. That's where I met Alicia, my ex. After '75 we came back down. Sometimes I still feel like I'm always going north in my head. Like I have to find some place inside where everything is white, pure white."

Storm stopped talking, and I lay there, rigid as a board, my fists tight. Finally Lily said that the stars were pure white. I suddenly saw them then, thousands of them, and I realized the moon had set. I looked over at her. She was rubbing her temple as if she had a sharp pain there. Then I heard the crickets again, and I felt Lily and Storm in my circle, breathing slower and quieter. I figured I could sleep then, maybe, and I hoped I didn't dream of that other David.

"Davey," Lily said, "look at the butterflies." It was early—we must not have slept more than four hours. Wisps of fog drifted in the trees.

"What butterflies? Go back to sleep."

But she kept talking at me, and she managed to wake up Storm, too. Then I did see them—hundreds of monarchs flitting above the wet hay. I was content to lie there, watching them drift by, but Lily wanted to follow them.

"You'll miss the turkeys for the butterflies," Storm said, laughing.

But she was already putting on her boots and brushing her hair with her fingers. In the morning light, I noticed a long, smooth scar between her eye and her hairline on the right side of her face. I knew it was none of my business, but before I thought, I asked her about it.

She shook her hair down over it and looked at Storm. "I have a story, too," she said. She looked back at the butterflies, but we didn't speak. "If you guys wanta sleep awhile, go ahead. I'll find my way back. I'll just follow the butterfly droppings." She laughed and walked away.

In a couple of minutes we went after her. Just when you thought it was the end of the monarchs, more flitted into view. As the sky reddened, their wings looked like lacy mirrors. I stretched and yawned.

"Watch it," Storm said. "A monarch'll fly down your throat and you'll never be the same." I laughed just as I heard Lily yelling our names.

We cut through low brush toward the sound of her voice. When I saw her, she stood by a barbed-wire fence with white signs every few yards: Military Installation—Absolutely No Trespassing—Deadly Force Authorized. A wide strip of smooth black asphalt ran between the barbed-wire fence and a taller fence made out of fine, shiny chain link. The signs on it had only one word—DANGER—and a bright red insignia shaped like a lightning bolt. I didn't want any part of the place.

Lily pointed with one hand and rubbed at her hair with the other. "Look, the butterflies, they're hitting the fence."

I'd already forgotten the monarchs. But they were rolling up the rise behind us, floating out into the black no-man's land between the fences without a flutter of apprehension. Most of them seemed to be rising up over the tall fence in a kind of windless grace, but about every fifth or sixth one hit the fence and disappeared with just a little white smoke and the lightest little psst sound, maybe, but my heart was louder than that.

"We've got to stop them," Lily yelled.

She and Storm climbed over the barbed wire and waved their arms like they were doing clumsy calisthenics. I followed them—to hell with the butterflies, I didn't want Lily and Storm to get near that tall fence. Before I could do or say anything, though, I heard an engine. A camouflage-green jeep appeared, doing what looked like fifty, between the two fences, and skidded to a stop. Three guys in uniforms that matched the jeep jumped out, their pistols pointing at us. We'd only been over the barbed wire for a minute at the most. One of the men wore plastic goggles with light brown lenses. I had the sense he was about Storm's age, but he looked a lot older. I couldn't stop looking at his left hand. Everything but his index finger was gone. It jutted out like a handle on half a fist. The other two guys were younger, not much older than me.

"You individuals are trespassing on federal property," the goggled man said, looking us over as slowly as if he were about to sketch us. "And we're going to have ourselves a little question and answer session here. I do the questions and you do the answers. Understood?" He waited.

None of us said a word. I nodded. "Good," he said, smiling, but it was a smile I didn't think I should trust. "My name," he said, in a fake courteous tone, as if he was about to extend an invitation to something nobody would want to attend, "is Ed." He holstered his gun and the other two did the same. "And now we'll have your names and addresses, one at a time." He pointed at me with his single finger.

"Altec. David Altec. I'm a senior at Missouri State in Springfield. I live on Bedford Street." My voice cracked. I felt stupid because I couldn't remember my address. No one had ever pointed a gun at me before. I remembered my father's guns, locked in his bedroom closet, and the ritual, every second Sunday morning, when he checked and cleaned them.

Storm and Lily followed suit. Their voices weren't steady either. Then the man wanted our ID—again, it was slowly and one at a time, me first. I handed him my wallet. He passed it to the guy next to him, who went through it piece by piece. Behind them a monarch puffed on the fence. They checked Storm's ID, but Lily said hers was in the truck.

"I'm glad you mentioned that, little lady," the man said, "because that's my next question. How the hell did you all get here?"

We all started talking at once, hesitated, and again, all started at once. I thought of that kid's game—rock breaks scissors cuts paper covers rock. A butterfly landed on the windshield of the jeep, folding and unfolding its wings. Finally, the third time, Storm spoke alone.

He'd collected himself. As he talked, I heard more and more of a sarcastic tone to his words, and I could see that he and the Ed guy were trying to stare each other down. He told them where the Blazer was, described it, gave the license number. He named the concert and said he had a ticket stub in the truck. He explained about coming to the refuge so Lily could maybe see a wild turkey and about waking up to the butterflies instead. He said it was just the spur-of-the-moment kind of thing people did in a free country, but he didn't expect Mister Ed to understand that.

As he told it, I realized it was exactly the truth, but it also sounded like the biggest bunch of bullshit I'd ever heard. Storm ended up pointing at the butterflies, like he was a defense attorney, resting his whole case on them. They'd thinned out—apparently we had diverted them, after all. Ed looked where Storm pointed. He hawked and spit on the fence. It hissed.

"I think you individuals are pretty much assholes," he said, "but I think you're pretty much harmless assholes, so I'll give you about sixty seconds to disappear back to wherever you came from. Unless, of course," he smiled for the second time, pausing between his words, watching our faces, "unless I reconsider and decide to check our fence here, make sure your butterflies haven't screwed it up. You know we got enough voltage here to fry an individual up like a piece of burnt bacon?"

Storm rotated his shoulders and started pulling on his beard. I thought of the story he'd told us in the starlight. Nobody said a word.

"I asked you all a question. What do you think, bigmouth? You've got all the answers, don't you?" He stared even harder at Storm, who still stared back. "You're the guru for the group, am I right? The little hippie gal and the want-a-be would follow you anywhere, am I right?" He paused again, rubbing the tops of his missing fingers with his good hand.

"I'll tell you what I think," Storm said, each word at the same angry pitch. "I think I don't need some small-time lifer jackboot feeding on my fear. And what's more, I think you need to show us your ID now. I don't care if you're from Air Force One— we're still in America here."

Ed didn't miss a beat. He soaked it in, worked his jaw. "I'm going to have to clarify things here, because, mister, you are one confused, crazy man. You don't even know where you are or who you're talking to."

He waved his hand, and the other two pulled their guns again and pushed Lily over by the jeep and moved behind Storm and me. I felt a gun barrel press against the base of my spine. Ed stepped forward and moved between us. Then with one unexpected motion, he reached up and hooked his lone finger into the loop of my earring. Mary Jo, Mike's girlfriend, had given each of us in the band gold earrings the Christmas before. Out of the corner of my eye, I saw he had Storm's earring, too.

He talked while he held us. "I'll tell you exactly what I have to do. My job. And part of that is to keep wild-eyed creeps like you off this site. You cross that barbed wire—you're standing in my land. You don't exist. You hearing me plain?" He twisted my earring, and my ear felt hot and pinched.

"I think you are. And when you step back over that wire, *I* don't exist. Go to the Cedrick County Sheriff—the State Patrol—they already know we're not here. Now I want you people out of here. And I want you to remember one thing, especially you, you loudmouth prick." He yelled in Storm's face. "You may have a ticket stub and chase your frigging butterflies, but in my country, you . . . don't . . . exist."

The man grinned like we really were invisible, only just didn't know it yet. Prayer words echoed in my head so loud I was sure everybody else could hear them. I had to say something, whatever this angry man wanted, so he'd let us go back to our lives. But it was Storm's voice I heard.

"If you're going to shoot me," he yelled, "do it now." I tensed up, my whole body cramping, waiting for my spine to explode. "Otherwise, get your goddamn hands off me." He shook his head hard like a horse shaking off a bridle and he screamed. I saw his ponytail waving, and a thin streak of blood from his ear sprayed across Ed's shirt. Through his goggles, I saw Ed's eyes widen up, like something he'd never intended had happened right at the end of his own arms. He lurched back from us like he was surprised for the first time, and the side of my head felt like somebody slapped me with a hot leather strap. I fell on my knees, both hands at my ear, feeling blood. Storm was next to me, his fingers wet and red. Lily ran over and knelt next to us. As the jeep pulled away, she screamed something at the men that I couldn't understand.

We got to our feet, helping each other, Storm first, then Lily, then me. As soon as I stood, I dropped back down. Lily hugged my head to her as they helped me up. We started to walk away, but Lily ran back. I watched her grope for our broken earrings on the asphalt. Storm was cursing under his breath, holding his ear. When Lily turned back toward us, I saw spots of my blood on her shirt. We climbed back over the barbed wire together, somehow. I didn't see any more butterflies anywhere.

• • •

We found Highway 13 and headed south. My ear throbbed like a high toothache. I couldn't look at Storm—I kept thinking that he'd caused the whole thing on purpose, that he'd wanted to get us hurt. Lily leaned her head on his shoulder. I felt alone, lost and alone between the dead-end bitter anger I'd just seen in Ed and Storm, and the numbing cul-de-sac carefulness I'd been running from ever since I'd left my folks' house.

Nobody said a word about the police. Ed had convinced us. I saw myself helpless, tiny, as if everything in the world except me had just tripled in size, the same way it seemed the first day I'd walked onto the university campus. After about ten miles, I saw a mileage sign for Collins. I figured we'd pass our breakdown spot soon, but I missed it, because the next thing I recognized was Roy and Maxine's house with Roy's truck in front. Without asking Lily or Storm, I turned in the drive.

Lily looked around at the little homestead. "What's this?" she asked.

"I want to pick up something," I said.

"We need to get back," Storm said, as if he'd just seen where we were.

"It won't take a minute." I pulled up next to Roy's truck.

"A minute might be too much," he said. "We sure don't need any more trouble." He rolled up his window and leaned back.

"It's kind of late to figure that out now, isn't it?" My voice rose in spite of myself. "Couldn't you have kept your mouth shut for once, Storm? What the hell did all that prove?" I opened the door and stood outside, one hand on the cab and one hand on the door.

"Take it easy," Lily said, "it's nobody's fault."

I slammed the door and stared at them through the window. Right that moment it seemed to me that nothing was nobody's fault. Or everything was.

"Davey doesn't understand what's at stake," Storm said, "what's been lost." He put his hand over his eyes like a visor. "That's all."

"No, that's not all," I said, leaning through the window toward Storm. "I'll be damned if it's all. Those guys weren't bluffing—we could've been killed." They both stared at me, their eyes as blank and glassy as if they had been, and I wondered if I looked that way, too. "Can't you see that, Lily? We can't save anything or anybody—not even a bunch of stupid butterflies. All we're doing out here is driving around."

She didn't answer. Storm closed his eyes under his hand.

I stepped away from the Blazer with the same scared but strong feeling I'd had the one and only time I'd run away from home. I opened Roy's truck and looked for the little Bible. That was why I'd stopped—for some reason, it seemed like the most important thing in the world to know if it was real or not. I fumbled at it, expecting it to be a slide-open box with something useful in it, but it was real. All those tiny pages filled with tiny words, the same words I remembered from the book that always rested in my great aunt's lap in the two years she lived with us before she died.

I saw Maxine crossing the yard. I moved from the truck and smiled.

"Oh, Davey, it's you, you boys back from the concert? We didn't figure we'd see you again so soon." I managed a weak hello.

"Have you eaten breakfast? Yesterday, after you left, Roy remembered that concert fellow you guys talked about. Roy's got one of his albums—he's a real nice gospel singer. What happened to your ear?"

"I snagged a fish hook in it," I lied to her. "Fishing in the Osage before dawn. Guess I shouldn't fish till it's light enough to see."

"It looks ragged—you ought to do something with it. Oh, did you want one?" she asked, pointing at her Bible in my hand. "You should've spoke up yesterday. I've got plenty. You all right this morning?"

She took the little Bible out of my palm and magneted it back into place on her dash. She opened the glove compartment and picked another one out of a small box filled with them, neatly stacked. "It's good luck, like a St. Christopher for the Catholics," she said as she handed it to me.

I muttered my thanks as she eyed Storm through the closed window. His hurt ear was away from us. Then he turned half toward us, and his face looked older than I'd ever seen it look— tired, washed-out, like it could crack and crumble any minute.

"Your friend looks flat worn out," Maxine said slowly. "I'd say he needs somebody to take some good care of him." I looked from him to her, and at the same time, I saw my parents' faces and Ed's glare behind the goggles, still burning into me when I closed my eyes. Just then Roy bounded out of the house, chewing something. He had two cans of Coke and an album in his hands, and I saw him, too, all of them, coming up out of the same years, and most of the time you'd never know it, but right then I did. And I knew, too, that whatever I was, it was something different.

"What's up with you guys? Had breakfast?" Roy said, handing me both the Cokes. All at once I knew I shouldn't have stopped, and yet at the same time, I wanted to stay, to let them feed me and talk to me and shelter me.

Roy beamed at me. "Here, look, this is an album by your singer. I've had it for years, but I forgot it." He waved a copy of *Saved*, Dylan's born-again album with the cover painting of God's big outstretched finger. It was the only one Storm said he'd never listened to. Roy said he wanted us to have it. I took it.

"Thanks," I said, feeling guilty. "My ear's killing me. I gotta go."

"The boy caught a fishhook in his ear this morning, Roy," Maxine said.

"You want some ice from the house? Here, put one of them Cokes up against your ear. They're good and cold."

I backed off and waved as I got in the truck. Lily was lying

down. She looked as wasted as Storm. She raised her feet for me
as I sat down, and I put them on my lap. I saw the line at her
temple again, clearer than ever. Storm stared at the finger on the
album when I set it on the dash.

"Do you believe it?" I nodded at the album. I handed him a
cold Coke with Roy's advice. He started a smile he didn't seem
to be able to finish.

"It's not why I stopped, but maybe we need it anyway," I
said.

"The album or the Coke?" Storm asked.

"Both. And Maxine's luck, too." I pointed at the dashboard
Bible.

He tapped the rim of the unopened can on the dash, like a
toast, and then pressed it against his swollen ear, finishing the
smile he'd begun. I knew then that he was relying on me somehow, whether he knew it or not. I rolled the Blazer out the
driveway, slow, and put the other Coke next to the album. I
saw one of the pictures from the night before. It was already fad-
ing in the sun—Polaroids always did that.

As we passed Collins, I looked at Lily lying with her eyes
closed between me and Storm. She'd folded our bent earrings
around the little chain on her neck, and one spot of blood on
her shirt had dried up over her nipple like a dark red dime.
Storm still had the Coke on his ear, and he was stroking Lily's
hair. I squeezed her fingers and steered with my other hand. We
drove for a long time in the silence of the highway. Finally, Lily
spoke.

"Where are we going?" she asked, her eyes still closed.
"Miller?"

I waited, and for the first time when it really counted, Storm
was silent, and it was me who spoke up, even though it was only
one word.

"Home," I said, way too quiet.

"Promise? David?"

Storm's head edged slowly backward until his eyes stared

straight up at the ceiling of the cab, his fingers white on the Coke can against his ear.

Then I knew I had to be sure, and I wasn't, not of me, or them, or anything, but it was my hand, there, on the wheel, and for the first time in my life I was really driving somebody somewhere, and even though the world had never looked so endless, I squinted out at it, squinted out hard at the highway ahead of me, and I said the only word I could hear in my head, without worrying whether I believed it or not.

They both slept all the way back.

Coffee

RUTHIE squinted at the late August sun behind Herman's head. Blurry and shimmery, the sun reminded her of an egg yolk jiggling on a plate, liquid and full and about to break open. She squeezed sun lotion onto her palms, rolling the thick milk of it between her hands, rubbing it on her legs and her stomach and as far down the back of her shoulders as she could reach.

"Herman, lotion up my back—would you, honey? I don't want my tan to turn all splotchy-looking."

Eleven-year-old Herman stayed where he was, sitting, half submerged in a pool at the river's edge. He spread his fingers apart and combed his hands slowly back and forth in the water. He turned his eyes back to the river.

"Your mother's talking to you, Herman. We can head home right now." She reached for her Snoopy key ring on the edge of her towel and jangled the keys at him. "I mean it."

Herman stood up, thin lines of water dripping from the string edges of his cutoffs. Ruthie was surprised at how tall he seemed. His twelfth birthday was still two months away. She pulled her hair into a quick bun with a ribbon and then rolled over on her stomach and untied her bikini top.

"Where's the oil?" Herman asked.

"Women use lotion," Ruthie said. "Little boys and men use oil."

Herman stared at his mother's back as she stretched out on the towel, adjusting her elbows and ankles to get the most sun. She hooked her thumbs under the bottom of her suit and stretched it down.

Ruthie knew last year's tan line still showed below the bottom of her bikini. She'd gained ten pounds over the winter they'd spent in Chillicothe where Clint, Herman's father, delivered propane in three counties. Ruthie and Clint weren't married, and the past winter was the first time they'd tried living together in over five years. Now she and Herman were back in St. Joe again. She liked it better, and she knew Herman did, too: he was a city kid at heart. But it worried her. In the last months she'd caught him, twice, sneaking out at night to meet other boys after she thought he was asleep.

"I'm waiting," Ruthie said, twisting her head around and squinting up at him. "The sun's still shining."

Herman picked up the lotion bottle. He stared at the cover picture—a little girl with a dog pulling her swimsuit down. Beyond Herman Ruthie saw a lone man, way down the river, walking upstream in the shallows and turning over rocks, one by one, as if he were looking for something lost in the water.

"Don't you start looking down pants, boy. If you turn out like your daddy, you'll be looking down pants and up skirts your whole life. And break a fool woman's heart like he does mine."

"She's just a little girl, Mama."

"Bottoms are bottoms, bubba. You just ask your father, sometime, how old you have to be to get in big trouble."

"How old are you?"

"Mama's told you how old she is before."

"I didn't listen." Herman smiled. No teeth showed, but his whole face crimped up, a big friendly crack running ear to ear.

Ruthie loved that grin—she called it his birthday grin. "C'mere and give me a hug, honey."

Herman knelt in the sand by Ruthie and bent his head down. She hugged it. She whispered a little white lie in his ear. "Mama's twenty-seven."

She was really twenty-nine, and she was scared of that next birthday. She felt it rolling up on her, big and wide as the river coming downstream. She'd spent her whole life around Chillicothe and St. Joseph or on the highway in between. Thirty was too big a number.

"So when I was born, you were . . ." Herman looked away, subtracting. "Sixteen?" he asked.

"That's right." She'd been eighteen really. She thought about her sweet-sixteenth birthday—the first time—in Roger Maitey's VW in the alley behind the Dairy Queen in Chillicothe. The only time with him. He was Clint's best friend then. She'd left a red stain, big as her palm, on Roger's back seat. Clint had threatened her with his belt for that—months later when he saw the faded remnant of it and got the truth out of Roger with his fists. It all seemed a thousand years before—not thirteen.

She looked at Herman's body and tried to remember the baby version of it, tried to remember it coming out of her, the same place where the men had come in. Ruthie was glad she'd grown up on a farm. She'd talked to St. Joe girls who'd never seen animals mate or give birth, and they lived uneasy and fearful: afraid of men and what they had in their pants. Even afraid of their own bodies. Ruthie's best friend Alice, a coworker at Shopko, was a single mother, too, ten years older than Ruthie, who'd had a bad female surgery just after New Year's and turned sour on everything. Drunk one night, she'd told Ruthie that to her mind being PG wasn't all that different from the Big C. "Like a two-legged tumor kicking out of control in your belly," she'd said, and the picture of that nearly made Ruthie sick. Ruthie had liked being pregnant, and she'd been wild with joy when Herman was born, thrashing and trying to keep anyone from touching him. The doctor had yelled at her to settle her down. And then sewed her up. And then handed her Herman.

He rubbed the lotion across the small of her back. Ruthie had a twinge in her stomach, and it made her remember the way it felt when Clint touched her body, either way, nice or rough. She got part of the feeling both ways, though she tried to hide the last one from Clint. He could turn rough enough without thinking she liked it. And it wasn't really liking it, anyway. It was way more mixed up than that—pain and hurt and pleasure all worked in together, the way Ruthie's mother worked herb leaves from the garden into her wooden salad bowl with strong, broad thumbs.

Maybe it was true, what her daddy said when she'd turned up pregnant at eighteen, unmarried—maybe she was just sex-sick. Maybe she liked it too much and just didn't know yes from no, white from black. She thought of Clint again and slapped at Herman's hand on her leg.

"Watch it, now. Have some respect for your mama."

Herman put the bottle down. "What do you mean?"

"Respect," Ruthie said. Then she tried to sing it out one letter at a time, like in the song, where that black woman sounded mad and happy at the same time.

The sound of splashing rocks startled them both. Ruthie turned over, tying up her top in one motion the way she'd learned to do in high school when the municipal-pool boys tried to make her sit up every time her top was undone. A man stood near them in the shallows, wearing only wet, shaggy cutoffs, like Herman's, but bigger. He turned over one rock at a time, stared, and then let it go, moving upstream half a step, the water turning sandy and murky behind him. Across his shoulder was an angry red blotch that turned pinkish red around the edges, like a birthmark that had never settled in. It reminded

Ruthie of a school map she'd seen a long time ago, but she couldn't remember what of.

Herman walked toward him. Ruthie saw the man's muscles knot and unknot as he upended the stones. He looked young, only a kid really, twenty, twenty-one at most, she figured. His hind end wasn't much bigger than Herman's.

"What are you looking for?" Herman asked.

"Crawdads," the man said, not looking up.

"I've seen crawdads before," Herman said, smiling his birthday grin again. "They swim backwards." He pointed back at Ruthie. "That's my mother. She's twenty-seven."

The man straightened and looked at Ruthie. She reached for the cigarette pack in her tote bag, then remembered she'd quit again last week.

"Is it?" His eyes rolled up and down Ruthie. He put his finger to his temple and gave her a little salute, like there was something secret between them, even though they were stark strangers. "Twenty-seven, huh?" he said, smiling at Herman and then bending to another rock.

"Why're you looking for crawdads?" Herman asked.

"To kill 'em."

"How come?"

"For fun." He turned around. "Why else?" He dropped a large stone. It splashed water up on Herman. The man laughed.

"Herman, come away from that man," Ruthie said. "It's not our river."

Herman stepped into the water and looked under the stone. Ruthie lay down again. She hated it when Herman disobeyed, but she'd learned not to press it in public. "Never punish in public," her daddy always said to her and her sister when they acted up. And they knew what that meant: they'd get a red-roaring licking the next chance he had. Her father had used a hard hand with his kids, and so did she, now, when she was mad, which was pretty often.

Kids needed it, though. If they didn't get it at home, the

world did it soon enough. That was about the only thing she and Clint did agree on. The saddest thing to see was watching a doted-on kid hit the real world all of a sudden. She'd seen plenty of that in the richer kids at Chillicothe High: never been spanked, never been denied a single thing they wanted, and then boom—the real world stepped in on them. Like lambs at the slaughter, all big-eyed and betrayed-looking.

Ruthie heard Herman talking again. "What's that deal?" he asked, pointing up at the man's shoulder.

The man rubbed his hand over the pink edges of the mark and then spit in the water. He watched it float away behind him.

"Coffee," he said, staring back at Herman.

"Shopko," Ruthie said when he asked where she worked. He'd gone on up the river and then walked back down to them about a half hour after Herman asked him about the mark. He'd come up on her carrying a six-pack of Falstaff and introduced himself—"I'm Shane"—as he offered her one and she took it.

"I'm a checkout girl," she said. "I quit them twice, and they took me back both times. Now I'm on six-month probation all over again. I worked in the Chillicothe store before I worked here. You ever been there?"

"I get oil and filters over there in the automotive section," he said. "K-Mart's cheaper on plugs and points, though."

"No. I mean Chillicothe."

"Never once. Did I miss much?"

"Not really. Me, maybe." Ruthie smiled at him, her eyes avoiding his shoulder. "'Course, most of the time I was there, you would've been a kid."

He matched her smile. "I grew up fast. I'd have noticed you."

"I don't wear a bikini at work."

"Now that's the customer's loss, I'd say."

Ruthie blushed. The river rolling over the round stones at her feet made a wet spattering sound like bacon frying on low fire. This kid was cute, she thought, even if there was something uneasy about him. And not just because of the burn-mark, or scar, or whatever. Close up, the mark was smaller than it looked when he was standing. It wasn't exactly ugly, Ruthie thought. It was the kind of thing you just looked away from without knowing why.

"So why're you really out here killing crawdads?" she asked.

"I told your boy. The fun of it. It's not like they're good for something. Me and my buddies used to do it down here summers ago all day long. Smash them between two rocks. Bango."

"That's gross." Ruthie smoothed a hair back beneath her swimsuit bottom when he wasn't looking.

"Just being honest," he said.

"So you're still a kid? Smashing crawdads in the river?"

"There's some boy left in me. I'll grant you that. But there's a lot a man in me, too. Which do you like best?"

"I didn't say I liked either one."

"No, you didn't say that."

Ruthie didn't want to let her eyes pass over his wet shorts, but now that she'd thought of it, she didn't stop herself.

"Herman, shake your towel out," she said. "We need to go home. The sun's too low to tan. It's soon dark."

"What about him?" Herman asked as he came up to them. "I didn't find no crawdads under any stones," he said.

"You just keep looking. They're scarce." The man turned back to Ruthie. "Only one beer? There's four more."

"It's a movie." Ruthie pointed at him, her eyes bright with the sudden memory. "That's what your name is. I knew it sounded similar. You have a movie name."

"My folks' favorite," he said. "The hero was a righteous cowboy type of guy. Just like yours truly." He popped the tops on two cans.

"Cowboys don't wear cutoffs," she said.

"Maybe not, but my girlfriends say I'm a straight shooter." He laughed and held one of the cans out toward her.

"You're shameless, is what I'd say." She took the can from

his hand, noticing a class ring on his third finger as their hands touched for a second. "Shameless Shane, that's what I'd call you."

They tipped their cans back and drank. From the river, the sound of Herman splashing stones drifted in the breeze.

Shane and Ruthie drank beer at her kitchen table. Herman was in his room with a Nintendo comic book that Shane had bought him at the Come-n-Go when they'd stopped for another six-pack on the way back from the river. Shane had asked Herman if he wanted to ride with him, but Ruthie had insisted Shane follow them in his car.

"I quit after this one," Ruthie said, raising the beer. "I have to be to the store by eight sharp. And Herman's school bus comes before that. It's the first full week."

"I start at seven," Shane said. He tossed an empty into a brown grocery sack in the corner of the kitchen.

"Where?"

"The Midas shop on 57th."

"You like it?"

"Putting on mufflers? Give me a break. Who'd like that?"

"I guess not. Herman's father drives a propane truck."

"Where's he at?"

"Not far enough. Chillicothe."

"And you don't miss him?"

"Not much. Maybe sometimes. Herman needs a father."

"I did fine minus one."

"What happened to him?"

"He's probably still sitting in the kitchen where I left him when I was fourteen. He was a drunk. Ditto the old lady. They didn't seem so sad to see me go either."

Ruthie looked at his broad chest in the white T-shirt he'd put on in the car. She was glad she couldn't see the mark through it. She thought about all the families she knew anything about. It was hard to figure any of them.

152

She moved to the stove and lit the back burner with a kitchen match. She took the top off the percolator and pulled out the basket with the grounds from the morning. The pot was half-full.

"I like it late at night," she said, setting the pot over the flame. "It doesn't keep me awake." She tapped the grounds into a sack in the sink. She pulled two cups out of the dish drainer. "You want one for the road?"

Shane tipped his chair down and dropped his legs from the table. He looked at his watch as he shook his head. He stared at an open milk carton on the table. "My folks never put one of these kid pictures out on me," he said.

Ruthie sat back down and picked up the carton. It was almost empty. The face of a little girl smiled out from the picture. She read out loud. "Mary Jo Rittenbury, Age Nine, Last Seen 9/14/91, Overland Park, KS." She shuddered. "These are no runaways, Shane. They're kidnapped kids, the kind they find floating in some faraway river with their heads cut off and their feet tied up." She sniffed the open milk carton and wrinkled her nose up. She'd left it sitting out all day. "It's turning," she said.

"Some are runaways. I know. Sometimes it's better out on the streets. Some of the real bastards live right at home."

"Don't talk that way. Herman might hear."

"So he does. You don't want to keep him a mama's boy forever, do you?"

"It's not exactly your business, is it?"

"He likes me."

"He may be the only one." Ruthie raised her chin, trying to look proud and distant. It was a pose she'd struck ever since she could remember. Her daddy had always teased her about it. "Don't lead with it, little Ruth, don't lead with it," he'd always said.

"Hey, Ruthie, don't be stuck-up with me," Shane said. "I'm a friendly guy. And I think you're a damn pretty woman. I thought that the first minute I saw you on the riverbank with nothing on but your bikini and your ribbon."

"While you were thinking about dead crawdads?"

"Boy, you don't let go of things, do you?" Shane leaned over and took her hand that was still on the milk carton. "Don't worry about the boy. Take some care of his mama for a change."

He leaned and kissed her. They edged their chairs closer together. He untied the ribbon and let her hair down. All Ruthie heard was the breathing—like the big flat leaves rustling in the poplar windbreak outside her parent's house right before a summer storm gathered up.

Ruthie let him slip his hand under her blouse. She knew it was too soon, but she didn't feel right about pushing him away. Men got their feelings hurt real quick, and then they usually got mad even quicker to cover it over. He fiddled awkwardly at the hook of her bra between her breasts, and she held herself perfectly still, waiting to see if he could get it undone and how he would touch her. Then she heard a noise in Herman's room.

"Shane, stop." She moved his hand away. "Herman's still up. I have to put him to bed."

"What about me, sweetheart? Big boys have a bedtime, too."

Ruthie turned her back on him and walked toward Herman's room. She started to knock, but then pulled her hand back. She opened the door.

"The little twerp," Ruthie said when she got back to the table. Shane was still studying the milk carton. The ribbon was laced between his fingers.

"What's up?"

"He was doing you-know-what. Looking at the J. C. Penney models in their swimsuits. He's getting to that age, I guess."

"Good for him," Shane said.

Ruthie shook her head. "You're all out of the same batch, aren't you?"

Shane put his hands up, his palms toward her. "Your coffee boiled up."

"Oh Christ," she said. Ruthie moved toward the stove, feeling worn-out and sunburnt all at once. "One more thing."

"I turned it off and wiped it up."

Her shoulders relaxed. "Thanks." She turned back to face him. "You like my ribbon?"

Shane looked down at his hand. "My favorite color."

Ruthie smiled at him and slowly pulled it from his fingers.

"You want me to talk to him, Ruthie? Set him straight?"

"No thank you, mister. I don't want to imagine what you'd tell him."

"The truth, maybe."

"And what would that be?"

"You want me to run through the facts of life for you? It might take a little show and tell."

Ruthie sat back down. She noticed what Shane wanted her to notice.

"You are shameless."

"It's just nature. Don't be so god-awful tough on us."

Ruthie looked at the picture of Mary Jo again, between them on the table. She scratched at the paraffin with her fingernail. The picture looked pitiful to her, like a little wanted poster, a little picture of something somebody wanted worse than anything but would never get. "Would you?"

"Talk to him? If that's what you want."

"Well, I can't. And anything you'd say can't be worse than what Clint might say." She picked at the wax that had balled up under her nail. "And his namesake, my father, swears sex is a sickness only Jesus can cure."

"Could I stay over then?"

Ruthie looked right through him. She felt her mind's eye rise up and look down at her: flirting in the kitchen with a man whose name she didn't trust. And her boy in the bedroom, thumbing through the swimsuit flyer in yesterday's paper.

"God damn," she said. It sounded like a flat statement of fact.

Shane winked quick and stood up slow, avoiding Ruthie's eyes. "I'll be back in a few," he said as he walked away from her.

When she heard Herman's door close, Ruthie picked up the milk carton and tossed it at the wall. A few fat drops of milk splattered on the little wall plaque Alice had given her: God Already Blessed Our Kitchen, Now You Do the Dishes. She went to the stove and took the top off the percolator and stuck her finger in. Lukewarm. She lit the burner again.

In the living room, she clicked the TV on. Jay Leno was doing a standup routine in a shiny suit. The sound was turned all the way down—Herman liked to watch TV with his Walkman on. She stared down the hallway and then tiptoed to Herman's bedroom door and put her ear against it.

"So, c'mon now, how much you know about it?" Shane asked.

"Just about everything," Herman said.

"I heard a rumor about a certain boy doing certain things these days."

"Maybe," Herman said.

"There's nothin' wrong with it, you know."

"Mom says so."

"How would your mama know what it's like to be a man?"

Ruthie's calf cramped up and she shifted her weight to the other leg. She did it slow so the floorboards didn't creak. She wanted to walk away but couldn't. She felt she'd spent half her life trying to know what it was like to be a man, as if that was the only way to figure out how to be a woman. She pictured the shine in Shane's black eyes while he talked.

"What's it like?" Herman asked.

"The best thing in the world. And downright terrible. Depends."

"What on?"

"On whether you're getting any, I guess."

"Any what?"

"Any what? I thought you said you knew all about it."

"I do. I just wondered what you called it."

"I call it lots of things. Sometimes I even call it heaven."

"Heaven?"

"Listen, Herman, a man finds himself a good woman and it's like rising up to heaven one night at a time."

"How old was your first time?"

"Fourteen."

"How do you get them to do it?"

"Different ways for every one. Be nice. Be tough. Tell 'em right out what you want. Beat around the bush."

Herman laughed his high giggle. Ruthie heard the newspaper rustle. She was afraid if she moved they would hear her. She wondered if Shane would stop even if he knew she was listening. She remembered one dark night spying at her parents' open bedroom door and her father turning his head toward her as if he knew someone was there. Her mother had been kneeling on the floor and her father was sitting on the edge of the bed. He'd kept staring at the doorway as the silhouette of her mother's head moved up and down. Finally he'd looked straight up at the ceiling, saying Jesus' name three times, and Ruthie had backed down the hallway on all fours, pretending she was a little animal. She told her sister that her mother and father were saying their prayers in the dark. She hadn't remembered that moment in years.

"Look at this one," Herman said.

"She sure is stacked up all right," Shane said.

Herman laughed again, lower.

"Listen. You're gonna be OK. That thing grows like a weed at your age. Just keep pulling on it, too, that helps. One day in a few years, you'll sidle up to some gal and see it in her eyes."

"See what?"

"That she wants it to happen to her. Something she just can't put away on her own. Once it starts, it's the easiest thing in the world to finish. You just listen to me. I been doing it almost ten years."

Ruthie straightened up. She pressed her fingers against her stomach. She thought of the first year with Clint when he'd insisted they do it seven times a week, every week, even when Ruthie was sick with strep throat. He had a pocket calendar and kept track every day, marking red X's with a thick magic marker. If they missed a day or two, he made her catch up. She'd found that calendar in a box the last time she'd moved back to St. Joseph. She still had it in a drawer somewhere.

"Every night?" Herman asked.

" 'Course not. There's lean times and fat. Just remember two rules."

"Which ones?"

"Nothing makes a woman madder or hurts her harder than a man turning her down. Every one's got a secret to teach. I don't care if she's fat, old, brown, or has polka dots, you just unroll your little drugstore glove, pull it on, and don't you back off from her. You reading me?"

Herman didn't answer. Ruthie wanted to yell "like a book" through the door. She pushed her fingers through her hair and remembered the feel of Shane's fingers on the back of her head while they kissed.

"Sure you do," Shane said, "and number two is—don't ever say those three little words 'I love you.' "

"How come?"

"Because nothing ruins anything quicker. I grant you'll want to, you may look in somebody's eyes and hear it like a song on the radio. But button it down and keep it to yourself."

Ruthie heard them both breathing and the newspaper pages turning again.

"So what else, boy? Here's your chance, we're talking man to man here."

"Is it true you can kiss it?"

"Who told you that?"

"Guys at school."

There was a long silence. Then Shane laughed. Herman began laughing, too, and Ruthie tiptoed back toward the kitchen. A commercial for a thigh reducer was on TV. Ruthie had seen it before. A close-up shot showed thin lines of cellulite running like faint scars down a woman's hip.

In a few minutes, Shane came back into the kitchen, grinning. He opened the last beer.

"He's a fine boy. Just needs somebody on his team to talk to once in a while. You ready for bed?"

"I could be," Ruthie said over her shoulder. She watched the yellow tips of flame disappear under the coffee pot as she twisted the dial to off.

"Well, we both have long Mondays to look at tomorrow. What's on TV?"

"Nothing. The usual."

"I think I'll spread out on the couch. All right?"

Ruthie turned to face him, standing up straight. She saw the milk stains on the wall plaque behind him. "Two things," she said.

Shane turned around, looking at the thin stripes of milk on the wall.

"I can count," he said over his shoulder.

"I don't want him to hear."

He smiled. "I can do half of that."

Ruthie smiled back because she knew she should. She didn't say anything about her half. "And people need protection," she said.

Shane patted the wallet in his back pocket. "I can do all of that," he said. He unbuckled his belt, staring at her.

"Will you leave your T-shirt on?"

Shane looked at her direct, surprise and something like disappointment in his eyes.

"That's three."

159

"I can count," she said. She felt icy inside, and tough toward him on the outside, yet she knew it was still some brand of flirting she was doing.

"If you want."

"I do," she said.

Shane went to the living room. Ruthie poured coffee in her cup. She watched it swirl in circles, the pot still in her hand. She remembered hearing about people looking at the bottom of empty teacups to read the future, or the past. She wasn't sure which.

"C'mon, sweetheart," Shane said from the living room. She heard him turn the TV up and saw the lights dim. Jay Leno delivered a punch line Ruthie couldn't quite hear. The audience laughed.

The circles in the coffee slowed, then stopped. Ruthie put the pot down on the wooden table and stared into her cup next to it. Without any milk, the surface of the coffee looked just like boiling oil, she thought, shiny and slick, a greasy black mirror. Ruthie stared into it, thinking about little Mary Jo Rittenbury. She'd be ten now, if she was alive. Ruthie saw a bad picture of her tied up in some small-town motel room, strapped to a bed. She saw the door opening and a tall bare-chested man coming in. She squeezed her eyes tight, trying to see the man's face, but it stayed in shadow. Other faces rushed by: her father, Clint, then Herman, his boy's head strangely perched on a man's body where it didn't belong.

She shook her head back and forth to shatter the vision and tried to remember the face she'd just seen, Shane's, the way he'd held his eyes so careful, and almost kind, when she'd spoken up about his shirt. She reached under her blouse and unsnapped her bra. She picked up her cup and moved toward the living room.

The Glass Boat

"SAY THAT AGAIN," said Ricker, the other night janitor at the Vo-Tech Center where Waldron Myers worked Sunday through Thursday, eleven to seven.

"I said I'm drowning their heroes. See how they like it."

"You're taking an aquarium full of suds to the University Art Fest? You're sailing too close to the edge, Wally. Give me a hand with this buffer. My back's out of whack."

Waldron took the heavy side of the floor-buffing machine. Ricker was almost twenty years older, and Waldron tried to give him a break when he could. He couldn't stand to think of himself there for twenty more years, especially, God forbid, on the night shift, but recently it had begun to seem first possible and then likely. He had good benefits. And there was the child support for his boy. The last thing in the world he'd want to be was one of those deadbeat dads they talked about on the news. He and Ricker lifted the buffer up the steps into

161

the Annex where the cosmetology and computer classes were held.

"Didn't you hear about it?" Waldron asked. "Back East somewhere? Jesus on display in a bottle. It was in *USA Today* a few weeks back."

"I keep telling you, this country's history, man. Hell in a goddamn handbasket is what we got here." Ricker turned the buffer on its side and cleaned the circular brushes with a coarse wire comb.

"That's what I'm saying. Some joker puts the Lord in a bottle of yellow water, and people line up to say it's OK—as long as they call it art."

"I never knew you were a religious man, Wally."

"I don't go to any set church, but you can bet your left boot I'm a Christian. Dad's folks practiced Lutheran. Mom used to be a Methodist." Waldron remembered both churches, and the alternating Sundays whenever his dad was home. He'd liked switching like that, even though it had seemed like a tension on both his folks. He'd never been sure how the faiths had been all that different, except in the decorations inside the churches. But they'd both had Jesus up on the wall.

"Used to be?"

"She went through a whole slew of different churches after his plane never came back. I don't keep track since she married that guy out in Los Angeles."

"Yeah. Well, hell. What do you say you do the bathrooms if I buff?"

"In good time. I'm gonna read the paper for a while. You just watch, Ricker. Those people will see how tight the shoe can fit."

"C'mon now," Ricker said. "Don't get curvy on me. How will you get something like that over to the campus? I think you need a vacation, man. Have you signed up for any time off this summer yet?"

"Last week in July. I'm going to drive down and see the ex

and the boy in Tulsa. Take him camping or something." Waldron had been camping once with his own father before he'd re-upped for a second tour in Vietnam, the one that turned out to be his last. They'd fished in a stocked sandpit lake, and late in the day about two dozen bullhead pulled the stringer loose from where it was spiked in the bank. Waldron had walked right into the water after them, but his dad had grabbed him just before the water got too deep. He remembered the feel of his dad's arm around his waist and the thrashing pull of the bullhead in his hands. It had seemed a perfect moment, there between his father and the fish, balanced just right between two big strengths.

"How old is he now?" Ricker asked.

"Nine. Just."

"You miss him pretty bad?"

"I miss somebody. I miss who I'd miss if I knew him better, I guess."

"Tough age."

"Don't worry about me. Anyway, I got this thing figured through. I'll drive it over on top of that '73 VW Bug I bought for fishing trips. It's almost ready to roll, three-quarters full right now. You oughta come with me."

"Sure." Ricker unrolled the orange extension cord down the hall. In front of the men's room, he dropped the coil and pushed the door open. "You need a contribution?" He stood in the door and cupped his crotch with his hand. "I always said you was a pint low." Ricker laughed at his own joke, and the laugh echoed down the empty hallway. The door cylinder groaned twice as he disappeared into the bathroom.

That's just the problem, Waldron thought. Everybody thinks everything is nothing but one big joke anymore. He gathered the paper off a chair in the instructor's lounge and sat down. Waldron looked at the "Doonesbury" panel, a fruity guy with AIDS dying in a hospital and his so-called friends laughing up their sleeves about it behind his back. He folded the paper to the National League box scores. He didn't know much about gays, or AIDS, and he didn't think he really wanted to. But he couldn't see laughing about them, either.

Waldron dialed his mother's number before he thought about the time.

"Wally? It's five in the morning. What's wrong?"

"Nothing. I just got off work. It's after seven here. How are you?"

"I'm sleeping, son. Nothing's wrong with little W.D., is there?"

"No, Mom. I talked to him on the phone just last week. I'll see him in July, maybe. I'm going down for a visit."

"Good. Why don't you come out and see Drew and me? You sound lonely."

"Maybe I am. I'm thirty this year, Mom. Did you hear about that obscene art thing with Jesus in the bottle?"

"Hey mister, thirty's the prime of life—you're just hitting a stride. You haven't been going to that Foundational church again, have you?"

"I just thought you might've heard about it. Especially in California."

"You always say that like it was some foreign country. More Americans live out here than anywhere else, Wally. Come for a visit, you'd love it."

"I'll see. I like it here in the middle just fine. I don't know how much time I can get off anyway. You didn't hear about it?"

"What? A new soft drink? Jesus in a bottle?" His mother laughed.

Waldron didn't laugh or answer.

"Just a joke, son. I don't know what you're talking about, really."

"No big deal. Hey, do you remember Dad's voice much ever?" Waldron wanted to tell her about his dream, but he knew he wouldn't.

"Whoa. It's too early in the day for that kind of question. I think the night shift's got you upside down. Remember when I worked nights at the Sheraton when you were in junior high? I moped around like the whole world was a party I'd never been invited to. Anyway, listen, I had to get over your dad. It took damn near half a lifetime."

"He died for us," Waldron said.

Waldron's mother paused. "Some people would say that. Do you want to say good morning to Drew? He's wide awake now."

"No—say hello for me."

"Waldron?"

"Yeah?"

"Your father's voice was beautiful. It was clear and light, not feminine-sounding like he worried about. It was something I loved to hear."

"Me, too," Waldron said. "I think." He hadn't known his father had worried about much of anything. Except doing his duty for his country. And staying alive in the war. And neither one had done him much good.

As he hung up, Waldron checked his watch. He needed to get some sleep, and he wondered if he'd have the dream again. The Art Fest started at two.

The dream had recurred at least once a week with only a few variations. But in all the dreams, Waldron had seen Christ drowning in urine, trying to swim to the surface, his arms and the rubbery cross they were nailed to flailing awkwardly in thick liquid. Waldron kneeled in a boat made of glass floating on a yellow lake, his eyes and nose stinging, and beneath him Jesus' suffering was magnified and distorted. Bubbles streamed from his mouth, and as they popped on the surface, Waldron heard his moaning voice, telling his agony—he said his wounds were on fire, the holes in his hands and feet, the gash in his side, the gouges ringing his head. He was begging Waldron to rescue him. But his voice was too familiar—it was the voice of W.D., Waldron's father, who'd been reported missing on a navy reconnaissance flight off the Cambodian coast when Waldron was ten. His status had been officially changed to killed in action the same year that Waldron had graduated from high school and married Karen.

Sometimes he dove into the lake to save the Christ. He'd wake up then in a sweat, his skin wet and burning, the life-size crucifix sinking away from him, receding to a speck in the dark room of his real life. Other times the dream would go on and on, with Waldron rowing harder and harder, the roiling bubbles sliding around the transparent boat in a slow slick foam. That was the worst of all, when the dream didn't wake him.

Once during the endless dream, the one that wouldn't wake him, the one where Waldron rowed and rowed, he wet the bed—the first time in over twenty years—a warm stain spreading from his knees to the small of his back. That woke him up. And that was when the idea came to him. Later the same day he'd gone to the secondhand shops looking for an aquarium tank.

Waldron poured in one more half-quart for good measure before he sealed the lid down with a thick bead of silicone caulk. He cinched three web straps tight around the two-by-four carrier and the tank. He looked at the little dolls of a prancing Mick Jagger and Tina Turner he'd found at the Goodwill on Bennett Street, and the two half-size ceramic busts of Jesse Jackson and Madonna he'd bought on discount at a shop at the mall. In the half-light of the garage, he stared at the smiles on Jesse and Madonna, the tight pants on Mick and the short skirt on Tina, the exaggerated lips on all of them.

As he pulled away from his house, Waldron couldn't quite believe that he was really doing it. The anger that had gotten him this far was draining away, being replaced by something new, something like fear. And in the same way that he hadn't been able to put any actual faces to his anger, he had no idea who or what he was afraid of.

He took side streets, easing away from stop signs and steering around potholes. Small gray rumpled clouds slid across the sky quickly, and Waldron watched shadows appear and disappear on the pavement as the sunshine clicked on and off like a light bulb. Rows of daffodils and jonquils bloomed along the foundations of houses, and the air smelled wet and almost too fresh—sour fresh—like after a light rain melts old snow and the first grass can't sprout quite fast enough. It was the time of day when Waldron was usually asleep. He wondered if he should have brought a jacket.

The annual Art Fest included films, poetry readings, indoor and outdoor gallery displays by students, craft booths, and street artists. Waldron had been to it once with Karen, his ex-wife, when little W.D. was just a baby. Karen had always wanted to go to the university events. After she moved to Tulsa she'd gone back to school for a degree in interpersonal communications. Waldron circled slowly around Campus Drive, thinking about Karen and how she'd changed since they'd come here together seven years ago. He didn't think he'd changed much, though, and he wondered if that was good or bad.

Near an open-sided tent by the Fine Arts Building, a crowd milled around a large sculpture: eight bicycles with nude mannequins riding them backwards. The front tires were nosed together, bound by black chains with heavy-duty links snaking among the delicate spokes. The mannequins wore only sunglasses, and their handless wrists shaded their eyes, as if they were looking for something far away. Waldron guessed he was in the right place.

He parked on the grass and got out. The tank hadn't leaked a drop, but it was so stirred up and cloudy from the drive over that it was hard to see the faces inside. Waldron realized he'd never thought further than just getting the tank on campus. He wasn't sure what to do next. He took out a canvas fishing stool and sat down next to the Bug.

"What d'ya call it?" asked a bald guy with six rings in his left ear.

"Huh?" Waldron tried not to look at the man's ear, but he had to.

"Your work. Does it have a name? It's interesting."

"I hadn't thought of a name."

The man circled the car, looking at the tank on top of it. The liquid was settling, and in the sunlight streaking through the tank, it looked like thin salty honey. Waldron had glued down the two dolls and busts so that one looked out of the tank from each side. Other people came near.

"You should name it, all the same," the man said. Waldron watched the people circle the car. A crew-cut woman in overalls bent close to the tank, eyeball to eyeball with the Madonna bust. She sniffed.

"What's in there?"

"Just what it smells like," Waldron said.

"Piss Bug," a young guy with a ponytail said.

"Pardon me?" Waldron said. More people were coming close.

"That's what you could call it, the Piss Bug."

"No, the car's irrelevant," the woman in overalls said. "Are you a fine arts major?" she asked Waldron.

"I work at the Vo-Tech." He hadn't expected to talk to anybody.

"Applied arts," she said. "I'm a welder myself."

"Why Jesse Jackson?" said an older woman in slacks. "Why Tina Turner?"

"Why not?" the welder answered.

"It's just a random romp in pop culture," the earring man said, "through the eyes of TV and tabloids."

"It's racist," the older woman said. Two Asian students on the Jesse Jackson end of the tank nodded their heads. Waldron didn't want it to be racist. He saw several blacks in the crowd. Ricker was black.

"Bullshit," the welder said.

"It's anti-racist," the earring man said.

168

"It may be racist and sexist," said a tall man in a sports jacket from the Madonna side of the tank. "But it's a self-conscious racism and sexism that makes its own point. In the final analysis, it's anticulture."

Waldron wished he had made a sign with a name.

A campus security cop ambled through the crowd. "Whose car is this?"

Waldron stepped forward. "Mine."

"You got an Art Fest permit?"

"No. But I'm on the staff over at Vo-Tech."

"Don't matter where you work. All exhibits need prior approval from the university. In writing."

"It's not an exhibit. It's my statement."

"Don't matter what you call it either. You move it or we impound it."

"The tank, too?" the welder asked.

The cop took a closer look at the aquarium. He bent over and squinted at the faces inside, and sniffed. He started laughing.

"You shoulda got a permit. You're a funny guy."

"No, no I'm not a funny guy. Don't you see?" Waldron's voice rose. "We're on the same side of this thing, you and me. I work nights. I'm no student. I'm taking a stand here." He was yelling and pointing.

Everyone was silent, looking at how angry and serious Waldron was. And then as he pointed to the tank, a rock hit the front of it, the Tina Turner side, breaking the glass. Somebody disappeared behind the Fine Arts Building, laughing. The security cop turned, took a quick step, and stopped. He looked at the tank like everybody else. It hadn't shattered, but the contents poured out of the jagged, half-dollar-sized hole the rock had made, splashing on the windshield and the hood, and dripping on the ground. An ammonia stench floated around the car. The dolls and busts looked smaller in the empty, broken tank. A couple of people clapped halfheartedly, and then the clapping spread slowly across the crowd. Waldron got the idea they

169

thought he might have staged the whole thing. Then the crowd drifted away, a few people snickering and shaking their heads, until only Waldron and the cop remained.

"Hit the road, man," the cop said. "I probably could ticket you for something, but forget it. Just get lost. Stay off the campus."

Waldron turned the wipers on for a minute and drove away in the wet VW. He tried to imagine how he would look to his son right that moment. Or his father. At a dumpster behind a dormitory he unstrapped the tank and ditched it. He stopped at the U-Wash and hosed off the car. He heard distant thunder like the echo of a steel door slamming shut in an empty concrete building. Ricker had been right. It was a stupid idea.

At home, Waldron fell on the bed, exhausted. He wanted to sleep. He felt that he'd never have his dream again, as if the rock that had drained the aquarium had shattered the boat and drained the lake in his dream, too, yet it didn't make him glad. He wanted to hear his father's voice again—at any price. But he didn't. The dream wouldn't come.

Instead, he woke up thinking about his son. He wondered how often Karen took him to church. He realized he'd never had a real talk with the boy about Jesus. Or about his own father, the boy's namesake. He dialed their number.

"Hi. It's me. How're you doing?"

"Pretty good. We're under a storm warning. You wanta talk to Wally?"

"Yeah. Hey, Karen, would the last week in July be good for my visit?"

"Sounds OK—I'll get back to you. Hey, 'Cheers' is on. Here's Wally."

"Hi, Dad." At the sound of his boy's voice, Waldron smiled. It was so high and pure. How much longer until it started changing? Two years? Three?

"What's up, WD-40?"

"Nothing much. Mom's worried about the weather on TV. Hey, I saw Raphael and Donatello and Michelangelo at the movies last night."

"Say what? What movie? What Michelangelo?"

"The Ninjas. Don't you go to the movies, dad?"

"Sure I do. I go to the movies." Waldron tried to remember the last time he had. Had it been with Karen?

"Next I wanta see *Dick Tracy*," his son said.

"Dick Tracy—hey, did I ever tell you about my crimestoppers notebook? I used to memorize the crimestoppers, kept a whole notebook of them."

"What are crimestoppers? I wanta see Madonna—she's great. I saw her videos. Madonna and Warren Beatty and Danny De-Vito. It'll be better than *Batman*. You coming down this summer, Dad? Will you take me?"

Waldron felt like his nine-year-old boy knew more than he did. He saw himself as a night janitor who knew nothing, had no sense of humor, couldn't begin to explain to his own son what he did believe in and why. Maybe the Piss Christ people were right, he thought. You either laughed or got laughed at. There was no middle ground anymore.

"Dad? You still there? 'Cheers' is on, Dad."

"Yeah, I'm here. Hey, I'm coming down to see you soon. How'd you like to go to Los Angeles with me this summer to visit your grandma and Drew?"

"I like Drew. I liked when he visited with Grandma. He's funny."

"Think you'd like a trip like that?"

"California? You bet. Can we go to Knotts Berry Farm? Sea World?"

Waldron wanted to keep his boy talking, keep him on the line a little longer, hear his sweet choirboy voice before it was lost forever.

"Sure, anything you want. You just name it, boy."

"I want to see the stars in the sidewalk. And the beach. I want to go swimming and watch the whales and the dolphins. They got ocean boats where you can see right through the floor into the water. I want to go for a boat ride. With you, Dad, OK?"

"Hey, I said anything, didn't I? You just wait, son—we'll have us a million laughs, you and me."

Little W.D. laughed. Number one, Waldron thought. Then the boy started yelling at his mother in excitement, and Waldron pulled the phone away from his ear. When he listened again, he heard only scratchy static. He started to press the reset button, but hesitated. He didn't want to be disconnected. Maybe Karen or the boy would pick up their receiver. They'd be surprised and glad to find him still on the line. He listened to the snapping, surging sounds of distance, as if he could hear into all the rooms of all the open phones in the world, and it made him feel he was alone and stranded back in the boat of his dream.

Waldron hung on, fearing the dial tone, as flat and final as the straight line at the end of a failed "Code Blue" on TV. He pressed his ear harder into the phone, hearing his own thoughts bubble up through the muffled and muted static, thoughts he'd never had before: he heard people laughing from way across a sea—or people stranded, frantic in some far-off stadium, pounding their palms with their fists, waving so hard that Waldron could hear them, laughing and clapping at each others' jokes and lives. People just like him. Little electric people shrunk by miles, even their voices at the mercy of machines. But still laughing and waving. Still drowning and clapping.

The Velvet Shelf

RAYMOND and Natalie didn't get to finish their after-dinner argument, sitting in aluminum lawn chairs on the pine deck behind her house in Billings on a dusky July evening, because two teenagers, a boy and girl, pushed open the sagging gate on the sideyard fence and handed Raymond a paper grocery sack, neatly rolled up, with Natalie's puppy, Blackie, dead inside it.

Once the teenagers handed over the sack, they both tried to talk at once, explaining how they'd hit the dog in the boy's VW, halfway down the block, on their way from Safeway with groceries for the boy's mother. As if to lend veracity to a tale they didn't want to be telling, the girl held the groceries in her arms: two rolls of toilet paper, a quart of milk, three grapefruit, a plastic bottle of ketchup. Raymond felt the heat of the puppy through the sack.

Natalie began to cry immediately, effortlessly, it seemed to

Raymond, something he'd envied in most of the women he'd been close to. Raymond had learned to cry, but it was something he'd had to cultivate, and he had to be alone for tears to rise, as if the water seeped slowly up from deep inside, like groundwater filtered through acres of gravel. Natalie's tears, like his mother's and grandmother's, seemed sudden and unbidden, artesian springs that surfaced without warning and subsided just as suddenly.

Raymond sucked air through his teeth, nodding at the boy and girl when they paused in their story. They'd asked the neighbor three houses down who the dog belonged to, and they'd come to the side gate when they'd heard voices in the backyard. Raymond thought of Jennifer, Natalie's daughter, who'd gone in to play video games, and was glad that at least his and Natalie's wrangling had spared Jennifer from hearing of the puppy's death from strangers.

"What was his name?" the girl asked, shifting the groceries in her arms. She dropped a grapefruit, and the boy picked it up.

"I got him for my daughter," Natalie said.

"Blackie," Raymond said. Blackie was a little terrier, six months old. Raymond called him ToyDog, a name he answered to as readily as Blackie—and the pup found every crack and crevice in the boards Raymond had propped around the base of the backyard fence.

"There's too much traffic," Natalie said, more to Raymond than the teenagers. "People don't watch."

"I was driving," the girl said, but looking into her eyes, Raymond believed she hadn't been. He followed her gaze as it shifted toward the boy: it was clear they were sweethearts.

"Thanks for bringing him back," Raymond said.

Natalie slumped against him as the teenagers walked away. He put his arm around her, bracing her, as he balanced the sack in the palm of his right hand, holding it away from his body as if he were a waiter with a platter. A breeze blew up the alley and through the box elder trees at the edge of the yard. It hadn't

rained in Billings in weeks, and the sound of the dry leaves reminded Raymond of the rustle of his grandmother's crinoline
skirts when she'd let him unpack her old clothes from the pine
chests in the attic.

"I loved that little puppy," Natalie said, her eyes wide and
wet, staring at the paper bag.

"I know," Raymond said, the muscles in his face cramping
up as if to protect his eyes from too much vision. Natalie looked
at him, and even amid her tears, put the tip of her finger between his thick bushy eyebrows, which had furrowed into a
wide fuzzy stripe. He'd seen that happen a hundred times in the
mirror since Natalie had first called it to his attention with the
same gesture, one that seemed to be second nature to her now.
He tried to relax his expression, the way he'd practiced in the
mirror.

"I've got to tell Jennifer," Natalie said, dropping her hand
from Raymond's face, her voice still stuck between choking and
coughing. "It'll break her heart. I don't want to see her hurt."

"You could let her think he ran away," Raymond said. But
he knew it wasn't a good idea. He remembered the first pet he'd
had that had died, a little white rabbit he'd named Peter that his
grandmother had given him for Easter when they lived in her
house at the edge of Forsyth, a hundred miles farther down the
Yellowstone River. One morning his mother had accidentally
let the back door slam on it and broken its neck. Raymond had
stayed home from school that day. Less than a year later his
grandmother had died of complications from diabetes, after losing her feet, and then her eyesight, and then her legs. After the
first operation, Raymond, ten at the time, had asked his grandmother where her feet had gone, and she'd told him God was
keeping them for her. Raymond had imagined an endless velvet
shelf in heaven, within easy reach of God's tall throne, and on it
he envisioned his grandmother's tired, bluish feet, wrapped in
silk and labeled with only her first name, Amelia—and somewhere nearby, his rabbit, Peter, whole and happy again. And

that was how Raymond had come to think of God, the one who kept track of everything lost, the one who gave everything back.

"Raymond, that would be more cruel," Natalie said. "I have to tell her the truth. You can't let someone wonder and worry like that."

Raymond thought of Jennifer again, tranced out in front of the Nintendo. They had time to compose themselves. He tried to remember where they'd been in their argument. Raymond had made no secret of his love for Natalie and that he'd like nothing better than to move in with her and Jennifer. Two of his friends at the college library where he'd worked as an archives clerk for almost a decade had advised him "to play it closer to the chest," but that was a way of loving foreign to Raymond, a game he believed he was too old to learn. Yet the more tangible he made his love for Natalie, the more distant and cautious she became. Tonight she'd said they needed to talk, yet he'd sensed that the argument she'd pursued after his comment about the money they'd save living together was only a diversion from what she wanted to say.

"Maybe it's not ours," Natalie said, looking around the yard. "Maybe it's someone else's."

Raymond didn't want to look at the dog. All dead things seemed of a single piece. One silent stoniness that lurked beneath the heart of life, a drab featureless slab, looming below all flesh and every movement like a frozen gray root. He knew he couldn't look at Blackie's body without seeing that first glimpse of Peter the rabbit, his head bent too far sideways, protruding between the door and the jam. And his grandmother, floating in white sheets in the white hospital room with the pillows the nurses had put under the covers in the place where her legs should have been. Or the others, too: a friend's sister, the parents of co-workers—those midday black-tie treks through the dim gloom of funeral parlors, the timid shuffles past pale heads set in satin like small anonymous boulders. He laid the sack

176

down on the grass and unrolled it slowly. All four of Blackie's paws were topped in white, and Raymond counted only three before he rolled the bag back up.

"Nattie, it's him. It's Blackie."

"You're sure?"

"He didn't suffer. There's no blood. The kids said he jumped up in front of them and the bumper just hit his head. They didn't really run over him." In his urge to comfort, Raymond caught himself from saying more: he's not really dead, he's just sleeping. That's what his mother had said about his grandmother: She's only sleeping. She'll wake up in heaven, whole again.

"You have such large hands," Natalie said, staring at his fingers as he curled the roll of the sack tight against the puppy, carefully, as if he were sealing leftovers from a potluck.

Raymond had another thought he didn't want to have. "I remember the first time you said that," he said. The first time Raymond had put his hand between her legs and cupped her there, that's what she'd said. Almost six months ago, and six months after they'd begun seeing each other. He'd pressed his palm against her, stretching his fingers out behind her, and he'd felt he could lift her up there, one-handed, or cleave her apart, lift her through herself somehow, as if he'd found a secret seam that held her all together.

"Bury him," Natalie said, "please." She gave no sign of remembering the first time. It had been her birthday, a cold cloudless January night when the wind chill had cracked fifty below and Jennifer had stayed at a friend's house.

"What about Jennifer?"

"That's why. Bury him, quickly, before she sees. I'll tell her what happened, but there's no need for her to see."

Natalie stood, wiping her tears on the tails of her blouse. Her navel looked like a blind eye, riding just above her blue jeans. Raymond picked the sack up again, keeping one hand beneath it. It was still warm.

"The garden would be a good place," he said.

"Anywhere. I'll go play Nintendo with her until you're gone."

"Until I'm done?"

"Raymond, I need to be alone tonight. I need to be here for her. And tomorrow's a nightmare—schedule changes are due." Natalie worked as a receptionist in the registrar's office on campus. She scraped her sandal on the edge of a flagstone. She'd stepped in one of Blackie's piles.

Raymond walked through the backyard toward the garden he'd helped plant over the Memorial Day weekend. He placed the sack at the garden's edge. The dusk thickened, and Raymond traced the dim, rusty line of the Rimrocks that surrounded the town like the lip of a wide, shallow bowl that held everything that mattered in the last twenty years of Raymond's life. He found the first star, a speck of white sand glinting in the eastern sky. Before he could make a wish, he noticed others. Amelia had always said it was bad luck to wish after you'd seen more than one.

A shovel stood upright in the loose soil next to a hill of climbing beans that would be ready to pick soon. The long crescent pods hung from the vines like flat green fingers. He grabbed the shovel and began to dig.

Raymond stood at his bathroom mirror, a plastic razor in his hand, the two things about his body he'd always most wanted to change both glaring in the reflection: his hands and eyebrows, both out of proportion to the rest of his features, as if they'd been borrowed from a much larger man. "When they lined everybody up for eyebrows, God just let you go through the line more than once," Amelia had kidded him. Raymond wondered, as he often did, what his father had looked like, if he'd borne these features like crosses, too, passing them to Raymond with no chance of showing him how best to carry them.

He smoothed lather over his chin and cheeks. Shaving usually relaxed him, but tonight the argument and the unfinished talk with Natalie nagged at him. Worse than that, ever since he'd climbed in his pickup and headed home, there had been the thought. Or not the thought, but his arguments with it, which served only to bring it closer to the surface of his mind: The dog hadn't moved. No, he hadn't really looked at it. But the bag hadn't moved. He rotated his watchband on his wrist, smearing shaving lotion on the crystal. He wiped it off—it had been twenty minutes.

He pulled the blade across his chin, moving from ear to jaw in straight careful lines, shaking the razor into the sink after each stroke. Whiskers floated in the soupy lather like iron filings. He talked to the mirror.

You're crazy. Of course it was dead. No, it's not absolutely impossible. What is? But if there were odds, it would be a thousand to one. He started on the other side of his face. A million to one.

The Raymond in the mirror spoke. "So people win the lotto. Only this winner gets the picture of a live puppy waking up at the bottom of two feet of soil. Not pretty." The mirror Raymond was blunt, never pulled his punches: he said the thought out loud. "It may be a long shot, but you don't know for sure it was dead. You should have checked."

Raymond jerked and cut himself. Bright blood ran down his chin like a single stripe of war paint on a Hollywood Indian. Raymond stared, waiting until it formed a drop and broke away from his face. He pressed a washrag against the cut, staring at the rough red circle on the porcelain and the tiny red specks that surrounded it.

He dug the hole again in his mind. Square sides, two shovel lengths deep. He'd dug below the garden loam, removing fist-sized stones and tossing them into the rockpile at the far end of the garden. He remembered several times, three times at least, looking over at the Safeway sack, silent and still on the lawn. He'd leveled the bottom of the hole and lowered the sack, but he hadn't wanted to throw soil directly on it, so he'd grabbed a short section of two-by-eight from a scrap pile and wedged it in over the sack. He felt silly, but it seemed cleaner, more respectful: a grocery bag wasn't much of a coffin, even for a dog. As the dirt landed on the white pine board, Raymond remembered sawing it from one of the four-foot lengths he'd used to build the shelves in Natalie's bedroom closet, a Valentine's Day surprise—she'd complained about having no place for her shoes. He packed the soil down twice with his boot, once when it was halfway full and then again near the top. He had to borrow a shovelful of loose dirt from the side of the bean hill to level the ground off. He put a circle of stones on top in case Jennifer wanted to know where Blackie was. He'd said good-night to Natalie through the screen door and let himself out through the side gate, padlocking it for the night. The memory ran out, and the other voice chimed in.

"So the pup had breathing room. You made it worse. It could be suffocating right now." The mirror Raymond wouldn't let up.

Raymond flipped the bathroom light out, standing in the dark. He closed his eyes and his mouth.

"You'd better check."

He flicked the light back on and faced the mirror. All in one motion, he filled his palm with shaving cream, wiped it across his left eyebrow, and pulled the razor into it until it got caught up in the stiff wiry hair.

"You are out of your mind," said the Raymond with one and a half eyebrows. "You need help. All this to avoid dealing with the chance you buried your girlfriend's puppy alive? Too long in the archives, buddy."

Raymond stared at the razor in his hand.

"And she doesn't love you," the mirror freak said. "Try burying that."

Raymond scratched off the rest of the eyebrow in short pulls, leaving a five o'clock shadow line above his eye. I'll check, he said. I'll check. He spread a thinner layer of cream and shaved the eyebrow smooth. The mirror man was silent. He looked subdued, silly.

Raymond laughed out loud, a nervous, unconvincing laugh that came from a place inside himself he wasn't sure he'd ever been to. He let the silence settle back into the room and then just as methodically shaved his other eyebrow off. He looked to himself as if he'd worn glasses night and day for years and suddenly taken them off. He washed his face and rinsed the lather, whiskers, and blood down the drain.

On his way out, he grabbed the cap he wore when he played second base for the library softball team twice a week from May to August, a brimmed blue cap with the team name, "The Bookers," lettered in gold across the front. He pulled it down low on his forehead. As he drove the seven blocks back toward Natalie's, he saw a half-moon, rising in the northeast. He had to tip his head back to see it, staring off in the direction where the Yellowstone rushed away from Billings, toward Forsyth, his vanished childhood, and beyond toward the Missouri and North Dakota. With the bill protruding just above his eyes, everything looked foreshortened, as if someone had lowered the ceiling on the world. He parked on the nearest side street and walked down the alley behind her house. He climbed the wire fence, feeling like a burglar or a peeper. On any ordinary night, Blackie would have been barking by now.

The yard and house were silent. With the coming of the darkness, the wind had died and the box elder leaves were still. He'd been gone little more than a half hour, but only Natalie's bedroom light was on.

He felt like he was caught in a movie running backward: watch the stones jump back into the man's hand, see the dirt spring up to meet the shovel. And he wished it could be that way. Watch the puppy come back to life, leap back to the curb, see the woman fall back into the man's open arms. When he felt the metal scrape wood, he shoved the spade into the dirt pile and knelt by the hole. He cupped four handfuls of dirt out and pulled the board up. The sack was dirty despite his precaution. He put a hand on each side of it, spreading his fingers out beneath it, and lifted straight up. It was as cool as the soil around it, and he knew immediately what a fool he'd been. Still, the other voice prodded him: open it, look at it, don't make the same mistake again. He unrolled the sack. He pulled the puppy out.

It was just slightly stiff. Except for its open eyes, it looked peaceful, like a photograph of a puppy taken through a lens that got the shape and colors right but filtered out everything vital. When he looked at it lying there on the dirt, the four white paws bunched together like a wilted bouquet of night-blooming flowers, he felt water rising inside him.

As he gathered the dog in his arms and stood up, he heard a loud crunch of gravel in the alley. He stood stock-still as a police cruiser jerked to a stop and the beam of a searchlight played across the yard. He tipped his head down so the bill of his cap shielded his eyes from the piercing light.

"Freeze it," a voice yelled as the cruiser's doors slammed shut, one after the other. Static blasted from the police radio.

In the bright light, Raymond couldn't see anything except the dog in his arms. Its eyes glinted like obsidian marbles.

The officers hopped the fence, one at a time. "Not a muscle," the same voice yelled as Raymond shifted the puppy in his arms. They walked directly at him with their pistols drawn. He felt himself shivering, as if the cold in Blackie had spread throughout his body.

"Hands on your head," a second voice said, "slowly."

"I can't," Raymond said, his voice and shoulders shaking. Lights in a neighbor's house had flicked on. The officers stood ten feet from Raymond.

"What is it?" the officer asked, pointing his gun barrel at Blackie.

"A puppy," Raymond said.

"Drop it," the second officer said. "I want your hands on your head."

The dog hit the dirt pile with no more sound than if Raymond had dropped a pillow. Raymond raised his arms and clasped his hands together on his head.

The two policemen walked closer. One put his pistol away and shone a flashlight in Raymond's face and then down on the dead dog. Then he stepped forward and frisked Raymond. He pulled Raymond's wallet from his pocket.

"What's your name?" He opened the wallet.

"Raymond Knight."

"What are you doing here?"

"I live here. Practically. I was burying the dog."

"A resident reported a prowler."

"I'm her boyfriend," Raymond said, pointing at the house. "I spend four or five nights a week with her. She just doesn't know I'm here."

The officer looked up from the wallet. He pulled Raymond's cap off and stared at Raymond's face and then down at Blackie. "I'll go check with the woman," he told his partner.

The second officer kept his eyes trained on Raymond and pointed his gun straight up at the sky, as if something up there might threaten them both. Raymond heard Natalie's muffled voice.

"Bring him over," yelled the first officer.

When Raymond climbed up on the deck, he saw Natalie behind the screen.

"You know this man?" the officer asked.

"Raymond?" Natalie said. He stepped closer to her.

"He says he's your boyfriend," the officer said. "He practically lives here, he says." The second officer laughed.

Raymond didn't speak. He stared at Natalie's eyes, but she was staring just above his.

"I'm sorry," Natalie said. "I'm sorry. I didn't know Raymond was here. I live alone with my daughter. I heard noises. Our puppy was run over."

"We noticed," the second officer said. He'd holstered his pistol, like his partner. "You don't need to file a complaint?"

"No," Natalie said.

The policemen stared at Raymond. The first one handed the wallet and hat back to him. Raymond held them at his waist between his hands. After a moment, the officers stepped away, talking as they crossed the backyard. Raymond and Natalie didn't speak until the car moved off down the alley.

"What in the world are you doing?" Natalie asked.

"Checking," Raymond said.

"You weren't spying on me, were you?"

"It was Blackie. I wasn't sure." Raymond's voice trailed off.

"Sure what?"

"That I buried him right." Raymond grabbed at the first thought that came. "Facing east."

"East?"

"It's in books at the library. The Crow. And the Cheyenne— all of them say it. So the soul finds its way to the door of the world or something."

"You and your books, Raymond. I don't know whether to believe you or not. I couldn't stand the thought of you spying on me."

"Why would I spy on you, Nattie? Why would I need to?" Raymond smiled, thinking of the times she'd undressed for him. He felt like he was talking to a lover from years ago, someone he'd run into on the street. The special pain of eyes averted from what they'd once loved. "I buried your dog for you."

"And I appreciate that. You've been very sweet. To both of us."

"Can I come in?" Natalie's face looked shadowed and untouchable behind the thin metal veil of the screen door.

"What happened to your eyebrows?"

"It's a sign of mourning," Raymond said. It didn't really seem like that much of a lie. "You never liked them anyway."

"I never said that."

"Can I come in?"

"I just got Jennifer to sleep before all this," Natalie waved her hand from him toward the garden and the alley.

Raymond looked back over at the dark garden. He didn't speak.

"This isn't the best time, Raymond, but I've got to tell you. I can't go on with this anymore."

"This?"

"Us. You."

"That's what you wanted to talk about tonight?"

"More or less."

"Why?"

"Raymond, I love you. But I don't love you. You know what I mean."

Raymond put his hat on and pulled the bill down over the place where his eyebrows should have been. "Why tonight?"

"It isn't just tonight. You must know that."

Raymond looked through the screen and over Natalie's shoulder into the house. He could picture the furniture, the dishes stacked in the cabinets, the food in the refrigerator, everything cozy and close as a nest.

"Is the door locked, Nattie?" Raymond stared at her hand on the inside of the screen door.

"Why?"

"I don't want to leave by the alley. What about my things?"

"You can pick them up later. There's no reason we can't stay sociable, Raymond. But not tonight. I'm very tired."

"Let me go out the front door. I promise I'll walk right through."

"Your word?"

"My word." My word is my bond, Raymond thought, remembering Amelia, the anchor of his childhood, who'd taught

185

him the strength in that phrase, that idea, and so many others, like a father and a best friend. Raymond scraped his shoes on the rope mat. Natalie opened the door and walked past the washer and dryer into the kitchen.

She stood near the table with her head down, as if she was about to cry again. Raymond walked toward her, taking it all in, the warmth, the absent sounds of laughter and love. He saw his things, here and there, insinuating themselves into the fabric of the house, but now, each stood out as surely as if they'd had price tags on them. She was right. Later was better.

He pulled his hat off and stooped and kissed the back of her neck quickly. "The best we could," he said.

Before she could speak, he walked into the dining room and then the living room. He unbolted the front door and stepped through, closing it softly, careful not to wake her daughter.

He put his cap on again, staring for a moment at his big hands like two awkward friends. He walked across the yard and down the street. The half-moon had moved until it hung halfway up the eastern sky. Raymond walked toward it, tipping his head up and back until he could see clearly the flat horizon of stone that hemmed both him and the town in. The water that had begun moving when he'd looked at Blackie rose slowly in him, imperceptibly, near the surface. Then everything, the moon, the streetlights, the specks of stars, and every bright memory he possessed, swam.

River Street

AS HE CROSSES River Street, Luther sees the shadow of
the bear, a giant gray silhouette looming on the plate glass window. He shifts his bedroll up tighter under his arm and taps the
rear deck of an old Plymouth that crosses in front of him as he
stands on the center line. He lets the cars come so close that he
can feel the breezes they make and smell their rusted, oily
smells. It makes him feel awake, wide awake and invincible.
Luther likes to jaywalk and thread between traffic as if he's some
vagrant matador teasing huge iron bulls. He has never been hit.

The bear's shadow disappears as Luther steps into the shade
the building casts across the littered parking lot. The old neon
sign is glowing in the midmorning light. Luther notices first the
letters that are burnt out, the gray neon tubes looking like
empty glass arteries connecting the lit purple letters that re-
main—**The Restwell Motel**.

Luther noses up to the office window and glares into the dim lobby. The stuffed bear dominates the room. It seems as big as an elephant. He turns and raises his eyes to the mountainous horizon ringing the town and imagines bears that big up there, pulling up trees by their roots.

He shudders. He has heard about grizzlies.

They tear vans apart in search of steaks. They rip open tents in the still of the night to get at women who are menstruating and eat them alive while their terrified, helpless boyfriends die of heart attacks. He is glad now that he didn't get off the freight train in the dark when it stopped in the middle of nowhere.

Luther lowers his eyes to the parking lot of the motel. All the cars are old except one with a broken windshield and a crushed fender, and they all have Montana license plates. One of the cars is jacked up with a front tire and wheel off, leaving the brake drum exposed. The motel looks like a long row of doors. Some of the doors have screens, some don't. Some of the doors have little numbers above them, on others they're gone.

Luther stands still, figuring out all the missing numbers. He likes to find missing pieces, letters, numbers. It keeps him alert, in control, on top of things. There are fourteen doors.

When the train stopped, it was black and cold out and the boxcar was at an angle. He realizes now it had been in the mountains, on a grade, maybe even in one of those long tunnels like the ones the diesel locomotives were always emerging from on the pages of the calendars Luther's mother kept in the hallway. He'd been sound asleep, as sound asleep as he ever got riding the trains, sprawled across some bundles of crushed cardboard cartons. The abrupt lack of motion woke him, and he peered out the open door of the boxcar into the blackness. He felt alone, completely, without relief, as if the train had been abandoned and he was the last to know, as if it would sit forever on the mountainside and the sun would never come up.

Quickly Luther pivots back to squint at the bear, somehow expecting it to have moved. The bear's mouth is wide open as if it were screaming something no one would ever hear. Luther decides to go in. He pushes at the lobby door twice before seeing the Pull sign.

The lobby of the motel is an animal mortuary, a frozen zoo. Dozens of glassy eyes stare out from the stuffed heads and bodies of deer, moose, elk, pheasant, cougar, sheep, ducks, and some animals Luther doesn't even know the names of. Above all of them towers the bear. Luther walks up to it. His head comes to its chest. He figures for a minute. He is five-foot-five. He can look up into the bear's open mouth. It must be over seven, maybe even eight feet tall.

He touches the bear's outstretched front claws—they feel like porcelain. He steadies himself on the bear, holding hands with it in a moment of terror. All the animals are screaming something. The train is stopped again. Luther can't remember where he is or what he's supposed to be doing. So he counts; it is an old trick, whenever he is in trouble or his head blurs like this, he counts or figures. Boxcars, phone poles, beer cans, women he's laid, fights he's won or fights he's lost, car antennas, wallpaper roses in dim light when he's trying not to come before a woman, anything that can be numbered or rhythmed out of chaos to a kind of clarity and order. Twenty-seven.

Twenty-seven stuffed animals in the lobby of the Restwell Motel that has fourteen doors, and he has eight bucks in his pocket, and the nine license plates all say Montana. The animals are beautiful to Luther then, numbered and secure, for just a moment.

He takes a deep breath through his nose, thinking he should be able to smell this much death, but all he smells is cigar smoke. A shiny stand-up ashtray is overflowing with cigar stubs between two old leather chairs off to one side of the bear. Luther sits down with his bedroll in his lap. He leans way back and looks around the room. The door he just entered has a strip of little tarnished bells on a red Christmas sash hanging from the handle on the inside. Luther can't remember them tinkling—no one seems to be aware he's here. He goes to the counter and leans on it. A metal postcard rack holds two postcards that both say Greetings from Montana. Luther takes the last matchbook from a plastic tray that says For Our Matchless Friends.

He returns to the soft chair and sits back down, pulling the largest cigar stub from the ashtray and lighting it. He smokes and counts the animals he doesn't know. There are four. Two little furry creatures and two birds that look like hawks but aren't.

He slides the sturdy old chair as close as he can get it to the bear and relaxes into it. He keeps checking the bear's face out of the corner of his eye. It doesn't move. Luther waits. He lights another stub.

As Luther finishes it, the manager comes out from the back room and around the counter into the lobby. He's gray-haired with clear blue eyes. His hair, like Luther's, is parted roughly in the middle, but it is much shorter. He wears gray work pants and a gray work shirt, a uniform a mechanic or a milkman might wear. Above one shirt pocket the name "Roy" is embroidered in red thread in looping longhand style. The man pushes a bucket on wheels with a mop stuck in a wringer that hangs on the bucket's edge. He notices the smoke hovering in the lobby and looks around at Luther in the chair. The cigar smoke rises in circles around the big bear's extended paws and exposed teeth.

"What the holy hell. Are you looking for something?"

Luther jumps up, sticks his hand out, smiles. He will charm Roy.

"Yes, yes I am. I pushed the buzzer, but it must not work. I was wondering about a room, Roy. I need a place to sleep. Do you have something cheap? Any day rates?"

"My name's not Roy. These were my brother's clothes—he's dead. The cheapest room is twelve dollars a night, sixty-five a week, no day rates. They don't pay." He pauses and ignores Luther's hand.

"That's a twin bed, black-and-white TV, and no phone. The

190

buzzer does work, by the way, and I don't care for people moving my furniture around." He steps behind Luther and pushes the chair back to where it had been. "I got work to do, so if you want the room, let's hear it."

Luther stalls. "Sixty-five a week. That's reasonable. That might be just the ticket for me." In his head he subtracts the eight bucks he has from twelve and gets four. Four dollars shy of a place to hole up at least for a night. But then he'd be broke again. He hasn't had a room for over a week. "Is there a cafe close by? I'm thinking about looking for work."

Roy's brother is pushing the plunger on the ashtray up and down, stuffing the stubs out of sight. He says nothing.

Luther asks about the bear. "Is that a grizzly? I've never seen one before, but I've read about 'em in the papers."

The man straightens up. "Good luck finding work here, pal. I need the money in advance. The place is run-down just now, as you might have noticed, and I can't be financing anybody's job search." He draws out these last two words slowly and ends them with a kind of smirk.

"Betty's Grill is two blocks down, open at five A.M. every day."

Luther smiles at him, thinking, waiting. "And the bear?"

"The bear is what I don't have time for, pal." He puffs his chest out at Luther. Luther suddenly realizes how he must look, fresh off the train and a four-day drunk in Casper. He runs his hand through his hair.

The older man relents. "No, it's a Kodiak, out of North Canada. Only place you can get 'em. Biggest bear there is—they make two of grizzlies. So do you want the room or not?"

"Well, yeah, I do. But I'm kinda short at the moment. I could give you five now and make some calls today and come up with something. Or wait—" Luther remembers the broken doors, sees the mop and pail and dirty water. "Isn't there any work I could do for the room? I'm handy enough."

"Hell's bells, man, you don't need a motel. Look, the Open Door is downtown, they got beds there. I have a business to run here, OK?"

Luther imagines the Open Door. He knows he had best move on. He looks from the old man to the bear and back, wondering if there's a bullet hole in the bear's body somewhere, one single hole where all the seams in the bear's empty skin meet and are sewed together.

He wishes he could freeze everything in the smoky dim lobby. The old man with his rolling bucket and the bear with his porcelain fingers and him with his foam bedroll. He imagines himself standing with his teeth bared and his arms outstretched like that, resting like that, screaming like that, maybe forever, maybe just for a while.

He heads for the door. He pulls at the sash and jingles the bells on it and smiles at the man. "Jingle Bells, Merry Christmas."

"Not in July, my friend, not in July. Oh for chrissakes, look, I've got a real fucking mess down in number fourteen. If you want to clean it up, clean it up good, you can spend the night and keep your five."

Luther knows how bad the room will be, but he doesn't care. "Thanks, yeah, you'll see, I'm OK, I know how to work. Do I need a key?"

Luther moves back into the room.

"No, the lock's busted. It's bad down there. Two guys and some broad really tore it up before they left two days ago, and I haven't had the stomach to do anything but look at it yet. You ever seen what some people'll do to motel rooms, the kinda mess they don't mind leaving? I'll take animals anytime, buddy." He waves his head around the circle of dead creatures.

"Anyway, look, throw all the crap into the haulaway out front. You can use this mop—have at it. Do a good job and you can stay till, say, two o'clock tomorrow. How's that?" He grins at Luther. "So you're a little short right now, huh? I'd say you're a little short—period." He laughs a small, practiced laugh, as if he's breaking the ice now that everything is straight and Luther knows who the boss is.

Luther senses that he must take this, maybe chuckle a little even, in order to get the room, some breathing space. "Some people say so."

Luther smiles like the animals on the walls. He opens the door partway again.

"Yeah, I've seen dirty rooms before. I know all about it. It's nothing to surprise me. I'll get started right now."

"I'll bet you have, I'll bet you have." He smiles slowly, still sizing Luther up. "My name's McInnes; people call me McInney. What's yours?"

"Brian," Luther lies quickly. His father's name. "So, McInney, how in hell do you get a bear like that anyway?"

McInney has already moved behind the counter. He turns his head back over his shoulder as he moves away from Luther. He smiles with his teeth and then looks away. "Go up and kill one."

2

A STALE smell slaps into Luther's face when he opens the door to number fourteen as if a thick sour blanket had been thrown over his head. He cleans mechanically, methodically, trying not to think of the people or the scenes that stretch backwards from all the debris and garbage. The room reminds him of a small beach he saw once near San Pedro harbor in LA, a strip of sand between two dirty jetties where garbage from the sewers and the boats washed up.

He finds a sack and stuffs it full of fast food trash—Colonel Sanders and Wendy's and Taco John's and two pizza boxes with soggy grease stains and uneaten crusts. One of the bags collapses as Luther picks it up—wet cigarette butts and ashes and an Evergreen chewing tobacco can spill across the floor.

Nine perfectly burnt-out filter cigarettes stand upright in a row on the windowsill next to a cup filled with caramel-colored water.

In the corner icebox are two opened cans of Pabst beer. Luther drinks them slowly as he works, conjuring up a meal at Betty's Grill as his reward for the cleaning, followed by a hot shower and a long nap. He wonders what kind of work he could find in the town, things he might say when asked about his work history, his job skills.

When he's sober, he can do a good job as a short-order cook. He likes the excitement sometimes of fixing four or five meals all at once, knowing hungry people are waiting on what he's doing.

A bloodstain in the center of the bedsheets looks like one of those inkblots the psychiatrists use in the movies. It has two symmetrical halves, as if somebody had folded the sheet and pressed it when the blood was fresh. Luther wads the sheets into the pillowcase. He pours the two partial Pabsts into a paper cup and throws the cans into his trash sack. He takes the sack to McInney's haulaway and puts the sheets on the sidewalk in front of the door.

He props the door wide open with the only chair in the room, a chrome chair with a speckled vinyl seat that matches the pattern on the Formica and chrome table near the icebox. The room still stinks, and Luther hasn't opened the door to the bathroom yet. He stands outside smoking one of the longest butts he can find, sipping his beer, gazing at the brown and green mountains past the railroad tracks.

The floor is linoleum. Luther goes back in and sweeps it with a worn plastic broom he found outside of number twelve. He slides the metal bed frame out into the center of the room. Under the bed is a dog-eared, rumpled magazine, spread-eagled open to a two-page close-up of a woman's crotch. It reminds Luther of some blown-up photos taken with a microscope that he'd seen in high school science classes, photos that looked like the ocean floor or fields of grain but always turned out to be interior views of kidneys or cross sections of tumors.

194

Luther brushes at the photo gently with his broom, cocking his head at an angle until the photo is right-side-up. He tries to sketch in a woman to fit the photo, a real woman sprouting out in all directions from the glossy pink and brown fuzz of the photo. He can't. He wants to sweep the image away—suddenly it seems like a bodiless mouth just about to speak, about to pronounce a judgment on Luther, sealing his fate, seeing him for what he is, a twenty-eight-year-old drifter sweeping up after someone else in a ratty motel room two blocks from the boxcars that he calls home.

Luther flips the magazine shut with the broom. But the cover is similar, just a shot from slightly farther back—the woman's legs are pulled up in front of her and you can see her ankles and the outlines of her breasts flattened into wide circles behind her knees. The title *Cherry* is spaced across the top, and beneath the woman's right leg the issue number and date: #12 June 1987. Luther puts the magazine between the TV and the wall on top of the fridge. He thinks of what his mother and sister—Joan and little Joan—would think. He wishes he were at their house in Sarcoxie.

His shoes pinch his tired feet, and he kicks them off one at a time. He stands in his socks, remembering McInney's remark about the Open Door—another shelter for the homeless. Luther never sees himself as homeless, though. He believes he's just between places somehow. And although as he stands in the gray-green light of the motel room he realizes he can't really remember clearly a time when he felt at home or even clearly picture one anymore, he thinks this rootlessness, this stumbling downhill feeling that his life has become is only temporary, reversible, just a phase he must pass through.

As Luther stashes the magazine, he notices the TV. The knobs are missing from both the volume and channel controls and the shafts are broken off flush. He sees the cord lying on the floor next to the fridge and bends to plug it in. Nothing happens for several seconds, then a small white dot appears in the center.

Luther glares at it for a minute as if it were an unblinking, blank eye he has to stare down. He decides to take a look at the bathroom.

Someone has been using the shower stall for a trash can. Three or four used tampons lie in one corner. Another is stuck on the wall a few inches from the bottom of the stall as if someone threw it there. A damp box for one dozen condoms is stuffed full of used rubbers. A TV guide and a garish red and orange paperback, both soaked through, lie side by side.

Luther tries to sweep everything to one corner of the stall, but the stuff is wet and sticks to the tile. He grabs the shower curtain and discovers why the stall stinks so much. Food chunks are splattered on the inside of the curtain where someone threw up. Luther realizes his hand is on the curtain and he jumps back away from it.

He feels a sharp stab in his foot and clutches for it. A few dark drops of blood well up from a puncture at the base of his heel. Luther stands on one leg. A metal ice cube tray, a broken plastic glass, half of a rusty pair of pliers, and an old, worn, wooden-handled ice pick are piled up in the corner as if somebody had emptied out a kitchen drawer.

The tip of the pick is wet and red. Luther grabs for some TP, but the rack on the back of the door is empty. He hops out front, pulls off his socks, and wipes his foot on the wadded-up sheet. The wound looks deep, but it won't bleed much. He smokes another cigarette butt and puts his loafers on over his bare feet and goes back inside.

The TV has a picture now. A game show is playing; the picture keeps jumping back and forth between an earnest moderator and two anxious contestants. Luther finds a piece of cardboard and sweeps the shower mess onto it and takes it to the haulaway. He throws all the drawer junk on the Formica kitchen table.

Then he sweeps the whole place quickly again, mops the floor with McInney's mop, turns the shower on and scrubs the stall and curtain with an old Brillo pad, and spreads the brown wool blanket out carefully on the bed. He figures the room is clean enough, maybe cleaner than it's been in a long time.

In the blanket there's a folded newspaper—Luther turns to the want ads. Under Help Wanted–General, he finds several delivery jobs that require a vehicle. There are some nurse aid jobs and several over-the-road truck ads that all ask for at least two years experience. Luther skips over the babysitter and child care ads and two apartment manager jobs offering rent reductions.

There are two ads for cooks. One of these is under a larger ad for Kenny's Keno Klub. It's advertising for dancers, a bouncer, a dealer, and a cook. Luther folds the paper up neatly to pocket-size with the Kenny's ad in the center. He decides to shower and sleep before heading down to check on the dealer's job.

After his shower Luther lies down; he's beginning to feel too sober to sleep very well, but the bed feels great. "The Price is Right" is on TV. Luther remembers watching it mornings he was sick and home from school lying on the rose couch in his mom's front room. Luther likes the women who display the prizes and help Bob Barker play little games. They look beautiful to Luther; they dress fancy like office workers. They're always real modest, and yet they have long, graceful legs that they cross and uncross carefully as they sit in the prize La-Z-Boys or get in and out of the winners' Camaros.

Luther realizes he hasn't had a woman for months, at least not that he remembers. He pulls his shorts down and watches the models on the tube. The redhead is pedaling an exercise bike that's up for grabs, and she demurely pulls her skirt down below her knees every time it rides up. The camera flips back and forth between her and the contestants standing behind their lit-up guesses. Luther pictures the woman living in his house, coming home to her after work and finding her like that on the bike, and having her undress for him.

3

WHEN Luther wakes up, there's a soap opera on the tube. A middle-aged man and woman are fighting. They keep rubbing their foreheads and turning away from each other as they argue. Luther unties his bedroll and pulls out his other clothes, a short-sleeved shirt and a pair of wrinkled cotton slacks. He shakes the shirt and pants out and dresses slowly, feeling cleaner than he has in a week. He puts the want ads in his jacket pocket and checks his foot. It's begun to swell as if it's infected. He heads down River Street away from the Restwell, trying not to let the loafer rub the sore spot on his heel. The sun is low; it's after three.

Luther finds his way to Kenny's Klub, asking directions when he stops to buy a pack of Winstons. A huge sign mounted on the roof of the building blinks back and forth from red to green—K K K. He goes into the club and orders a beer and asks the bartender about the jobs. The bartender sends him to talk to a Mr. Strint, the afternoon manager.

Strint is at his desk when Luther walks in. He's a thin man with a receding hairline and a crew cut. The short hairs along his hairline are set forward at a jaunty angle like the prow of a ship. Strint tells Luther the dealer job was filled last week when Luther shows him the paper. Strint unfolds it.

Strint laughs lightly. "Did you happen to notice the date on this paper, Mac? July 22—that's last Friday. You're a week late and a few dollars behind, heh, heh."

Luther slaps his forehead amiably. He figures he can still make Strint like him even though he's started out badly. "I'll be damned—I was so excited about the dealer position, I didn't even check the date."

He smiles blankly at Strint, letting his mock sincerity soak in.

"I dealt in Reno one winter. Have you got anything else? How 'bout the cook job?"

Strint looks Luther over more closely. "Yeah, that's open—

it's kind of an all-around job, chief cook and bottle washer, if you catch my drift. Most of the cooking is fried stuff, burgers, mushrooms, fries, onion rings, nachos, et cetera. The rest of the time you stock and clean up." He waits a little, giving Luther a chance to interrupt him. Luther keeps smiling.

"There's some heavy work. Still interested?"

"Sure, I've got experience as a short-order man."

Strint opens a drawer and tears off an application form from a pad. "Fill this out, if you would. Then I'll show you around, and we'll see what we can do."

Luther fills out the app slowly, not because it's difficult but because he's trying to make up good lies about his past. When he gives it back, though, Strint barely looks at it. He puts it face down on his desk.

"C'mon, I want you to know what you're in for."

Luther follows him down a hallway. Strint holds open a swinging door and waves Luther in front of him. They go through part of the kitchen and into a stock room. "What's the matter with your leg? You don't have a disability or anything, do you?"

Luther realizes he's favoring his foot as he walks. "No, no way, it's just a blister on my foot, that's all."

Strint and he are standing in front of the freezer locker door, across from stacks of crates filled with clean glasses. Strint looks at Luther's feet.

"That's a good way to come up with a blister, wearing shoes with no socks. You got socks, don't you?" Strint steps back from Luther; his expression changes—his smile gets bigger but less relaxed.

"Oh sure, it's just so hot today. Yeah, I've got some socks back at the motel."

Strint nods, then is silent for a moment. Luther tries to think up a question about the job to show his interest. He wants another beer. He's beginning to dislike Strint.

"Look, tell you what—you go home, get off that bum foot

and take care of it; I'll take a look at your application and give you a call if we can use you. OK? You got a number where you can be reached, right?"

Luther senses the job is gone. "Yeah, it's on the paper," he lies. "I think I'll have a beer and then go get my weight off my foot, like you said." Strint is moving past him already. Luther follows him back out into the club. Strint talks to the bartender a minute and then disappears. Luther orders a beer and takes it to the darkest booth in the room.

The crowd changes and grows as the afternoon wanes. Luther notices no light comes in the door now when people enter. Happy Hour is Two-for-One; he orders four beers and four shots just before eight when it ends. He lines them up on the table along with his cigarettes and his last buck. He figures maybe tomorrow noon he will hit the Open Door—they can probably help him out of a jam. He alternates beers and shots; whenever somebody in the club laughs loudly, Luther laughs too. He feels OK— he tells himself he's making the best of a bad situation. That's one of his mother's favorite sayings. *Make the best of a bad situation.*

He talks to a few people that wander by his booth on their way to the johns. For a while an Indian with waist-length hair joins him. Luther and he talk about Custer's Last Stand. When the Indian tells him he's a direct descendant of a Northern Cheyenne warrior who fought at the Little Big Horn, Luther agrees wholeheartedly that Custer really was an asshole. The Indian calls himself "Joe Just Joe" several times like it might be dangerous for him to say more. He wants to shake hands with Luther, and they do that over the table for a long time.

Luther introduces himself as Roy, remembering McInney's dead brother. Joe talks about some secret negotiations between the FBI and the CIA and the Northern Cheyenne Tribal Council that he is privy to. He says it all has to do with titanium deposits on his tribe's Montana reservation, a mineral needed for rockets that's found nowhere else in the States, according to Joe.

Luther loses track of it all as he sips his beer. The next time he looks up, Joe is gone.

A huge man comes into Kenny's Klub about eleven. He is burly and tall with a full beard and a pot gut. He has big boots on with wafflestomper tread—Luther thinks of Paul Bunyan. For a minute he wants to yell out, "Hey Paul, where's your blue ox?" He figures that might get a laugh with some of the drunks, but he thinks better of it.

The man's voice reverberates across the room. Luther hears him ask the bartender about the bouncer's job, and the bartender tells him all the positions are filled. Luther wonders if this guy's using a week-old paper, too.

The man stays at the bar, drinking vodka and telling the bartender loud stories about himself and women he's punched. Luther can't tell at first whether he means punched like hit or punched like screwed, but he figures out it's like screwed because the guy keeps talking about "getting his nut off" and "ole Conrad slipping the meat to her" and "getting good skull." At one point the man looks over at Luther's corner. His eyes are angry and wild; he looks unpredictable like an animal, like a dog straining against an invisible chain.

Luther starts to leave the Klub when he runs into Joe again. Joe asks him if he's tried the house drink yet—the Buzzsaw.

"No, what the hell's that?"

"The Bitterroot Buzzsaw, man, part bourbon, part rum, and part pussy juice—it's guaranteed to make a Montana logger out of you. C'mon, have one with me."

"How much are they? I've only got a buck left, Joe."

"Two bucks a Buzzsaw, but that's cool, I'll front you half of one—I had one of your shots, in case you don't remember."

Luther doesn't remember, not exactly, but he joins Joe at the bar. Joe orders "Two BB's" with a flourish. Luther drinks his while Joe tells him about William Casey, the CIA director, making secret trips to Montana right before he died.

"If people knew what I know about Casey and this whole

titanium thing, it'd make that Iran-Contra thing look like small potatoes, Roy."

Luther nods and drinks. The big man at the other end of the bar has run out of stories and is sitting by himself, spinning his vodka glass around and around. He grimaces as he cleans his teeth with a toothpick.

4

LUTHER'S downtown. He's drunk to the point where inside him is a painless, spaceless place and outside is a quiet, almost calculated look. He's heading in the general direction of the Restwell, glad he has a bed and a shower and a night of shelter even though he's busted. He passes a stairwell in front of a restaurant. Loud music is rising from it, a big bass beat drowned in some kind of organ music.

Luther leans on the railing, letting the music blow around him like a hot wind. Downstairs, a sign on a table by the door says Killer Bees 2$ Cover, but it's one-fifteen and the band is well into its last set—the table is abandoned. Luther walks nonchalantly into the bar. A reggae band is playing, and the dance floor is full. All the people sitting down are nodding their heads or tapping their hands on their legs. Luther sits at an empty table near the bar.

After the next song, a woman returns to the table. She smiles at Luther but doesn't speak as she sits down. She takes the purse and jacket that Luther hadn't noticed off her chair before she sits. Her face is sweaty and flushed. She stares at the stage while the musicians confer between numbers. Luther watches her watch the band.

He thinks she is pretty, too thin maybe—her arms very thin and white. She's wearing a sleeveless white blouse and blue jeans. She has no rings on any of her fingers. Luther watches her foot swinging in front of her. She's wearing nylons and low red heels. Her hair is poufed, spun; even after the dancing it seems tight and held in place. The band starts another song Luther doesn't recognize as the woman pulls a cigarette out of a pack in her purse. When she fishes for her lighter, Luther strikes a match from the book he found at McInney's and holds it out to her. His hand weaves a little, and the woman has to move the cigarette around to get it lit.

"Thanks," she says without meeting Luther's eyes.

As she turns toward him, Luther notices a red splotch on the side of her neck and under her jaw, either a birthmark or a burn scar, about the size of a small child's hand. It reminds Luther of the shapeless red bloodstain on the sheet in number fourteen.

When the song ends, Luther asks her if she wants to dance.

She looks at her cigarette and hesitates, as if it might be important for her to finish it, and then says, "Sure."

Luther follows her to the dance floor. She still hasn't looked directly at him. She leaves the cigarette burning in the ashtray on the table. Luther realizes as he follows her that he hasn't danced in years and never to this kind of music. He likes old classics, what he calls straight-ahead rock'n'roll, the kind of old-time rock'n'roll Bob Seger sings about in his song. Luther shuffles around on the floor, trying to move as slowly as the other dancers around him.

At one point the woman leans over and yells at him to ask if he likes reggae, and Luther nods and smiles. He doesn't feel the sore on his foot much now, yet he favors it some as he bobs in and out of the steady beat.

The woman seems to be enjoying herself. Everyone, including the band, is drunk or high. Luther closes his eyes several times during the song. He feels like he could go to sleep in the midst of it all. When the song is finished, he does like the woman does—stands and claps real hard while looking at the band.

The lead singer is talking into the mike, something about really liking the crowd here, and then something about how they want to slow it down one last time. Before Luther realizes it, he is dancing slowly with the woman in his arms. The song keeps repeating its title, "No Woman No Cry," over and over, along with other words Luther can't catch.

The woman in his arms feels strong and full of energy. Her fingers on his back are long and narrow. Luther feels her small breasts beneath her blouse and bra. He asks into her ear what her name is as they circle slowly around together.

"Belinda," she says back, and Luther repeats, "Belinda." She doesn't ask him his name.

He's too nervous touching her gently like this not to talk, so he starts asking her questions. She tells him she's a clerk at Randy's Full-Service Hunter's One-Stop across town. When they talk they have to put their mouths right next to each other's ears. In her heels she is the same height as Luther.

She says Randy's sells guns and ammo and does custom taxidermy in the winter, and stocks and guides hunting parties in the summer. She says she's worked there since the summer after she graduated from Windgate High, five years ago. The song goes on and on. Luther catches himself saying the title words "No Woman No Cry" along with the singers right into Belinda's ear. She tells him he has a nice voice.

When they sit back down, Luther feels suddenly panicky. He wants to see her again and find out more about her job and her life and dance slowly with her some more.

She acts like nothing at all has happened between them.

The crowd brings the band back for an encore number by clapping in unison for a minute or two. Belinda has picked up her coat and purse. Luther starts talking too fast at her.

"My name's Joe. I like reggae—I do—that beat's terrific. Maybe we could meet again sometime down here."

Belinda doesn't say anything.

"Actually, I work here in town too. I just got a job dealing cards over at Kenny's Klub. Do you know that place? I'm fairly new in town. Maybe we could go somewhere and talk?"

Belinda turns to him as the band climbs back on the stage and the rhythmic clapping fades away. She caresses the mark on her neck with her thin fingertips.

"Ah, maybe. You're a dealer, huh? Look, I've got to go to

the restroom—beer always goes right through me. I'll be back in a minute and we'll see. Mother Nature calls."

She smiles at Luther, and he almost blushes at her euphemism. He hasn't heard anybody say that in years. He watches her walk away. He can't believe his luck, meeting someone this sweet so easily.

The band finishes with "I Shot the Sheriff." Luther vaguely remembers it had been a big hit when he was in high school. He stares at the booming, six-foot-tall speakers, his eyes closing. As he hears the song's opening lines echo across the bar, he remembers the face of a Tulsa cop who'd hit him once. He shakes his head and instead tries to picture Belinda, leaving work at her hunting shop and waiting for him to pick her up in a car. Luther didn't know what he'd done to be hit for. They would talk about where to eat dinner, maybe Ponderosa Steakhouse or Pizza Hut. Luther smiles. He might get to know Belinda so well she would tell him about the mark on her neck. It would be important to her, and she'd be shy to talk about it. The band sings something about planting seeds. If Belinda told him about her mark, then he could show her his photos of Joan and Joan and tell her about growing up in Sarcoxie and about his father choking. But he doesn't want to think about that face either, not his father's final grimace or the cop's furious glare as he raised his night stick. Luther begins to wonder where Belinda is. The guitarists lean into the mike and repeat the last lyric as the keyboard player and drummer end the song with a crescendo. Luther's glad the song's over—the words hurt him and make him mad at the same time. He claps as long as anybody in the room when the band bows. He waits for a few more minutes, watching the barmaids pick up glasses and bottles, but when the lights come on, he goes back up the stairs to the street.

5

LUTHER decides he will call Joan and little Joan from the pay phone in the lobby at the Restwell when he finds the front door unlocked, but the Kodiak distracts him again. It seems even larger and more unearthly at night in the shadowy light. He wonders how long it takes the taxidermists to do a job like that—McInney might've even had the bear stuffed at the shop where Belinda works. He figures McInney must be in bed so he slides the chair he likes over beneath the bear and sits in the darkened lobby.

He pulls his money envelope from the pocket of the ragged corduroy sports coat he bought at the Goodwill in Rapid City. He'd worked at a Sonic drive-in there for two weeks, running counters. But all that's left is the check stub. And his photos. He makes sure his two photos are still there, two little pictures, one of himself and his mother, and one of himself and his sister.

The photos have been relaminated several times in hardware stores—they have a gauzy, blurred look. Both of them were taken in a little photo booth in Chicago, where they had all gone on a three-day holiday weekend one time in Luther's senior year in high school in 1978. He loves those little booths—every now and then he takes his picture and sends it back to Joan and Joan from wherever he finds himself. Milwaukee, Kansas City, Topeka, Pueblo.

He knows these places aren't really exotic or even that far away from his home in the Ozarks, but he likes to think of Joan and Joan imagining him roaming around the nation like this, free and wild. Luther wonders if they're still mad at him, if they've saved the last picture he sent from Sioux Falls.

The only light in the room comes from the bright Vacancy sign burning in the window and from a night light on the counter. Luther feels calm by the bear, calm and still. He figures it's been almost exactly twenty-four hours since the train stopped in the mountains last night—he counts through the hours to make sure—it feels much longer than that. He stares over at the pay phone on the wall, trying to compose some sort of apology to say to Joan and Joan if he gets through to them.

McInney comes out from the back rooms, carrying a can of beer. He's wearing slippers and a bathrobe and glasses. He looks much older than before. Luther can't imagine him killing the Kodiak.

"What are you doing out here?" asks McInney, but the gruffness of the day is gone out of his voice. "You did a good job down in fourteen." He swigs from his can.

"Thanks, you weren't lying about the mess, were you." Luther sighs, almost the kind of sigh people only do when they're with somebody they can trust. "I was gonna use the phone, if it's all right. I want to call home."

"Where's home?"

Luther begins to say Missouri, starts to change it to Mississippi, but then switches back. "Missouri." McInney doesn't press it.

"Well, go ahead and use it. It's not free though, you know. I'll wait and lock up after you're done."

As Luther goes to the phone, McInney grabs a rag from the counter and begins polishing the brass ID plates beneath a row of mounted deer and elk heads on the far wall of the lobby.

He gets the operator and places a collect call to his mother's phone number. Station-to-station. He fidgets with the flap on his jacket pocket while the phone rings. His sister answers. The operator says she's got a collect call for anyone from Luther. Little Joan asks from who and the operator repeats Luther's name. Little Joan says to the operator to wait just a minute, and she puts her hand over the phone. All Luther can hear is a muted static and the soft sound of McInney's rag, polishing the trophy plates.

Little Joan comes back on the line and tells the operator that she can't accept the charges. The operator says she's sorry but the party won't accept the call. Luther is straining to hear into the receiver. For a second it seems there's an endless, hollow tunnel from the Restwell to Sarcoxie and he's falling down into it. He hears the dial tone again.

Luther looks over his shoulder at McInney at the far wall and the bear in the center of the room. "Hi Mom, it's me. How're you doing? How's little Joan?" He pauses, counting seconds by one-thousands as if he's hearing her reply. The phone is swallowing him; he's struggling not to drop into a two-thousand-mile shaft that goes nowhere. "Yeah, I know it's late. I didn't think about it till after the phone was already ringing. You know I never get these time changes straight. I was thinking it was earlier there." *One. Two. Three. Four.* "Right. Well, I didn't have anything special, really, I just hadn't called for a while. I just wanted to check in and see how you all were. Is Sis there?" *One. Two. Three.* "Sure, I guess she would be asleep." *One.* "No, don't wake her. Look, I'll call tomorrow in the day-time, and we'll have a good talk." *One. Two. Three. Four. Five.* "OK, me too, love you too. Sorry I woke you up. Bye."

Luther hangs up the phone as if it were made from eggshells. He sets a careful smile on his face, a smile for the bear and McInney. But when he turns around, McInney is gone. He lights a cigarette and stands staring out the lobby window for a long time, thinking of nothing but smoke.

6

LUTHER is still standing in the window when a yellow car pulls up. A large man gets out and looks around the motel parking lot. Luther recognizes him from Kenny's Klub, the one who called himself Conrad. He looks just as big but maybe drunker as he comes into the lobby and looks at Luther; he doesn't seem to recognize him from earlier.

"Evening. I need a room. Whatcha got?" His eyes catch on the Kodiak as he speaks. "Brother, that sonofabitch's bigger than me. That's one hell of a lot of bear." He moves toward it.

Luther loses all sense of caution; an idea flashes in his head— a way to get some quick bread and get out of this town.

"It oughta be. It's a Kodiak, biggest bear there is." Luther tries to mimic McInney's confident tone. "I have one room left

I could let you have. It's twenty bucks—checkout time's normally noon, but since it's so late you can stay till two if you need to. Fair enough?" Luther holds his breath for a second as Conrad turns around from the bear.

"I guess so. I don't feel like looking around at this hour. I'll take it, yeah." He pulls his wallet out and takes out a twenty. Luther sees more bills.

"Number fourteen. It's unlocked—the key broke in the lock, and I haven't got it fixed yet. Damn locksmiths want an arm and a leg. No need to register since you've got cash." Luther steps up near Conrad and takes the twenty without looking him in the eyes. He goes around behind the counter with it. Conrad puts his wallet back. He tucks his shirt in and pulls his pants up while he looks the bear over again. When he goes out, the little bells on the sash jingle, and Luther hopes McInney stays asleep.

Luther watches from the lobby while Conrad moves his car down to the stall right in front of fourteen and goes inside. Then he remembers his bedroll stashed under the metal bed in the room. It's not much, a worn piece of foam and an old cotton sleeping bag with a broken zipper and a piece of plastic to keep dry with. He doesn't like leaving it behind, but it's not worth the twenty he's got in his hand.

He figures he better hit the road pretty quick. His foot is beginning to hurt like crazy again. He unfolds the rag McInney left on the counter and puts it inside his shoe like a sock. He laughs to himself about his quick thinking and his scam. The big lady-killer and the big bear-killer.

By the time those two find out, Luther'll be long gone. He imagines the look on McInney's face if he goes down to fourteen in the morning and finds Conrad. Luther is sure they would never get along, those two. On the way out of the lobby, he grabs the two postcards from their metal rack and stops and winks at the bear. God helps those who help themselves, he thinks. It was one of his mother's favorite expressions—*God helps those who help themselves.* He closes the door carefully to keep the little bells from ringing.

When he gets to the middle of the parking lot, right under the sign, Conrad comes out of door fourteen. Luther freezes, as if this might make him invisible. Conrad calls out to him. He sounds friendly enough.

"Hey, buddy, there's something you forgot to tell me."

Luther considers running right now—that fat giant couldn't catch him, he's sure, but that would be showing his hand. A pickup truck cruises by. He doesn't want to call attention to himself. He can carry this off.

"What's that? I was just getting ready to turn off the sign for the night."

"The TV don't work. Will you take a look at it for me? I like to run the TV when I fall asleep."

Conrad has come closer as he speaks, now it might be chancy to run. Conrad is still smiling. Luther goes with him into the room. He probably just hasn't plugged it in.

"Probably isn't plugged in," says Luther as he steps into the room ahead of Conrad. "There's really not much on now anyway, I imagine." He bends down and plugs in the cord. As he straightens up, Conrad grabs his arm and twists it up hard behind his shoulder blades in one motion. Luther doesn't make a sound.

"OK, you little asshole, what the hell's the deal here? I get down here, and I remember all of a sudden seeing you at Kenny's Klub tonight, borrowing money off a goddamned Indian no less, and now you're running a motel? You're not trying to fuck with me, are you?"

"No, no way, not at all. I work here. I just—"

Conrad twists Luther's arm up higher. "How 'bout you don't give me one more ounce of bullshit, boy, or I'll pull your goddamned arm off—all right?"

Luther tells Conrad the truth then, some of it anyway; he tries to convince him that the room's twenty bucks anyway and the only one getting cheated is McInney.

"I don't give a shit about no McInney. I want my twenty back." He reaches into Luther's jacket pocket and retrieves the dirty envelope with the pictures and the twenty. He throws Luther onto the kitchen chair. He puts his twenty back in his wallet.

"I can't believe a little shit like you fuckin' with me. What a deal. Well, well, who are the bitches with Mr. Littleshit here, Cinderella's two ugly sisters?"

Luther lunges for the photos. Conrad shoves him back down.

"No. wait, these two look familiar. Maybe I seen them in the magazine there, eh?" He points to the *Cherry* magazine he's opened on the table. As Luther turns to see it, his eye catches on the ice pick in the pile of junk in the corner against the wall. He pretends to be staring at the naked picture for a minute as he tenses up. He grabs the pick and swings around.

"Let me the hell out of here. Just give me my pictures and get out of my way. We're all even. You got your money."

Conrad looks shocked, but he doesn't budge. His eyes are glued on the point of the pick. "Well, go on, pal, do what comes natural. Or I will."

Luther has no idea what to do next. His bluff has failed. He hesitates for a second and tries to think. Conrad kicks him in the shin so hard Luther snaps back. Conrad squeezes his wrist and grabs the pick away from him.

"I think you're gonna wish you hadn't done that, my friend. Let me think about this." He looks at Luther for a long moment. "Tell you what. See if this don't sound fair. You tried to screw me, so now I screw you. Tit for tat. You been on the inside. I can tell by looking. You know how it's done, don't you? You can give ole Conrad some skull, can't you?"

Conrad unzips his pants as he talks. "Or would you rather I had you sit on this ice pick," he holds it point-up in Luther's face, "and rotate some. What'll it be?"

Luther says nothing, feels nothing. Fear is over almost before it begins. He knows what will happen now; he has been on the inside; he does know how this happens. Conrad holds the pick in one hand right next to Luther's head while with the other he grabs his shoulder and pushes him down in front of the chrome chair. He sits down and rubs himself while he looks back and forth from the picture on the table to Luther's eyes. All the time he holds the pick an inch from Luther's ear. When he's ready, he pulls Luther to him. Luther closes his eyes. He begins to count. The TV has come on.

7

LUTHER lurches away from Conrad's chair. He goes to the bathroom and spits into the white bowl he'd cleaned earlier in the day. Conrad moans, rubbing his fingers on the pictures in the magazine. He keeps saying, "Oh you sweet bitch." He grabs his bottle of vodka and follows Luther into the bathroom.

"Got indigestion, my little friend? Musta been something you ate." Conrad begins to laugh and then offers Luther the bottle. "Here, wash it down with a shot of white magic."

Luther takes the bottle, staring at Conrad's huge boots.

"Go ahead, kill it." Conrad reaches in his pants pocket, gets his wallet, pulls out a dollar bill. He drops it at Luther. "Here you go. I don't usually pay to get my nut, but you did OK, and I don't like to think about anybody being completely busted. Not here in the good ole US of A. Look at it this way, now you got exactly one more dollar than when you tried to rip me off. Take it and get the fuck outa here."

Luther clutches at the dollar and the vodka bottle. He can't move. He feels like he has been in this motel room all his life and he will never find a way out.

Conrad waits a minute for Luther to move. Then he says, "Suit yourself, pal, but I gotta piss now." He hovers over the bowl next to Luther. Water splashes in Luther's face. He tries to raise his head back far enough to see all the way to Conrad's eyes. When he finally finds them, they are closed. He realizes how drunk Conrad is.

"Don't forget to flush when you leave, little buddy." Conrad finishes and closes the door behind him.

Luther gets cold sitting on the floor of the bathroom in the dark. He finishes off the vodka and feels warmer, drunker, stronger. He closes and opens his eyes several times, trying to see. It doesn't even occur to him that it is dark—this lack of vision must be his own.

He feels weighted down, and his eyes blur and burn, like he's underwater. Like he's swimming in the Sarcoxie municipal pool in the summer as a boy, holding his breath, trying to stay at the bottom of the pool, holding onto a drain grate, listening to the muffled sounds of the kids at the surface. Finally he stands.

He listens for Conrad, hears deep, thick breathing, the beginnings of a slow snore. He wishes there were a window in the bathroom that he could crawl out of. He flicks the light on and sees one, there, on the wall, in front of him, above the sink. He leans toward it, but then sees only himself, gaunt, drunk, dirty, humiliated. Humiliated by his own reflection. He grins and a quick glimpse of the TV commercial with the vapid face of the apartment-house neighbor grinning from the medicine cabinet mirror floats in front of him, but he has a sure keen sense that behind this mirror and its image lies something dark and humorless—a phantom built up from the black impossibilities of a lifetime.

Luther considers smashing it to see. He wants to break something, anything. He wants to make a terrible mess that someone else will have to clean up. He watches the face in the mirror shake itself back and forth in confusion; he flicks the light switch off; the face disappears. He stands in the dark with a dollar in his hand, hearing Conrad's stifled snore.

He steps into the motel room. There has to be a way out, a door opening to somewhere. Conrad is asleep at the Formica table with the shiny hollow metal legs, his head bent forward over his forearms, the open magazine beneath them. The soundless TV flickers light across the room. Luther sees the door and heads toward it, feeling like he's rising to the surface of the pool, years before. If he can make it outside and take a deep breath, he will be all right. He can go on with his life, find a train or a highway out of this town. Forget Conrad and Mc-Inney's dead screaming bear and this room he's drowning in. He opens the door, gasps in a breath, stares into the cool summer night.

The outline of the mountains frames the distance. But it looks like high walls to Luther, painted with pleasant murals, yet dimensionless and impossible to penetrate. He looks down the row of identical numbered doors, across the hoods of the look-alike cars, to the bay windows of the lobby. The Vacancy sign illuminates the bear.

He takes one more deep slow breath, as if about to dive underwater. He goes back into the small room and closes the door.

Luther feels lucid now, even in only the faint flickering TV light. All the light in the room is coming out of his eyes, and he can make it brighter and brighter at will. Conrad snores into the Formica table. His great bulk, moving slowly and rhythmically with his breath, is the largest thing in the room. The TV goes black for an instant between commercials, then one of those record ads comes on where the names of old standby tunes ride up the screen, one after another, over a backdrop of teenage lovers strolling along a lakeside holding hands. *Teen Angel.*

The pictures are sweet; they could be advertising diamond engagement rings or long distance phone calls. *Two Hearts on Fire.*

He thinks of the couples in the mountains, safely in love, sleeping soundly in the woods before the moment of terror when the grizzly stalks into their campsites and ruins everything forever. The lobby bear looms before his own eyes, large as this whole day and night that suddenly seems different from all the others, separated from all the others.

Luther struggles to establish a date, a number in his head for this different day. He rocks back and forth on his heels, reeling, reading the song titles as they glide by. *All in the Game. The Sea of Heartbreak.*

Luther tries for a moment to break the spell of darkness he feels surrounding him. He opens his eyes as wide as he possibly can, wider and wider to let out all the light that's shining through his head, that's hiding in his skull. A skull in a motel room peeling light from deep beneath its eyes.

The TV blacks out again for a second, and Luther sees the dollar still clutched in his fist and Conrad slumped at the table. Conrad's back is swirled with long fine hair, and the knobs of his spine roll up his back like the little coned symbols for mountain ranges on a map. Luther follows the line of knobs as it rises from Conrad's pants up to the hairless, tanned, wrinkled spot at the base of his skull. And without knowing that he had even seen it lying on the floor by Conrad's overturned boot, Luther reaches for the ice pick.

The room fills with a bluish pulsating light that keeps rhythm in Luther's head with the screaming red noise of Conrad's steady breathing. Luther moves like a hunter, like an animal, shifting his weight away from the sore spot on his foot and steadying himself. He puts the shaft of the ice pick in his left hand like a drill bit in a boring guide, the point just flush with the edge of his curled little finger. His hand hovers above the bare spot at the top of Conrad's neck, tilting the pick around in small circles, projecting a perfect angle into Conrad's sleeping brain. He holds the dollar bill between his teeth, gritting them into its inky bitter taste, and steadies his left hand as it squeezes the pick. He feels as if he's about to pry the lock of the world apart; he feels alert as a diamond cutter.

The commercials have ended on the silent screen above the refrigerator, and a late night rerun of a musical lip-synch show from LA has come on. Two would-be country-western singers, a boy and a girl in fringe jackets, are mouthing secondhand lyrics into the camera.

Luther compresses his right hand into a fist; he tightens his arm and wrist into a hammer. He waits while Conrad's breath builds louder, as if a freight train were roaring right into the room, and then he swings the hammer as hard as he can, driving the pick straight into the base of Conrad's brain.

There is a sound like something brittle breaking underwater, like something murky and viscous giving way all at once. Conrad's arms shoot out across the table. He makes a gull-like squawk. Luther feels tiny hanging from the end of the pick as if Conrad is a gigantic, dragon-sized puppet that he must somehow control. Luther remembers pithing frogs in his high school biology class; he levers the pick back and forth and up and down. Conrad's arms and legs keep convulsing as Luther rotates the pick handle, and a dense acrid smell fills the room.

The TV camera is panning the audience as they clap and cavort wildly for the country-western adolescents who act shy and bow repeatedly in their fringe, the boy's guitar swung casually around behind him. Luther jumps back from his murder.

The pantomime of applause on the screen continues and people in the audience wave at the passing camera. Luther feels as if they all have seen him. He yanks the cord from the wall and the grinning teenagers disappear.

Luther has torn the dollar bill with his teeth. He jams it into his pocket and feels himself on the train again, stopping with its cold metal crunch in the still night. He feels naked and freezing cold as if he had stepped completely out of his own tired skin. He climbs into the bed and pulls the brown blanket around him in one motion as he rolls to the wall. He lies there rolled up, face down, and tries to think of a word, any word. He can't. All he can see in his mind is McInney's bear, keeping watch in the lobby, and all he can hear is a small, steady dripping, something leaking, something pooling, as if the night itself were melting.

8

ABOVE the eastern mountain rim, the sun rises in smog— sick, burnt orange, like a rotten eye someone forgot to close.

Luther awakens in dim light and knows what he has done before he swivels his head around to see Conrad's body glued to the cheap metal furniture in the motel room. He crawls to the window and peeks out at the sunlit street. The neon sign hums. The missing letters blink on occasionally. A police car cruises down River Street. Luther sucks in his breath.

He pulls the blanket from the bed and throws it at the foot of Conrad's chair, covering the pool that's congealed there in the night. He slips Conrad's wallet out and takes all the money—a twenty, the same one he had earlier, and two fives. He replaces the wallet. He grabs Conrad's keys from the end table. He sees the pick protruding like a handle from Conrad's neck. He shakes it, and the body moves. A small trail of blood, the only blood, runs straight down the bumps of his spine like a hardened stripe of red paint on the side of a paint can.

Conrad is stiff; the ice pick is stuck fast in his neck. Luther pulls harder. Conrad's body straightens up, and the whole chair pivots back on one leg before the pick finally slides free. Luther dodges away as the chair and Conrad settle against the wall by the table. Conrad's eyes are glazed open. Luther scrapes the ice pick on the edge of the blanket and puts it in his pocket.

Seeing the shallow open eyes of the dead man spins Luther back into a dream, a nightmare where every thought surfaces slowly like the sluggish, emotionless voices on a record played at the wrong speed and every action slogs forward in syrup-thick air. Conrad's hands are clenched, one outstretched on the table, one in his lap. Luther grabs a coffee cup from the white metal cabinet below the fridge and puts it on the table, working Conrad's fingers around it as if he were about to take a drink. He puts the ragged magazine in Conrad's other hand and folds a stiff thumb down around it.

Luther backs away toward the door. He wonders if this is how the undertakers feel as they manufacture calm expressions on the faces of the dead. He tries to imagine what the taxidermists think about as they seam their stiff, dried skins together.

He counts the money again, thirty-one dollars, wraps it around his pictures of Joan and Joan in the torn envelope, puts his jacket on. He opens the door, and a strand of sunlight catches on Conrad's blank stare.

Luther follows the empty gaze up toward the TV. He reaches down and plugs the cord in. A tiny dot appears first, and then a pattern of horizontal lines widens out from the dot, like the eye of a sci-fi computer opening after a long electronic sleep. Across the bottom of the screen is written *Good Morning from KSPS. Our programming day begins at 7 A.M. with Action Local News. July 29, 1987.*

Now Luther has a number; he files it away amid all the numbers of the days, files it in his catalog of lost and counted details. He knows the date is too late to help Conrad—knows Conrad is beyond being or feeling alone—yet he leaves the TV on as he closes the door, imagining the local newscaster coming on cheerily at seven, sending silent and phony greetings into the dead space of the room, into the vacant eyes of the man in the chrome chair.

Conrad's car, a yellow 1971 Duster with sanded, paintless spots the size of hubcaps on the doors and fenders, starts easily after Luther pumps the accelerator a few times. As he rolls down River Street, he notices the edge of a road map on the seat next to him beneath some sacks and wrappers from Tastee Freeze. He shoves the garbage onto the floor and accordions the map out to its full size.

On one side is Idaho; he turns it over to Montana. Spaced out evenly all across the dark line of Montana's northern border are the big letters C A N A D A. Luther stares at it. Canada looks roomy and blank, empty enough to hold him and hide him. Even on the worn map, it looks free and fresh and open. Maybe he should go there. It's close—he could be there by nightfall. Tomorrow could be his first day in Canada. He follows the red and blue signs for the Interstate, turning left off River Street.

A block later a construction site catches his eye, a small building with block walls half up. Luther parks and walks toward the walls, remembering the summer after high school he'd spent working as a hod carrier in Missouri. He'd liked the work and the alkaline smell of the mortar as he'd pushed brimming wheelbarrows of it and tossed sloppy shovelfuls of it over his shoulder onto mortarboards up on the scaffolding. Once in a while one of the bricklayers would drop something down inside the walls accidentally, a small tool or a full pack of cigarettes, and they would try to fish it out with a long piece of wire hooked on the end. Lots of times they'd have to abandon it.

He glances over his shoulder as he approaches a head-high wall with broken blocks and hardened globs of mortar all around its base. Scaffolding faces it, and Luther pictures the workers climbing up on it soon to begin their day. He swings himself up on the scaffold, careful of putting too much weight on his sore foot. He peers into the wall to see if it's plugged up and then drops the ice pick down, handle first. He hears hollow clicks as it bumps the edges of block on its way to the bottom.

Luther squats for a minute on the scaffold, trying to imagine staying and asking the brick foreman for work, hiring on and becoming part of a crew, getting a paycheck and going to the bar every Friday afternoon with friends. He thinks of the crew that summer in Missouri and how they'd told him he was a hard worker. After he'd pulled a muscle in his shoulder and couldn't do much, the foreman, Vinus Turner, had suggested maybe he was too small for hod carrying and told him it was a dead end anyway.

Luther thinks of the ice pick, the steel shaft that had probed inside a brain and drained the life from it, lying for years inside the hollow wall. He wonders what the building will be. It isn't very big, one story, maybe the beginnings of a branch bank or a Mr. Sizzler.

Luther believes nobody will ever find the ice pick. He feels smart and safe for a moment. He thinks that he's keeping his wits about him. That's a favorite phrase of his mother's. *Keep your wits about you.*

9

T W O blocks later the car stalls out. Luther gets it started again, but it runs only long enough to pull over to the curb. The gas gauge needle is below the "E." Luther's eye catches sight of the neck of a whiskey bottle beneath a pair of ragged coveralls under the fast food trash he'd shoved on the floormat. He fishes it out and downs two good gulps as he tries to think of what to do next.

He hops out of the Duster and locks it, walking away from it casually as if he was just headed to an appointment. He remembers he's got thirty-one dollars now. He wonders if he should head to a gas station or back to the train yard. The whiskey makes his head stop aching, and he forgets his foot. He steps down off a curb hard and winces. He looks back at the yellow Duster.

It's a block away now—a long way off. Luther decides to abandon it. He tosses the keys underhand into an open haul-away at the edge of a parking lot and walks on. He tries to move slowly—suspicious people move too fast. It's beginning to dawn on him that he's still in the same town with Conrad's huge corpse—the corpse he created in the middle of the night on his way to the door.

At the next corner, an old woman carrying a thin cane waits for a Walk sign. She taps the pavement with the tip of her cane as she waits. Luther gets close to her. She's humming. The woman's sweet, low sounds and the steady rhythm of her cane on the pavement soothe Luther. He follows behind her, trying to think. In the middle of the next block, as Luther slows even more in order not to overtake her, she turns suddenly into a small walkway.

Luther looks around slowly. St. Francis Church. He watches

the woman disappear behind the tall doors that close noiselessly in her wake. He rubs his eyes with the palms of his hands.

He wonders what would be different now if he had come here yesterday morning instead of to the Restwell. His vision is all yellow and black dots from rubbing his eyes so hard. He limps into the church, shrinking from the light of the street.

Dim. Dim even in the time near dawn. And cool. Cool and the smell of candles, candles burning in unison, dozens of small flames, each similar and cool and dim on low shelves.

Luther stands alone in the entryway. His head blurs even more in the shadows. He begins counting the candles, watching the flames rise and fall in the mild, airy eddies of the church's calm interior. He steadies and raises his gaze above a wooden rack full of pamphlets. A small crucifix draws his eyes.

He sees Christ hanging quietly on his cross, the cross hung on a wall, the wall, no doubt, tacked onto studs suspended from broad beams and rafters that hang, somehow, upside down from out of dark earth. And Luther feels himself hanging, then, hanging from the floor, hanging from an inverted world as if he had long nails through his shoes, his feet.

The spike through Christ's right hand reminds Luther of the ice pick—the ice pick and its hole—the hole in Conrad and in the bear and in Jesus—all the holes tearing into and out of Luther, an emptiness where the morning light leaks away.

Luther stumbles forward, tearing the nails from his shoes, shuffling away in confusion from the crucifix until he finds a niche in the side wall of the church. He tries to cry there beneath a stained window that turns the sunlight into portraits of saints. He crosses his hands over his chest, clasping his own arms.

A light catches his eye, a light disappearing. Just ahead of him, a small green light like a single Christmas tree bulb blinks off over a curtain in a nearby booth.

Luther focuses on the confessional, a booth with three doors, each with a small bulb above thick, pleated brown curtains.

Now only the red bulb over the center curtain is on, and the old woman whose hum Luther had followed parts the curtain and steps out.

Luther thinks of the photo booths where he takes his own picture in front of True Values or WalMarts or HiVees, and he wonders if Joan and Joan have kept any of the dozens of little photos he's sent from around the country. He tries to picture his mother and sister together at home in Sarcoxie in the living room beneath the lace curtains, thumbing through an album with his face on every page.

"Father Andus will forgive you. He can help. Go and tell the Father." The woman's voice is as straight and smooth as her humming. She pauses in front of Luther in his reverie, a small, shabby man smelling of whiskey. "He forgives us all."

The woman taps away with her metal cane before Luther can answer. He watches her circle around the back of the pews and then take a candle and walk up the center aisle, solemn and proud like a bride. Luther feels himself bobbing on the surface of the morning like a half-full bottle, on the verge of filling all at once and sinking fast, and yet he doesn't even know in which direction sinking would be.

He crosses quickly to the confessional and pulls aside the curtains on the booth the woman just left. He falls into a kneel and exhales loudly. The green bulb on his booth blinks on. A wooden window slides open behind a pegboard partition in front of his face.

A tired, reedy voice intones a prayer that sounds to Luther like a song in a foreign language, like the time in Texas when he had turned on the car radio in the middle of the night and heard a Mexican love song struggling in and out of static. Luther feels small again, boyish, as small as when he had dangled from the handle of the pick in Conrad's neck, but now he feels as if he's in a great, warm palm. The confessional smells like oiled walnut wood, like the furniture polish Luther's mother always used before company came over.

The voice behind the wall speaks his own language. "How long has it been since your last confession, my son?"

"Father, Father." Luther chokes on his answer, immediately and undeniably sure no one has called him "son" since his father died. His mother calls him Luther or little Luther sometimes, never "son."

"I've never confessed, not really. My folks weren't Catholic, but we did go to church. They did try an' teach me."

"I hear pain in your voice, my son, have you sinned?"

"Yes, Father, I've sinned." Luther's mind brims suddenly with images of his father and the night his father died on the kitchen floor in the house in Sarcoxie beneath the floral-pattern, plastic kitchen curtains. He had been drunk for days, silent, morose—he never screamed or beat his family, but he would retreat into a chair or a corner and not move except for drinking for hours, evenings, days. Luther's mother had tried that night to get him to eat, and he'd wanted nothing but steak, steak and potatoes, and she'd cooked steak and potatoes and fed him there at the kitchen table as his head drooped, and then he had choked. Choked because he'd forgotten to chew, even the small bites on his plate Joan had cut up for him like she still did for little Joan, forgotten to chew and choked to death on the floor in front of them. Luther, who had been putting a model airplane together in his bedroom because it was a quiet, out-of-the-way thing to be doing, came running, and for the first time ever, his father had been violent, flailing and scratching and fisting at them, letting no one near enough to help, like the warnings Luther had learned from his swimming teacher the summer before about the dangers of rescue, the threat of a drowning victim in their blind desperation, so likely to kill, and Brian had slapped Joan across the room finally and socked Luther so hard in the chest he was winded and kicked at them all with his pointed boots until his mother crawled over to the phone, and by then he'd been bright blue and unconscious, his hand sliding down a cabinet door he'd torn from the hinges, scratching the paint.

"You may confess your sins, Jesus will open your heart."

Luther trembles, holding his hands together, compressing them hard as if he could squeeze a tiny, solid prayer from between them.

"Father, I've done something terrible. I wish I could take it back, but it's too late now, it's too late, listen, I've killed, Father, I've killed—I've killed . . . a bear."

Luther's shoulders relax. His hands loosen. He hears his own voice rising from the well inside himself, the well they call a heart, the well Luther now knows he will never see to the bottom of. He pulls open the curtain before the priest can answer and crawls from the confessional on all fours.

10

AT THE Discount 66 Drug Store Luther buys an envelope and a stamp. He takes them to the counter in the back and orders coffee. He folds the thirty dollars up in the envelope. On a napkin he writes a letter to Joan and Joan with a pen he borrows from the waitress. She watches him write slowly as she fixes toast. The inkblots blur into the soft napkin, making Luther's block printing look delicate and veiny.

Hi—I'm at the airport, in a hurry. Don't blame you about not taking the call last night. I just wanted to say I got a new job with an outfit that guides hunters into the mountains after big game. For now I'm the cook, but maybe I can learn tracking or get a bushpilots license. Lots of possibilitys for me here. Sending this for now—don't think I'll forget what I owe you both, the bail money from Jeff City and all, now that things are looking up. Money's real good—we get hasard pay and over time. Heading for North Canada in a few minutes, don't know when to return. I love you both and look at your pictures everyday—Your Luther.

Luther seals the envelope and finishes his cup of coffee. He puts it in his pocket and feels the two postcards from McInney's.

He takes them out and lays them on the counter. He loses himself for a minute in the picture of the rushing blue river filming over rough rocks and foaming into the bright air beneath the green mountains.

When the waitress offers to refill his cup, Luther puts his hand over it. "Thanks, I've had enough. Here's your pen back. By the way, could you tell me where this Bitterroot River is at? The one in my postcard here?"

He swivels the card around so it's right-side-up for her.

The waitress sets the coffeepot down for a minute as she clips the pen back on her ticket pad and looks the postcard over.

"Sure, it's right outside of town here. It flows all the way down the valley right into the Clark Fork out west of Alder's salvage yard. Do you know where that is?"

Luther nods, not really hearing, but feeling that the river is nearby somehow and noticing the direction the waitress waves her hand in.

"Thanks," he says. "It looks real shallow."

He gathers the postcards and his photos up into his pocket.

"It is, mostly." She slides the change from Luther's dollar off the edge of the counter into her apron.

He walks briskly from the drugstore down Market Street in the general direction the waitress had pointed. Within a block he sees a bridge rising over a river. He pauses at a mailbox in front of an appliance store to mail his letter to Joan and Joan.

The appliance store has its front double doors wedged wide open. Luther squints into the store as he walks by. On the far wall, beyond the microwaves and VCRs and dishwashers and entertainment consoles is a bank of color TVs, all of them on with the sound turned way low. They are tuned to several different channels. Luther thinks of Conrad again, alone at the Restwell, empty, stiff, absent.

For a moment Luther wishes that all the dead people in the world were stuffed like the animals in McInney's lobby. Stores and malls and coffeeshops and parking lots brimming with stuffed people with their eyes open and their mouths open, with their arms upraised and their hands extended, like they're always just about to comment on something or touch somebody, but they never do. Luther believes it would be more honest like that than hiding all the death down underground, more honest and more real than turning death into nothing more than distance and disappearance.

He crosses the street before the bridge, walking against a Don't Walk sign, remembering the Plymouth that brushed against him twenty-four hours ago. He lumbers up the grade to the bridge.

The sidewalk is rising, but Luther's still above land. An access road winds below him down to the riverbank and a parking lot. A small sign says Clark Fork River.

Luther realizes this isn't the river in the postcard, the Bitterroot, but he doesn't care. It's a beautiful river with fast shining water, and Luther believes that the names of the rivers don't matter anyway. He remembers arguing once with a geography teacher about why the river below St. Louis was called Mississippi rather than Missouri. All the rivers flow into each other, sooner or later, and it just boils down to somebody having to make up their mind when they're writing up the maps. He can call this the Bitterroot if he wants to. He walks out over the fast water, looking down carefully as if he's figuring on a good place to fish. *Bitterroot River*, he says to himself as he turns his back on the traffic.

He wonders if people fish from this high up, whether it's possible to pull a fish up in the air all that way even if you did hook one. Luther imagines dangling a line and hook from the bridge in midair. He winces. What if a bird snapped at the line? For a minute he pictures this—bracing a long thin pole against his hip as a bird rises into the blue air, flapping its wings frantically to be free of the earth, pulling out the line faster and faster. The thought of capturing something so free and fast and graceful reminds him of all the mounted birds at McInney's.

His foot throbs inside his shoe. A woman in a beige Celica slows down and looks him over. He stares back at her and then leans backward over the railing until he can see to the top of the bridge canopy. He begins to climb.

Halfway up the girders, he pauses. A patrol car stops below him. He climbs again as the patrol car backs up and parks just off the bridge. The two cops start walking toward him, yelling. Traffic starts to slow down as people notice the cops and then him, high on the tall steel web.

Luther pretends the bridge is his own as he climbs it, made from an erector set on Christmas morning in Missouri twenty years ago. He loved to build things with the erector set and then lie on the floor with his eyes as close to the rug as possible and go into the erector-set world he had made. He thinks of the past as just like that erector-set world, bolted and screwed together out of small parts that could just as easily have been put together differently, that could be broken down and rebuilt into shape after shape.

The cops wave and yell. Another cruiser stops. Pedestrians gather at both ends of the bridge. More cops are directing traffic across the bridge, keeping everything moving. Luther is on all fours on top of the bridge, afraid all at once to stand up, afraid all at once of falling.

He kneels there at the top, removing one hand from the girders and then the other. He wonders if the cops are here about Conrad or just because he's disturbing the midmorning traffic routine on the bridge. In the wind he hears a deep, mechanical voice. One of the cops below has a megaphone and an amplifier.

What are you doing? Come down, there's someone down here who wants to speak to you. He says it slowly, over and over.

Luther cocks his head like a curious animal listening to the kind but mysterious voice of a human who is trying to convince him to do something. Can they possibly be talking to him? He knows no one down there wants to speak to him, but yet *he* wants to say something, something to someone, something better and truer than all he's said to the priest or Joan and Joan or Conrad or Belinda or McInney.

But he's speechless, hunched there, higher than anyone, realizing he has a chance to scream now, scream when it counts. He feels the past drift around him and the erector-set bridge in the bright morning wind, and his speechlessness takes him back to his sophomore class play in high school.

He had amazed himself and his mother by getting a part in one of the corny Shakespeare plays, but the drama teacher replaced him after the opening night because Luther had frozen up and forgotten his two rhymed lines. The main actor, a prince, had covered for him after a moment, and most of the audience hadn't even caught his mistake.

But Luther remembers those other actors, turning their eyes on him, one by one, in that brief moment everyone gave him to recover himself. Someone had even whispered a cue, but it was no good. Yet now he clamps his eyes shut like vises for those lines—if he could scream them now, maybe the crowd of strangers at his feet would leave him alone, would go back to their cars and forget him.

Luther opens his mouth and lets the wind blow into his head—he feels it drying his tongue—he hears no sound. He bares his teeth and opens his mouth even wider into a grimace and lets the wind blow right through him.

Two policemen climb toward him, and he feels dizzy as they get closer and closer. They don't say anything even though Luther sees their lips moving just as if they were yelling at him. He stands up shakily with his knees bent and traces the river until it disappears in the western distance. He knows that it leads to the ocean somehow, no matter what it's named between here and there. He wishes he had Conrad's map right now. He wonders just how shallow the water really is.

The nearest of the cops is right below him. He reaches out as if he's going to grab Luther's foot. Luther imagines that touch on his swollen, bare foot. He can imagine it as both soothing and searing.

Then he looks away from the police and the bridge, and the wind blows him back to another day, maybe the best day of his life, one summer late in high school up at the Buffalo River in Barton County. He and some friends had been swimming and climbing the rock ledges above deep pools in the river just downstream from the state park swimming beach. There was a perfect place to dive from the highest overhang, but everybody was afraid to go first once they looked out over the edge. Some of the girls they'd been watching at the beach started waving at them, showing they were watching back, and Luther had felt the sun shining on him, and he'd stood up straight and leaned over the rock, eyeing the water calmly as if gauging its depth like one of the pros at Acapulco on "Wide World of Sports."

Then with all eyes on him, he had leaped as far away from the rock as he could, curling himself up on the way down and then quickly uncurling, stretching out into a clean straight dive that would have impressed anyone with its graceful audacity.

Photo by Celeste River

About the Author

PHIL CONDON was born in Wyoming and grew up in Nebraska. A journeyman bricklayer since 1976, he holds an MFA in fiction from the University of Montana. Before he started writing at the age of thirty-eight, he worked off and on as a landscaper, firefighter, cabdriver, slaughterhouse worker, office clerk, and delivery truck driver. Twice nominated for a Pushcart Prize, Condon received a 1993 National Endowment for the Arts Fellowship. He's currently writing a novel set in 1969. Since 1987 he's lived near the Clark Fork River in Missoula, Montana.